# *P.S. YOU'RE DEAD. . . .*

*"This is a binding contract. Failure to adhere to it will bring certain death. The Committee hopes it will not be necessary to uphold its end, but in the event that it is, the Committee will act without hesitation and without remorse."*

Eamon wasn't getting anywhere with it. He thought the anti-male, pluralistic, we-the-committee phrasing pointed in the direction of some militant feminist group, something like that. Bunko was of the opinion that the chain letter was the work of only one woman, a head case at that. But how could they tell for sure?

The envelope provided a small handwriting sample and another clue that was far stranger and far more important. On the front was the address of Dooley's bar, neatly printed with a forceful, leftward-leaning slant. On the back was a custom-made wax seal, lip-shaped and ruby red.

Eamon Wearie thought it looked just like a kiss—a deadly kiss.

**Books by Sean McGrady**

Dead Letters
Gloom of Night
Sealed with a Kiss

Published by POCKET BOOKS

# SEALED WITH A KISS

## SEAN McGRADY

**POCKET BOOKS**

New York   London   Toronto   Sydney   Tokyo   Singapore

An *Original* Publication of POCKET BOOKS

POCKET BOOKS, a division of Simon & Schuster Inc.
1230 Avenue of the Americas, New York, NY 10020

Copyright © 1995 by Sean McGrady

ISBN: 0-671-86941-8

First Pocket Books printing April 1995

10  9  8  7  6  5  4  3  2  1

POCKET and colophon are registered trademarks of Simon & Schuster Inc.

Cover art by William Sloan/Three

Printed in the U.S.A.

*For Ingebjørg, always*

She was very frightened and didn't know how he was going to go about things but she snuggled close to him. Then the hand that felt so big in her lap went away and was on her leg and started to move up it.

"Don't, Jim," Liz said. Jim slid the hand further up.

"You mustn't, Jim. You mustn't." Neither Jim nor Jim's big <u>hand</u> paid any attention to her.

—Hemingway, "Up in Michigan"

# *One*

Lieutenant Eamon Wearie had some trouble believing that Christy Gertz was only fifteen years old. Even if the blond beauty, originally from Havre de Grace, Maryland, but most recently of Redondo Beach, California, was known as Baby Face.

"I got paid through Lou the Dog," she said with veteran matter-of-factness.

"Why was Ackerman called Lou the Dog?" Bunko asked.

"Believe me," she said, shaking her head, "you don't want to know."

"How did Ackerman pay you? Cash? Check? What?"

Bunko barked out questions while Christy, seated in a plastic chair, supplied answers into a camcorder, which was set on a tripod in the bare-bones interrogation room. Eamon leaned against the back wall and—as was his way—stayed out of the picture.

"Mostly cash," she said. "But sometimes with a little candy thrown in. Coke, sometimes heroin. Lou

1

was always trying to hook us into that shit. Thought it might make it easier to get us to do things, you know."

"What things?"

"You know. Girl on girl. Two guys at a time. Sick stuff."

"And Lou Ackerman knew you were thirteen years old at the time?"

*"Knew?* That's what the little prick was looking for."

"What do you mean by that, Christy?"

She made a disbelieving face that said, Get real. Like, don't you guys know anything?

"Louie liked them with their training bras," she sneered. "Now do you get it?"

"How did you meet Ackerman?"

"Through Tony Zee. It was his job to find the local talent. I was with my best friend Trina at McDonald's when this guy came over and asked if I'd ever done any modeling. Acted like amazed when I told him I hadn't. Told me I was like the most beautiful girl he'd ever seen. Used every line in the book. You got to understand, man, nobody had ever said things like this to me before. And he wasn't that bad, you know. In this leather jacket and tight jeans. And he had this totally awesome Trans-Am besides. Asked me if I wanted to take a ride. Trina warned me, telling me I was crazy, that I didn't even know the guy. But I was so naive then. I just didn't know how it worked."

"Who else besides Ackerman and Tony Zee knew your true age?"

She ran through the list of names, a rather long list of porno producers and publishers, many of whom would soon be indicted for trafficking obscene videocassettes and magazines through the mail. Some would also be charged with violating the federal Child Protection Act. This was not to mention the distributors and retailers and other middlemen who had profitted through callous indifference and determined ignorance.

Just a kid, Eamon thought, just a damn kid. Even if she did look like Heather Locklear or something. Her face was painted garishly, powdered and rouged to hell, a teenage girl's idea of what passes for sophistication and worldliness. She was in hot pink Lycra bicycle shorts and an oversize Bart Simpson T-shirt that still managed to reveal plenty. Ordinarily Eamon would have been attracted. Ordinarily he was the typical male animal, reducing and objectifying and thinking what a great piece of ass. But there wasn't anything ordinary about Christy Gertz or the circumstances that had brought her to his attention. Her ordeal, her whole situation saddened him. And shamed him; just being a man, part of it somehow.

"Well, I guess that's a wrap!" Bunko boomed, like some damn Hollywood director.

"'Bout time," she said disgustedly. "Too many hours of this shit."

"Seems like days," Bunko agreed. "But I've got to ask you to sit still a few minutes longer. I want to check with my boss to see if there's anything we've forgotten to cover."

They wanted to get it all on tape. As a precaution. Just in case somebody decided to put Christy in their own special version of a snuff film. By coming forward she wasn't lacking enemies.

For some reason it was awkward with Bunko out of the room. Eamon took out his Marlboros and lit one up. He was aware that she was staring at him. But he didn't want to chance the contact.

"Hey, aren't you even going to offer me one?"

"Sure, sure," he said, fumbling with the pack.

"Now aren't you going to light it?"

She held his arm steady as he reached out with the light.

"There, that's much better," she said, blowing smoke.

He merely nodded.

"You don't look like a cop," she remarked. "Or whatever it is you do."

"Postal inspector," he reminded her.

"You're way too good-looking for that shit, if you don't mind my sayin'."

She licked her lips blatantly, sexually.

"Have you seen any of my movies? Then you don't know what you're missing, do you?"

He was plainly uneasy with this turn.

"Maybe we could get together later on," she said invitingly. "You know, just you and me."

He demurred.

"What, you married or something? Is that what it is? Because I don't care, if that's what's got you worried."

He had to keep reminding himself that she was only fifteen.

He was relieved to hear Bunko returning. His partner was just outside arguing about something with Masterson. He could only catch bits and pieces, something about their upcoming vacation.

"Son of a bitch," Bunko fumed, reentering. Then he turned to Christy without any of the gruffness. "You're free to go now, honey. We appreciate you coming in and taking the time with us."

Ignoring Bunko, she turned her attention back to Eamon. "You have a pen, good-lookin'?"

She took his ballpoint and asked him to hold still. Then she wrote her phone number on his hand.

"This way you won't forget about me," she said in a very small voice, before taking her leave.

"What the hell was that all about, sport?"

"Got me, Bunk."

"Lemme tell ya something, you start datin' teenage porn stars, there will be some talk in the office."

"Anything to break up the monotony."

"Statutory rape charges oughta do the trick, sport."

"So what the hell were you and Masterson jawing about? Could hear you all the way in here."

"Wants us to postpone our vacation. Something's come up."

"No can-do, Bunk. We got two weeks coming to us. And I've made plans. Supposed to visit my folks on the Carolina coast. Already packed the suntan lotion and fishing rods."

"Then welcome to Disappointmentville. It's not just a direct order, it's a state of mind."

"What's so important that it can't wait till we get back?"

Bunko sighed. "A chain letter."

*"A what?"*

"Some guy got a very weird chain letter."

"Oh, *that* sounds really big," Eamon let out sarcastically. "What happened? He forget to make copies to send out to thirty-seven equally gullible friends? And now something really terrible has befallen him? Just like the chain letter said?"

"Something like that."

"Let me guess. He lost his job, his marriage broke up, the dog ran away, and his car broke down all in the same week, right?"

"Not exactly," Bunko said numbly. "More like he was murdered."

Eamon met Heather Bass, an attractive legal secretary who was somewhere in her late twenties, at the Chesapeake Crab in the Light Street Pavillion, which was just another overpriced cafe overlooking the sluggish brown water of the Inner Harbor.

It was late in July and this was their third date. Heather was still dressed for business, in a pearly blazer and immaculate linen skirt, not exactly suitable attire for a night at the old ballpark. After dinner they were going to join Bunko and Franny at Camden Yards. Eamon found himself examining her regal accoutrements, the golden necklace and diamond earrings, that emerald ring and Cartier watch, the absolute expense of it all. It never ceased to amaze him how these glorified secretaries and receptionists —the type with whom he so often found himself— managed to pull it off on such modest salaries.

She ordered the predictable glass of white wine and he opted for a bottle of Rolling Rock. She was certainly pretty enough, a tall, judiciously built brunette, whose hair was set in a rigid, impenetrable stack.

"So how was your day?" she asked.

"Fine. Spent it with an underage porno star."

"How nice for you," she laughed, thinking he was just kidding as usual.

The waitress came for their orders. Heather couldn't seem to make up her mind and told him to go right ahead. He went with a bowl of gumbo and the beer-battered shrimp. "Oh, I still don't know," she said, slightly flustered. "Why don't you order for me." So he did, guessing she liked it on the light side. A house salad with the grilled salmon.

"Oh, I like that in a man," she cooed, clearly pleased.

He didn't know what it was, what was bothering him. She was earnest and pleasant and their talk was polite and informed. She seemed to hang on to his every word, and he knew she'd already made her determination about him. They barely knew each other, but already she'd asked how he felt about marriage, at least the idea of it, the subject taken in its most general and informal terms. When he'd related that he had nothing personal against the institution, an expression of unconcealed delight crossed her unblemished face.

He was divorced. Not nearly ambitious enough. And anyone could tell you he spent too much time spinning on his bar stool. Eamon always tried to be up-front about these things. But no matter, Heather was already busy giving him the desired makeover, believing in her heart of hearts that she was just the woman to right this wayward postal inspector with the dreamy blue eyes and dark, unruly hair. Actually, he was just a little too nice looking, she thought. That might lead to problems later on. But she liked the fact that he had a good, sensible job. And besides, it wasn't like he had a bunch of kids and child support payments.

That was the thing about Eamon Wearie: women never failed to notice his potential.

It was a sticky, oozy summer night—a Baltimore special—smelling of beer and peanuts and thirty thousand perspiring humans. Oriole Park was a wavy, ecstatic sea of brightly colored polo shirts and baseball caps. It was a tie game going into the bottom of the ninth. Cal Ripkin chanced a big lead off third base with one out. The crowd leaped out of their seats with every pitch.

Everyone except Heather, that is.

She just sat there on Eamon's by now very wrinkled gabardine sport coat, looking unamused and very tired. For most of the evening she'd put on a good face, stomping and cheering along with everyone else, but it was difficult to maintain such false and manufactured energy. Baseball really wasn't her thing. Oh, at first she seemed knowledgeable enough, readily tossing off some prime stats, but Eamon soon realized that she'd merely memorized these surprising tidbits in a calculated attempt to show interest in her man.

Somehow that disturbed him. He just wished it could have come more naturally, that they could just make do without the artifice. Like Franny and Bunko over there. Franny—a tough, funny, cigar-chomping crime reporter for the *Sun*—seemed like the perfect match for Bunko, the tough, funny, whiskey-slurping ex–private eye with the heart of gold. They were bouncing up and down in a frenzy screaming, "Suicide! Suicide! Suicide!"

Heather looked on with a blank face.

"Suicide squeeze," Eamon explained. "They're calling for the bunt."

For some reason he found his attention wandering from the action at home plate to the floodlit green of center field and beyond to the dark towers and spires of the city, that great remoteness. Feeling more and more removed, Eamon wondered what he was doing there, what he was doing with a woman like Heather Bass.

When Baines dragged one toward first and Ripkin came scooting home with the winning run, the crowd erupted into molten happiness.

Eamon and Heather gathered up their things, practically oblivious.

They went back to his place, the tiny row house in Fells Point that he shared with his mondo bizarro tenant, Daniel P. Pinkus. Fortunately, judging by the darkened windows, Pinkus was sound asleep.

Heather excused herself to go to the bathroom.

She wasn't quite right for him. In the long run they were both wasting their time. He knew it, even if she didn't. They would go to bed together anyway; that was the sad part.

Heather reappeared in a lacy lavender teddy, an erotic morsel from the pages of Victoria's Secret. He wondered if she'd been wearing it under her work clothes—or had she managed to conceal it in her pocketbook? She looked choice, all the more edible. Just the same, her calculations did more to disconcert him than to arouse desire.

She only wanted to please him, and that just made him all the more unhappy and distant. She didn't seem to care about her own pleasure.

"What do you want me to do for you?" Heather asked, combing her fingers through his chest hair. "I'll do anything you want."

Eamon knew what he wanted, all right. But he didn't think she was going to go away that easily.

# *Two*

It was the time of day he liked best, early morning with the coffee on and the *Sun* opened to the sports section. The first light of day filtered into the breakfast nook, which encompassed two Oglivie chairs and a drop-leaf table from IKEA. In the ephemeral quiet he read about last night's Oriole victory, savoring the details even though he had been in attendance.

Heather was just a queasy memory; he had dialed for the cab at about three in the morning. He wondered when he would learn. Now he would have to figure a way out, to let her down easy. He was getting too old for this sort of thing. He would turn thirty-four in just a few days.

Daniel P. Pinkus appeared like an unwanted apparition. Biblical scorn was etched into the bearded, unforgiving face.

"You're just another fornicator," he finally launched without humor. "From the valley of Sodom and Gomorrah."

It was a bit like looking into the face of Jesus. The

long, flowing hair, the terminally tortured eyes. At six in the morning, no less.

"Dan, give it a rest," Eamon said, practically immune. "Can't you see I'm trying to enjoy the paper?"

"It's just another secular diversion from that pagan world of yours," Pinkus replied coldly.

The poor guy hadn't been the same since enrolling in seminary school. He wanted to be a priest now. It was his latest diversion. Pinkus was a career student, one of those lazy, unaccountable humans who had never held a job, who'd never known the simple joy of holding their own in the real world. He'd buried the better part of a decade studying animal behavior at Chapel Hill, on the laboratory-rat fast track, only to drop out a few months short of his Ph.D. He'd wasted a few more years at the Maryland Institute of Art, painting crucifixions, of all things. Now this—The Calling.

"You're doing the Devil's work," Pinkus continued from his pulpit. "The pleasure of the flesh is most fleeting, but the sins of the flesh are everlasting. Think about that, sinner."

"Dan, could you just give it a rest already?"

"You are nothing but a heathen, a blight on His holy kingdom. And you will perish in the fires of damnation if you continue with your wicked, unrepentant ways."

"Dan, did we keep you up last night? Is that what this is about?"

"You are a user and discarder of women. You have taken that which is pure and wholesome and sullied it with debauchery. My son, now is the time to find Jesus Christ, your one and true and only savior. Now is the time to turn your back on the Devil's empty temptations."

"I feel so, so cheap," Eamon cracked.

Pinkus just glared.

"Hey, Dan, relax. I used a condom."

"I didn't realize that a condom could protect the soul," Pinkus intoned solemnly.

"Jesus, that's enough," Eamon snapped, clearly exasperated.

Pinkus suddenly switched gears. "Not bad, huh? I really had you going with that hellfire stuff, didn't I? What did you think, did I lay it on a little too thick, or were you, like, duly chastised?"

Eamon could only shake his head in miffed wonder.

The three postal inspectors hunkered around Eamon's no-frills, standard-issue gunmetal desk, in the harsh fluorescence of the Command Post, taking apart the chain letter, line by line, clue by clue.

Greetings:

After careful consideration you have been chosen as the recipient of a rather unusual chain letter. If you do what is asked, you may avoid the terrifying consequences. Remember, there is nothing random about your selection. You have earned this dubious distinction in any number of thoughtless, penile ways—through your degenerate, penile actions or your snideful, unrepentant penile words—and unless you make immediate amends, there is nothing we can do to prevent the Committee from carrying out its rightful, God-given mission. Unfortunately, due to the ineffectiveness of the male-sponsored government and other ineffective male agents of social change, we have had to usurp this rather difficult judiciary role. And because there is such a backlog of cases, the Committee does not have the time or disposition for a lengthy appeals process. We accept, in the name of the greater good, the possibility that mistakes may be made in our haste to right the wrongs of a centuries-old, patriarchial, penis-dominant society. You are asked now to atone for your transgressions by immediately doing the following things:

11

1. Immediately relinquish all worldly goods. This is viewed as a necessary first step to starting anew.

2. Immediately make some kind of public statement to acknowledge your wrongdoings and the harm that you have caused. The Committee will be checking the newspapers closely.

3. Choose one person that you feel has also earned the justifiable wrath of this chain letter. Then send it on. You will be held accountable for your choice and your ability to follow through.

This is a binding contract. Failure to adhere to it will bring certain death. The Committee hopes that it will not be necessary to uphold its end, but in the event that it is, the Committee will act without hesitation and without remorse.

By sheer necessity they focused on the physical evidence, on that single sheet of typewriting and its Baltimore-postmarked envelope. Even though the letter had been Xeroxed, they were able to determine the original watermark with ultraviolet. The letter writer had used recycled paper from Environmentally Sensitive, a Connecticut manufacturer that sold its product only in the New England area. And it didn't take them long to discover that a five-year-old IBM Selectric had been the weapon of choice.

The envelope provided a small handwriting sample and another clue that was far stranger and far more important. On front was the address of Dooley's bar, neatly printed with a forceful, leftward-leaning slant. On back was a custom-made wax seal, lip shaped and ruby red.

Eamon Wearie thought it looked just like a kiss—a deadly kiss.

"I'm tellin' ya, this thing's got nothing to do with Eddie Dooley's murder," Bunko complained to Masterson. "Besides, me and Wearie are due some serious vacation time."

Del Masterson, their boss, was having none of it. "I

want you two clowns on the case ASAP, which means N-O-W. You can take your summer vacations in February, for all I care."

Masterson, a former FBI tough guy, who kept a .357 Magnum strapped to his chest at all times, was the original Dirty Harry. Quick to take offense and quick to draw, he had dispensed with too many rules and too many suspects. The trigger-happy veteran—whose reputation for insubordination was exceeded only by his legendary exploits in the field—had finally, most unceremoniously, been shipped off to Postal.

Bunko knew enough to proceed with caution. "Del, perhaps we should sit on this awhile. A wait-and-see approach."

"You have your orders, Lieutenant Ryan," answered Masterson.

"I just have a small problem with the psychological profile," Bunko said evenly, not wanting to set him off. "That chain letter was done by a woman, most probably someone who has recently undergone some kind of emotional or physical trauma."

"Whatever you say," Masterson said gruffly.

"I don't think you follow," Bunko said, getting testy himself now. "Homicide thinks that Dooley was knocked off by professionals. Nothing to do with chain letters or deranged women. Spoke to Detective Kelsey myself and—"

Masterson cut him off, turning his attention to Eamon. "What's your opinion, Lieutenant Wearie?"

"Basically the same as Bunk's," he replied, showing solidarity. "Of course, it's also possible that that anti-male, pluralistic, we-the-committee phrasing points in the direction of some militant feminist group, something like that. In any event, I can't see this chain letter having anything to do with the hit put on Dooley."

"To hell with both of you," Masterson boiled, the color rising in his face as clearly as the red in a Fahrenheit thermometer. "To hell with your mumbo-jumbo psychological profiles. Sometimes you just have to go on gut instinct. Which takes a certain amount of guts, which I'm not so sure you girls have."

Bunko kept his mouth shut, even though he was bristling with indignation. Eamon was glad for that. The last thing he wanted to see was these two dinosaurs getting into it. Del and Bunko were about the same size and age, two triceratops from the primordial ooze of the Truman Administration, two hefty, fifty-year-old carnivores who still washed their T-bones down with Johnnie Red and still didn't quite buy the Surgeon General's warning on their cigarette packs. They were too much alike, Eamon decided, and that was probably why they didn't like each other.

"Del, let me *tell you* something," Bunko shoved out with sudden force. "The way Dooley was taken out suggests professional action and nothing short of it. Detective Kelsey told me there was no sign of a struggle, nothing amateurish about it. It was real clean, a single bullet to the head, no witnesses, no cash taken from the register, nothing left behind. So don't give me any bull about gut instincts and your wild asinine hunches. Go to Pimlico and play the ponies if you want to make a big dumb G-man bet. Just don't involve us, *okay?"*

*Uh-oh,* Eamon thought. *Godzilla versus Megatron.*

"Professional action, my ass," Masterson snarled, jabbing a finger into Bunko. "What would you know about it? I've seen mob hits. Up close and personal. I know how the John Gottis of the world operate. And they could give a rat's ass if the job was nice and tidy. They shoot people in broad daylight all the goddamn time. With plenty of witnesses. With cops a block away. Without a trace of fear in their hearts."

Bunko took a last hack at reasoning with him. "Look, Del, this Dooley was a betting man. And, according to Detective Kelsey, he was also behind on the vigorish. Kelsey thinks the Shylock wanted Dooley's bar to even things up. And when Dooley refused—well, you know these guys, they play for keeps."

"You don't know what you're talking about, you lard ass," Masterson slammed back. "The shy doesn't want to kill the golden goose. Dooley's no good to him dead. You don't have a clue, do you, Ryan?"

Bunko felt the red-hot coals of hate in his belly. The man was born mean, junkyard-dog mean. He'd seen it before, drinking with the bastard at three in the morning, the way Masterson would start up with some unsuspecting drunk, insulting and baiting until he got a rise out of the poor sap, just so he could press some worthless advantage. Bunko wasn't going to give him the satisfaction this time; he just let those coals smolder down.

Masterson waited, girding himself for Bunko's return of serve; finally, with no volley in sight, he dispensed with them. "Okay, girls, you have your orders."

Suddenly it occurred to Bunko what was really going on here. "Christ, I get it. How could I be so stupid. You knew Dooley, didn't you, Del? You drank at his place, that's it, isn't it?"

"So what if I did?" Masterson said huffily.

"So plenty. This isn't Postal's business. And you know it. Let the homicide team take care of it and leave us out, for Christ' sake."

"Homicide's had it two weeks already. And you know what that means. Means that lots of other folders have been gathering over Dooley's. And that ain't right. Eddie was a friend of mine—or pretty damn close to it. At least the son of a gun poured his turn. That's more than most. So you and the pretty boy get on it. Because the closer you get to solving it, the closer you girls come to having a vacation."

That was the end of it as far as Masterson was concerned. Eamon and Bunko watched him make his way across the Command Post, their eyes blazing bullets.

When he was safely tucked in his office, Bunko sputtered, "Who does he think he is? Clint Eastwood? The damn son of a bitch."

Eamon said, "If he calls me the pretty boy one more time—"

"What are you complaining about? Referred to me as a lard ass. Lard Ass and Pretty Boy. Sounds like some new action-adventure movie, doesn't it?"

"Doesn't sound like any movie I want to be in."

"At least you always know where you stand with the man," Bunko said resignedly.

Dooley's, the bar, was in the Mount Vernon area, on a little side street off St. Paul. Twenty blocks up from the Inner Harbor, it was a quiet, pleasant enough part of town, mostly three- and four-story apartment buildings in sedate red brick with a smattering of restaurants and Laundromats. The mercury gripped ninety-five degrees Fahrenheit, where it had had a stranglehold for weeks now, which was probably why there were so few people about.

They were grateful for the cold burst of air-conditioning that greeted them inside. It was a real joint, a boozy haven for working stiffs and ordinary Joes, replete with blinking beer signs, ancient sports memorabilia—yellowing Colts pennants and ghostly photos from the winner's circle of Pimlico Past—and a certain comfortable, not entirely unintentioned shabbiness.

The bartender and two elderly customers had their eyes fixed on the television above the bar. Amazon women in strange neo-gladiator outfits were attacking each other with volleyballs. ESPN on a Tuesday afternoon. The bartender, a balding, bearded, tattooed, three-hundred pounder, made walking one end of the bar to the other a time-consuming, substantial feat.

"Can't get that damn air working right," he said

16

wearily, wiping his wet brow, even though the room was sufficiently chilled. "So what can I get you two gentlemen?"

"You Eddie Dooley's partner?" Bunko demanded in tough-guy style.

"I been all through this already," he said, tired of it. "How many times do I got to go over it? Don't you guys talk to each other? I must have spoken to ten cops by now—"

"Postal. Lieutenant Ryan. And this is Lieutenant Wearie. Sorry to be going over the same old ground but—"

"Del send you over? Yeah, he promised to do something. I'm Charlie Pike. But everybody calls me Chewy. Let me get you boys something. On the house, of course."

He tapped them a couple of Old Bohs. They both took a long, satisfying hit.

"Tell me," Bunko said, "you think this has anything to do with that chain letter?"

"Could be, I don't know. Weird stuff. Like out of some 'Twilight Zone' show, know what I'm saying? The way the envelope was sealed. The whole way it sounded and everything. But who knows for sure?"

"Detective Kelsey thinks it was because Eddie was behind on the vig."

"Oh, that's a bunch of it," Chewy said, shaking his head profusely. "Eddie didn't owe much. Couple a G's. No big deal. Nothing for him. Besides, you don't know Rudy. He's the shy. Sweetheart, know what I'm saying? Lovely man, a regular here."

"Who'd want to kill Eddie, then?"

"Beats me," he said, still shaking his head.

"What about the other regulars? Any grudges? Anything like that?"

"No, everybody loved Eddie. We hadn't raised the prices in ten years. Besides, where else would anyone go?"

17

"What do you mean?"

*"You know,"* Chewy said, as if they were really supposed to know.

"I don't follow."

*"You know,"* he repeated. "This area. Very you-know-what."

"Gay," Bunko concluded.

"There, you said it. Not too many bars like this one left. Place for real men to go to, know what I'm saying?"

"I hear you, chief."

Eamon said, "Do they ever come in here?"

"You mean the fruits? No, the word was out, know what I'm saying? Eddie couldn't stand their type, wouldn't serve them nohow. They go to their own places, that's the only way."

Eamon said, "Then it's possible Eddie wasn't very well liked in the gay community?"

Chewy rubbed his clammy bald head with something like consternation. "Yeah, I guess so. It's funny, too, because a couple nights before Eddie got whacked we had what you might call an incident here. Two women, know what I'm saying? Eddie was behind the bar. Told me all about it. These girls that look like boys with the short haircuts and all. Two of them starting in with the tongue action, you know. Eddie tells them to go to planet Venus, know what I'm saying? One of 'em really starts in with Eddie, yelling all sorts of nasty lesbo things, throwing her drink at him, that kind of thing. Eddie had to physically remove her: just picked her right off the stool and threw her into the street. The regs just loved it, cheering and everything."

Bunko tried to get him back on track. "Okay, but what about your end of it? You were partners, right? Fifty-fifty? What's going to happen to Eddie's share?"

"It's all mine now," Chewy said with a wide grin.

"Forgive me for saying so," Bunko said, "but you don't look all that broken up about Eddie's death."

18

"I'm just not good at showing emotions, know what I'm saying?" He was grinning like a loon now. "See, you guys just don't understand. Eddie and me was best friends. Did everything together. The track, bowling, watching TV. Like Ralph Kramden and Ed Norton without Alice and Trixie to spoil it. Even bought a house together. So when we made up our wills we just left everything to each other. Kind of like a bet, see? Always kidding about who'd die first and who'd wind up with the works. So I'm the big winner. Now do you get it?"

Bunko smiled at the man-child, the way you would at any crazy person. "I think that's all we need for now, Mister Chewy."

"Me and Eddie, like that 'Honeymooners' show all over again," he was saying as they made for the door.

They were met by the stultifying heat, by the stench and stillness of many days without so much as a wispy breeze.

"Feel like I'm melting," Bunko said, already perspiring heavily. "How do you do it, Wearie? You look cool as a cuke in that crisp new tan suit of yours. That presidential tie. Christ, give me a break."

"It's called poplin. A nice, lightweight summer fabric. My other secret is that I use something called an antiperspirant."

"Oh, real funny," Bunko said, his face a mad trickle. He hadn't even bothered with the sport coat today; the blue shirt was soaked at the armpits and his tie had all the splendor of a dishrag. "I'll have you know that I use deodorant, pal. I slather it on like suntan lotion, and still I sweat like a goddamn pig."

"How nice. Women must really go for you."

"We can't all be pretty boys."

"And we can't all smell nice either."

Bunko led Eamon into a deli, where he grabbed two quart bottles of Miller High Life from the cooler.

"Geeze, Bunk, maybe we ought to be getting back to the office."

19

"Think of it as our lunch hour, if that makes it any easier for you, kid."

They walked a few blocks to Mount Vernon Place, to that elegant, old-world square, a meticulously landscaped park boxed in by richly imposing, nineteenth-century brownstones. The tasteful, practically subdued mansions, occasionally enlivened by Corinthian columns or a beaux-arts facade, stared haughtily down on a small patch of green redeemed by fountains and bronze statues of lions and revolutionary generals. Too many of the benches were taken up by homeless men and women who had passed out in an incoherent haze of cheap wine and hard times. General George Washington, atop a 160-foot column of marble, surveyed it all with a solemn, noble face.

There was nothing like cold beer in the hot sun. They felt a rush of good feeling with those first, quenching slugs from their perspiring bottles.

"So what did you think of this Chewy?" Eamon asked.

"Who cares, kid? This ain't our problem. Nothing to do with us."

"Kind of funny about him living with Dooley, though. Especially considering that Dooley was such a homophobe."

Bunko said, "They're the worst ones, kid. The ones that deny what's inside of themselves and take it out on everybody else."

"That chain letter still troubles me. Strange about the watermark, that you can only buy that paper up in Connecticut and Rhode Island and—"

"Give it a rest, kid. Can't you see I'm trying to enjoy my beer? Hey, did I tell you what me and Franny wound up doing after the game last night?"

"Let me guess, you burned incense and read Tibetan poetry to each other? No? Experimented with cross-dressing? Not even close? Try your hand at some New Age channeling, did you?"

"You're just not funny," Bunko said gravely. "In all

good conscience I can't encourage it. Anyway, you would only see through my pale, halfhearted attempts at laughter."

"I'll bet you and Franny just did what you always do: filled the Jacuzzi with Jack Daniel's and practiced drowning."

"You're not even close. We went back to her place and—"

"Please Bunk, I'm not sure I want to hear this. Remember, I'm very impressionable. It doesn't take much to traumatize me."

"Would you just shut up and listen for a change? We didn't do anything. That's what was so nice about it. There was no need to have any sex. We just lay there together, feeling very close and all that."

"I can't believe it. A night without hot oil and Reddi Whip?"

"You know you're a hopeless jerk, don't you? I haven't a clue to what these women see in you. What about this Heather girl? She's good-looking and seems very nice to boot. So how's that going?"

"It's going, going, gone. That's where it's going."

"You're such a fool, Wearie. You don't know how good you have it, do you? You insane young bastard, you."

"Hey, I'd love to listen to some more of your constructive criticism—that's what it is, right? constructive?—but we better be heading back."

"Christ," Bunko said, after downing the last of his beer, "I've got a better idea. I know a place not far from here that's got a totally legendary happy hour. Sure, it's a gay bar, but with your pretty-boy looks that could quickly work to our advantage."

"We're still on shift and you know it. Besides, we've got to get cracking on this Dooley thing."

"Screw that," Bunko said, already heading in the direction of that bar. "As far as I'm concerned, we're on vacation."

# *Three*

〜♥〜

"Let's go over it again," Eamon said, picking up the chain letter from his desk. "There's bound to be something we've overlooked."

"Give it a rest, sport," Bunko said. "There's nothing to it, like I keep telling you. I've seen a million of these things. Bunch of idle threats by people who don't got day jobs."

The big guy was crumpling up paper into little balls and taking jump shots at a wastebasket fifteen feet away.

"Thanks for all your help," Eamon said. "Maybe you ought to take a break, ice down the arm. You must be getting tired."

Del Masterson was across the Command Post, ten gunmetal desks away, chewing out Santos. He smashed a fist into Santos's desk for emphasis.

"What's eating him?" Eamon asked.

Bunko said, "We got tossed off the front page, that's what's eating the humorless bastard. The murders forced him onto page forty-six of the *Sun*, right next to the legal notices."

Masterson had called a news conference yesterday to announce Lou Ackerman's indictment and the indictment of seven other miscreants connected with the Baby Face case—that fifteen-year-old porn star who'd been exploited through the mail and in so many other ways. Eamon knew there was nothing Masterson liked better than publicity, anything to make the FBI boys take notice. But Masterson couldn't have foreseen that his news conference would come on one of the busiest news days of the year. Two prominent members of the Maryland bar—Judge Harold Draper and Assistant District Attorney Molly Webster—had been assassinated. The murders were big news in Baltimore and even across the country. The speculation was that the mob had taken them out because of the Butanni trial. Two Butanni family lieutenants had been successfully prosecuted by the woman DA and given requisite stiff sentences by "Hang 'Em High" Draper.

Eamon was almost glad: that's how sick he was of Masterson and his .357 Magnum-size ego. He should have been down in Carolina, fishing off his dad's new Searay. He needed some time off; he was getting damn tired of the city and this soupy heat and having to put on a necktie every morning. He got up and walked over to the window—that long slat of soundproof, dirty glass overlooking Dead Letters—the only window in the joint. Below, three stories down, worker ants loaded conveyor belts and scooted by on red, white, and blue dollies. Even in a heat wave it was cool down there in the nation's largest warehouse, cool and dark and tomblike. Actually, it didn't look so bad, loading boxes and parcels in the anonymous shadows; sometimes he wished for a job like that, something without the complications.

"Hey, Romeo," Bunko called over, interrupting his reverie. He was pointing to the phone. "Line eight."

"Yeah, Wearie here," he said, picking up.

"How come you haven't called me yet?" Some girl.

The voice sounded awfully familiar. "All I do is wait by the phone for you, good-lookin'."

Jesus, Baby Face herself. Little Christy Gertz from Havre de Grace.

"How are you?" he said, his voice neutral.

"I miss you, gorgeous," she said.

"Christy, is there something we can do for you?" he said, trying to sound all business.

"I'll bet you could do lots for me, gorgeous," she replied like some kind of phone-sex operator. "I need you, I want you—"

"Christy—"

"Do you know what I'm wearing right now? I'm in just my—"

"Christy, I don't want to know, you understand? We better end this conversation before—"

"But I could really use a friend," she suddenly choked back. "I don't got no one to talk to."

"What about your family?"

"My mom and stepdad threw me out. Told me I was just a worthless slut. I'm at my grandma's now, in Dundalk. She's got that Lou Gehrig's disease and she can't move no more. The only reason she lets me stay here is because I go to the pharmacy and market for her."

"Do you have any friends your own age?" he asked, feeling bad for her now.

"Nobody wants to have anything to do with me when they find out the truth and all. Anyway, don't you think I'm a little too advanced for kids my own age?"

Hell, he thought, she might even be too advanced for him.

"Listen, Christy, I'm pretty busy right now and—"

"Can I call you again? Please?"

She was practically pleading. He didn't know what to say. "I guess it would be all right," he said, already regretting it.

When he got off, Bunko said, "When are you going to learn, kid? What's it going to take?"

Eamon ignored him. He needed some air, and he needed it now. He took the freight elevator down into the bowels of Postal Depot 349, and got behind the wheel of the Bob Hope Special, an electric golf cart that, like so many other things, had somehow come to be beached on the mysterious shores of Dead Letters.

He drove into the cool, dark nether regions, away from it all.

It was a narrow, mile-long, serpentine road that stretched through a vast, windowless wasteland. There was too little light, just the occasional dangling sixty-watt bulb, and way too many obstructions, from toppled cartons to giant, uncontainable letter slicks. Chaos reigned supreme, just as it seemed to do everywhere else in the world. There just wasn't enough manpower to right the awful sense that it was all out of control: Two dozen career postal clerks were no match for the armies of dead letters, raggle-taggle troops that came in at the rate of two hundred thousand a day, seventy-three million a year. Somehow the outnumbered, beleaguered clerks managed to return some twenty percent of the Manila soldiers, which was no small feat, considering the fact that so many of them were wounded beyond all recognition. For the letters weren't just rerouted and detained for easy-to-figure reasons. Oh, to be sure, they got their fair share of smudged addresses, misspellings, missing stamps, and nonexistent ZIPs. But that didn't take into account the ravages of war—postal warfare, that is—the mangled letters that were crunched out of malfunctioning sorting machines, or the many cardboard boxes that had simply fallen apart en route, their unlabeled contents spilled like so many Leggo pieces. But that was not the worst of it, as far as Eamon was concerned. Here, he was thinking of the real casualties, those letters that had arrived charred and waterlogged and coated with retardant. Letters that had perished in the flames, in fires that lashed out of control in post offices and skyscrapers and elsewhere. There were the letters that had been ill-fated passengers on skidding, brake-jammed mail trucks. Letters that had been aboard doomed airplanes, letters that had gone down with the ship. There was something altogether ominous about this mail, the way it couldn't be separated from the greater human tragedy.

But at Postal Depot 349 it didn't much matter how the letters had succumbed. There was no differentiation, no hierarchy among the dead. In that way, Depot 349 was just another potter's field, a burial place for luckless strangers, a place of no return. Acres and acres of the dead, without so much as a daisy. And it was that barrenness, that sense of eternal neglect, that left Eamon to understand the sad, unvarnished truth, which was, simply, that no one cared enough. It was everywhere, from Sector 1040, which was a solid football field of undeliverable IRS returns and refunds —so much of it pertaining to deceased taxpayers, a whole other twilight zone of the dead—to Sector 1225, otherwise known as the North Pole, last stop for all of the mail addressed to Santa and his little helpers. The North Pole was a sorry, awful place, what with its threadbare artificial spruce and its mountains of entreaties from America's children. Eamon had read enough of those letters to Santa to know that they weren't toy-laden shopping lists, as one might expect; instead he'd found out that there were a lot of neglected, hurting kids out there, kids who were just as likely to wish for someone to love them or a house in which to live as they were for Teenage Mutant Ninja Turtles.

He drove on through the wasteland.

He passed the Catacombs, which held the air-regulated vaults, and which in turn held the earliest-dated mail, stuff that went back to the 1840s, to the advent of the adhesive stamp.

As he approached the Holding Station, the long rows of picnic tables messy with letters and mailbags receded and gave way to the big ticket items, the boxes and crates that were stacked three stories high in monuments of geometric instability. Holding was a treasure trove, a welcoming shoal for all sorts of expensive merchandise that seemed to wash ashore like so much flotsam and jetsam. For some reason a lot of electronic equipment was always floating in: computers, VCRs, televisions, cameras. Usually damaged goods, stuff that had been insured and paid out against. Sometimes, though, there was nothing wrong with the loot, just that the companies had gone out of business or had screwed up the labeling all to hell. Often a language barrier turned out to be insurmountable: crates of porcelain marked with indecipherable Chinese characters, Persian rugs sent in Arabic, blue sable coats wrapped in Russian. There were plenty of reasons why something might come to be detained in the Holding Station. Sometimes all it had to do was look suspicious. Like those M-16s intercepted on their way to Belfast, on their way to the IRA. Or that Hawaiian pot that had been packed with macadamia nuts to throw off the scent.

Without a doubt, Holding was a magnet for the most unusual and valuable of the Dead Letters haul, a surreal shoppers' paradise. Unfortunately, it also drew a disproportionate number of the DL clerks. They seemed much more interested in the big cargo than in the anonymous sacks of mail; it was no secret that most of them would rather have located a lost shipment of Rolex watches than found a return address inside someone's lost letter. And that was the reason for all those eyes in the sky, strategically placed security cameras that weren't there ten years ago. Nobody seemed immune from temptation. Besides

27

the two dozen DL clerks, Depot 349—the United States Postal Service's Eastern Seaboard Mid-Regional Bulk Management Depot—employed over a thousand army regulars who were responsible for the loading docks, sorting machines, conveyor belts, and regular mail service. But it was the bad apples among the DL clerks that particularly rankled Eamon Wearie, for in some ways they were the worst violators of the public trust. They were the select few, men and women who, by a special act of Congress, no less, were paid to open the mail. God, Eamon thought, now you'd think that'd be an interesting job on its own, just getting to eavesdrop on your fellow citizens like that. But, admittedly, he knew better; even entering a sealed world of secrets and secret lives could get boring in a hurry. In fact, it usually took just six months for the new recruits to lose their initial enthusiasm; all one had to do was tear into a couple of thousand insincere Dear John letters—"But we can always be friends . . ."—and gingerly worded requests for a loan—"I wouldn't be asking, but . . ." —to notice a firmly set pattern of unoriginal, ungodly repetition. Nobody seemed to speak from the heart. Very few even took the time or trouble to cloak it in their own words. Still, though, Eamon got annoyed seeing that cluster of clerks in the Holding Station.

They were of a sort, these shapeless, sexless, trudging, Confederate-gray drones. It wasn't unusual to find them napping on the job, literally snoozing away in some quiet, forgotten cubbyhole. In fact, he wasn't surprised when he came upon Frankie Boyles and his cronies at a makeshift card table. There were four of them—Frankie, Billy Cash, Gleason, somebody he didn't know—playing poker on a wooden crate marked Animal Feed. Eamon turned the cart around, in no mood to play the heavy.

No doubt he'd have another occasion to face off with Boyles. Frankie Boyles just wasn't going to go away on his own. All his shenanigans with the Projection Room, turning it into some kind of private porno theater. Projection was only supposed to be used to help identify all the errant videocassettes that poured into Dead Letters. So many of those amateur videotapes nowadays. Everybody recording their weddings and golden anniversaries and baptisms and bar mitzvahs and what have you. That was the whole point of the Projection Room: to play them on the big-screen television, in a fast-forward attempt at spotting a name or an address, be it the family's, the church's, or even the catering hall's. But Frankie Boyles, as Eamon well knew, wasn't all that interested in retrieving people's lost celluloid memories. Oh, Boyles hunted through them, all right, but with his eye cocked for bigger game. He was after the stuff that came in shades of blue—homemade porno movies. And by the looks of things there were obviously a lot of people out there who got their kicks by videotaping, not to mention mailing off, their sexual exploits. It was common knowledge around the Depot—although it could never be proved—that Boyles had a little side business making dupes of popular X-rated finds. The guy was a bona fide creep. All you could hope for was that one of those security cameras might catch him in the act, making some kind of career-ending mistake.

Eamon stamped his thoughts Return to Sender, Return to Sender.

It was his birthday, his thirty-fourth. He felt sad for all the old, familiar reasons. He was still alone in the world, still searching. His parents were the only people likely to remember him this day. He hated birthdays, just like he hated Christmas and the Fourth of July; he just hated to be reminded that another year had passed, that's all.

Goddamn.

He drove back through the years, clearly marked

with sign posts, looking for his beginnings: 1967, 1966, 1965, 1964 . . .

The letters were aligned by state and then county in the year that they were officially declared dead. It was strange to realize that ZIP codes hadn't even come into use when he was born. He picked out a letter, any old letter, from the bin labeled Flushing, New York.

He was born there on the twenty-seventh of July.

It was addressed to Martin Bradley at 1212 Bitner Avenue.

Over it was stamped No Such Place.

Eamon tore it open with only the mildest anticipation.

Dear Marty,

I don't know how you can't take some responsibility for this. You were there with me in that motel room. Remember? Remember all the crap you told me about how much you loved me and how you'd always be there for me? I was so stupid, I actually believed you. Now I'm in so much trouble. But this isn't even about blame. I need some help paying for this. I'm going to need about three hundred to cover this—and Marty, I need it right away. I think it's the least you can do. Give me a call the moment you get this. That is, if you didn't lie about your address the way you lied about everything else. Hurry, I'm real desperate.

It wasn't even signed. Eamon thought it probably could have been written by any number of women that year. And lots of women every year since.

After work he went down to the Marlin, his bar. He didn't tell anybody it was his birthday, even though it would have got him his share of free drinks. That was about the only thing it was good for, he thought bitterly.

He came home just in time for "Jeopardy!," his favorite show. He hadn't expected to be greeted at his door by Heather.

"What are you doing here?" he asked, a little irritated. He just wasn't up to it tonight.

"I wanted to surprise you," she said, beaming.

"I wish you hadn't," he said glumly.

"It was no trouble, really," she said, still not understanding.

"No, that's not it," he began to explain. "I was going to talk to you but—"

"About what?" Concern started to edge in.

"Oh, I don't know. This doesn't seem like the right place for it. Or the right time, for that matter."

"No, I want to hear it, whatever it is," she said, getting all steely.

"You're not going to like it. And I feel very bad about it. Because you're a very nice and intelligent person. And I do like you, really. But I just don't think this is going to work out between us."

She looked like she was about to cry. But she didn't. She didn't seem able to say or do anything.

He said, "I'm really sorry."

She said, "You, you . . ."

She made as if she were going to pound her fists into his chest. But she couldn't connect, stopping just short of him.

Finally she just said, "You terrible, terrible man," and ran out into the street, away from him. He yelled after her, but by then it was too late.

Oh God, he thought, that could've been handled better.

Then he walked into his house to find out just how true that was. His living room was festive with balloons and streamers. Daniel P. Pinkus and the two cats sat on the couch with gloomy, miserable looks on their faces. All three of them were wearing little party hats. The birthday cake was on the coffee table, a

31

lovely white confection that went a long way to confirming Heather's opinion that he was a terrible, terrible man.

"Way to go," Pinkus said. "Really, nicely done. I mean, there aren't too many men who could ruin a surprise party and break a nice young girl's heart all in the same night. You haven't lost it. The old Wearie touch."

# *Four*

❦

The heat, it was unavoidable.

The nights were almost as still and sultry as the days. Eamon had a unit in his bedroom, a loud, energy-juicing thing that kept him cool and awake at the same time.

He lost his appetite for bacon and eggs in the morning. Even his desire for coffee waned—but, hell, he needed his daily caffeine supplement.

He was sipping his first cup of the day with the paper opened up before him, scanning American League box scores, when the call came in.

"Better get a move on, kid," he heard Bunko saying through the static of the portable phone. "Looks like our favorite chain letter has been going around. We're supposed to meet at the courthouse in half an hour. Superior Court, downtown. They found one of those freakin' letters in that dead judge's chambers. And then, to top it off, they found another copy in that dead woman lawyer's briefcase."

"Jesus, I thought those were mob-related hits."

"I gather the homicide boys still hold that opinion. But just the same, this has obviously got to be checked out. See you in a few. Oh—I almost forgot. There's a lot of press and TV people camped out at the courthouse. Don't mention the chain letter. If anyone recognizes you and asks, just tell them it's routine procedure, that we're just sorting through Draper's correspondence, looking for clues, whatever. Emphasize that it's no big deal, got it? *Ciao.*"

Eamon understood Bunko's concern. They'd worked plenty of high-profile cases in the past, and they were sure to bump into scribes and hairdos they knew. Hell, Bunko was even dating a member of the fourth estate. And if you had any brains, you learned to shut up. Nobody ever did himself any good by talking to a reporter. As if to underscore this very point, he spotted a small item buried beneath the avalanche of stories about the murders of Judge Harold Draper and Assistant District Attorney Molly Webster. The article, deep at the bottom of the *Sun*'s front page, had to do with the "Postal Inspection Service's roundup of suspected pornographers in the notorious Baby Face affair." Lou Ackerman, described as "a prominent local businessman," vigorously denied any wrongdoing or any knowledge of Christy Gertz's real age:

> "This girl gave us a fake driver's license. How are we supposed to know how old she really is? Believe me, we didn't exploit this kid. She wanted to be in the adult entertainment business. Believe me, she was a sex-hungry vixen that loved every minute of it. She should've paid us, I'm telling you, she loved it so much."

They stood on the courthouse steps waiting for Detective-Captain Brian Kelsey, a thirteen-year homicide veteran, whom they had never before met.

"How will we know him?" Eamon asked.

"I'll know him when I see him," Bunko said, unconcerned.

It was already broiling at nine in the morning. It didn't help that they were out in the open, on the stone steps in front of the giant Parthenon-like hall of justice.

Eamon said, "I presume you told Masterson about these new developments."

"Yeah, he could hardly contain himself. You know how Clint Eastwood gets when he smells a big, glamorous case."

"What about Franny? Did you tell her anything about our little murder chain?"

"She ain't going to run with the story. At least not the part about the letter. Listen, she would have found out sooner or later. You've shared enough hotel rooms with me to know I talk in my sleep. That's how my first marriage broke up. Described the affair I was having right in between the snoring. My wife went ballistic after I mumbled, 'Don't worry, baby, my wife's too stupid to ever figure it out.'"

As it turned out, Bunko was able to spot Kelsey right off. He just looked like a cop, that's all. There was the beige suit that had been made without the benefit of natural fibers. The paisley tie that had been fashionable several seasons before. There was the haircut that would have had many another considering legal action. Taken as a whole, Kelsey was a burly, buzz-sawed redhead in a tacky suit, who was sweating as badly as Bunko.

"Jesus, it's brutal out," Kelsey said, mopping his brow.

"You said it, brother," Bunko agreed, loosening his tie.

"I don't get it," Kelsey said to Bunko, examining Eamon. "How does your partner do it? The man looks as cool as a snow cone."

Bunko said, "Don't you hate him already?"

35

Kelsey said, "I know, I got a partner just like that. Detective Seppala should be here shortly."

"So what's the story, anyway?" Bunko demanded. "Do you guys still think it's Butanni family business? Or something crazier?"

"We think that chain letter's got something to do with it. I mean, yeah, the judge and that DA did a bang-up job in that racketeering trial. But the Butannis don't want this kind of heat. They knew how hard we'd come down. Besides, these two were almost celebrities because of the Cowel trial."

The Cowel trial had happened a few years back. Eamon and Bunko had watched some of it on television just like everybody else. Governor Cowel's son, Graham, had been accused of raping someone he'd met at a party. The trial was a sensationalized affair, a media feeding frenzy that churned up lurid revelations and daily headlines. The victim, a young woman who had not been lucky enough to call a convent home, found herself just as much on trial as the defendant. But what else was new in America? Graham Cowel, a young man with a permanent callow smirk and a high-powered attorney, was found not guilty. But that wasn't the interesting part. The interesting part had to do with the presiding judge and prosecuting attorney, none other than Draper and Webster.

"Jesus," Eamon said, "do you think there's any way it could have anything to do with that Cowel thing?"

Bunko remarked, "Little late for retribution, isn't it?"

Kelsey said, "I don't think you can count out anything at this point. Not when you consider that—" He stopped, seeing his partner. "Good, here's my better half now."

There had to be a mistake, that was Eamon's initial thought. Detective Seppala was just too beautiful to be a cop. The dark-maned, ocher-skinned woman, looking as cool as advertised in an ivory linen suit, practically shimmered in the haze. Introductions were made. Eamon didn't even realize he was staring until Bunko elbowed him in the side. "Get a grip on it, kid," he said under his breath.

They made their way into the courthouse, to Judge Draper's chambers. It was the solemn standard, this imposing office with the mahogany desk and leather furniture and oil portraits of Jefferson and Oliver Wendell Holmes.

Kelsey took charge. "We've collected all of the death threats and other questionable correspondence that Draper and this Webster received in the last six months. I'd sure appreciate it if you boys would go through it, see if there's anything that might be connected to that chain letter."

"No problem," Bunko said.

Eamon hardly heard. His eyes were full of her. Bunko thought he looked catatonic.

"If there aren't any objections," Kelsey continued, "we'll divide up the field work and all the rest of it."

Bunko said, "Yeah, I figure we could start by checking out some of the more extremist wackjob women's liberation groups."

Seppala glared at him. "I know what you're saying, Inspector, but there must be a better way of putting it."

"I suppose so," Bunko allowed.

Kelsey said, "There's a lot of peculiarities that I better fill you in on. We got two witnesses who saw what happened to this woman DA. Molly Webster's walking up Redwood at eight in the morning when somebody comes up and shoots her in the head with a Sig Sauer P226, which is a German nine-millimeter. Our very observant witnesses recall somebody in a trench coat and dark glasses and Humphrey Bogart hat walking swiftly away. Only one problem: they can't tell if it's a man or a woman."

"Jesus," Bunko said, "sounds like a pro to me."

Seppala said, "Although the assassin was dressed

like a man we think it's possible that it was a woman. The disguise seems a little overdone, especially when you consider how hot it was that morning."

"That's not the only thing out of whack," Kelsey said. "We found the judge in his Federal Hill brownstone. He was shot in the head too, but with a Glock 19. Which, incidentally, is the same gun that killed Eddie Dooley. Ballistics confirmed it this morning."

Seppala said, "Draper was found in his study with his pants down around his ankles. Not only was there a bullet in his head, but there was also a pair of nylon stockings wrapped around his neck. We don't know what to make of that yet. Except the last place he was seen alive was at Silk Stockings, which is this upscale nightclub at the Inner Harbor."

"Yeah," Kelsey interjected, "and Draper left with this blond babe that night. So far we haven't been able to find her. But she'd been hanging out there fairly regularly, according to the bartender."

"Maybe we should try some surveillance," Bunko suggested. "See if she returns."

"Well, maybe you're right," Kelsey said. "The bartender has instructions to call us if she shows, but perhaps we should go the extra mile."

Seppala said, "I don't think this is a case of one person acting alone. The chain letter keeps referring to something called the Committee."

Eamon nodded along and tried to act as if he were following her every word. Except he didn't have a clue; his face was plastered with a giant, idiotic grin. He liked the clear, cool precision of her voice, its full and confident enunciation. He liked her very smell, a tantalizing whiff of Parisian spring that cut through the stale mustiness of the judge's office. He noted the little things: her large, wet, violet eyes; the lipstick that somehow matched those wondrous Liz Taylor eyes; the fact that she wasn't wearing a wedding ring.

"Well, we better get cracking," Kelsey said. "Incidentally, we've put some feelers out, but so far we haven't stumbled across any more chain letters from this crazy Committee. Okay, we'll be in contact throughout the day."

Kelsey and Seppala left them there with Draper's and Webster's fan mail—with that ugly pile of death threats. Judges and assistant DAs, from the looks of things, were not the most loved people in the world.

"Snap out of it, will you?" Bunko said to his partner. "We don't have no time for you to be floating through the tunnel of love."

"Wasn't she something?" Eamon said from the gondola.

"Yeah, a regular goddess. Now let's get to work. Remember, we're looking for any kind of match. It could be the typeface, it could be a choice of words, what have you."

Some of the threats had been mailed from prison. Many more were the work of nameless, addressless cowards. And of these, quite a few made elaborate use of magazine cutouts and paste.

"Jesus," Bunko complained, "these guys never learn, do they? It's always 'Dear Scumbag' or 'Hello, Fuckface.' That's so stupid. Nobody with any brains or common sense is going to read any further. My feeling is you start off polite, show some good manners. You know, like 'Dear Sir' or 'If it please the court.' Then right in the middle of it you take their heads off with something like, 'And by the way, asshole, I'm going to kill your children and eat your dog.' Do you see my point? It's more effective that way."

Eamon said, "Whoever did the chain letter knew that. You remember? It just went 'Greetings,' man."

He was in his bedroom, sealed off in air-conditioned comfort, drinking beers and listening to Van Morrison's "Moondance," which was probably his all-time favorite album. Nicole, his college girlfriend, had turned him on to the many pleasures of

39

Van, and he remembered the luminous dial of his old stereo and the way they would snuggle together in his single bed in that bare, institutional room, just "Into the Mystic" and Nicole's sweet baby-powder smell.

Eamon needed a woman. Not just any woman, but a keeper. He wanted to lie in the dark again, entwined and connected and absolutely sure. He thought about Seppala again, not Seppala the cop, but Seppala the Roman-Greco goddess. He thought about smooth, dark legs and round, purple eyes and all the mysteries in between. He didn't even know her first name. And he felt funny kissing *Detective Seppala*—even if it was just wishful thinking at this point.

He was annoyed when the phone bleeped. It was almost eleven, too late for calls.

"Yeah, this better be good," Eamon said, full of menace.

"It's me, Christy. I hope I didn't wake you."

"No, it's okay," he told the fifteen-year-old. "How did you get my number, anyway?"

"You're in the book, good-lookin'. Didn't you know that?"

"Christy, I don't know if this is such a good idea."

"You said I could call. You promised."

"Yeah, I did," he said, defeated. "What's up?"

"I'm lonely. I'm just so lonely. I got no one to talk to."

"Look, loneliness is a part of life. That's just the way it is."

She said, "I bet you never get lonely. I bet not."

"Sure I do, all the goddamn time," he said, the defenses down.

"Maybe we could, like, help each other out."

"Hey," he said, changing subjects, "did you see that we indicted Lou Ackerman? That man's on his way to prison, you just watch."

"I'll believe it when I see it," she snapped.

"I don't think he's got a prayer, kiddo."

"You don't know about people like that," she said,

the voice of hard experience. "You don't know how it works."

"Well, I'm not going to argue with you about—"

"Eamon, will you be my boyfriend?" she asked, going soft again.

"Christy—"

"I just need somebody to love me, you know? Didn't you ever feel that way?"

"Yeah, sure," he said, tired to his very soul. "We're all looking, you know. That doesn't change, not if you're fifteen or thirty-four. That's the pain of it."

"I still wish you'd be my boyfriend. We don't have to do anything if you don't want. We don't have to do all that."

"It can't happen," he said earnestly. "It just can't. I'm sorry."

"You know, it wasn't my fault what happened to me. I didn't want to do what those men made me do. Lou the Dog is full of shit. I read what he said in the paper about how I loved havin' sex with everyone. That's not true. I didn't want to do all those things. You have to believe me."

He was silent, just out of his league.

"I never told anybody how it really happened," she continued, close to tears. "You know how it happened, don't you? Lou had a gun. That's how they made me do all those awful things."

"Why didn't you tell us that before?"

"Nobody ever believes a slut," she said.

# *Five*

Judith Shank was not an attractive woman by anyone's standard. Unfortunately, the hefty, acne-scarred six-footer in farmer overalls with the Brillo-pad coiffure looked like too many people's idea of a militant feminist lesbian, which she was.

"No, we didn't orchestrate this one," Judith said, examining the chain letter. "But believe me, I wouldn't mind taking credit for it."

Bunko and Eamon were at NMTE headquarters—Now More Than Ever—a cramped storefront on Eager in Mount Vernon. This was their third stop of the afternoon; they'd already hit the Maryland Lesbian Alliance and paid a call on the Baltimore Women's Center For Political Action. An overhead fan spun lazily on a 103-degree day, rustling up propaganda pamphlets but otherwise doing nothing to alter their sticky discomfort.

"Do you have any idea who might be behind this?" Bunko asked, perspiring like a sprinkler.

"Even if I did," Judith said, starting to chuckle, "I wouldn't tell you two petunia heads."

"Why is that?" Bunko asked tightly, his neck a fine lobster red.

"Because you're the enemy."

"Beg your pardon—"

"Oh, yes, yes, don't deny it," Judith said with religious fervor. "You two with all your white spermy power. You get whatever you want, don't you?"

"You're out of your mind, lady," Bunko said. "I haven't had what I wanted since I was eleven years old. All I do is work and pay bills and contemplate suicide."

"Oh, don't give me that," she snorted. "What do you take me for? A petunia head like you? Don't you think I see what's going on? You male white children have all the good jobs, all the money. You can have sex whenever you want—"

"Just a fuckin', cotton-pickin' minute here!" Bunko roared, holding his hand up like a traffic cop. *"Sex anytime I want?* What, are you nuts? Let me tell you something, Martina Navratilova: that is one thing that is unequivocally, without a doubt, always and forever left up to the female of the species. And as for your equally bizarre notion that we have all the good jobs and money—"

"Well, maybe not you personally," Judith admitted.

"Damn right, lady. By the time I pay the alimony, the mortgage, and the electric I'm lucky to wind up with bus fare."

"See, you are a petunia head, then."

"Maybe I am at that," Bunko said, sighing.

Eamon wanted to bring them back to the business at hand. "So you've never seen this chain letter before?"

"Why do you think I know anything anyway?"

Eamon picked up a pink mimeograph that had blown to the floor and began to read: "NMTE advocates the use of force and any other means necessary to overthrow the White Male Supremacist Government and its sperm-confused policies of domination and oppression and systematic rape and . . ."

*"Oh, that,"* she said, as if they were silly even to bring it up. "Just part of our fund-raising efforts. If we didn't jazz those things up, we'd lose out to our competitors. You know, there are quite a few freedom-expressive groups in our area and only a limited pool of donor resources."

"Thanks for your time," Bunko said, tired of the whole assignment.

They walked back out into a world that was the virtual equivalent of a Finnish sauna. Bunko said, "Remember when we used to have an ozone layer? Christ, those were the good ol' days."

"Don't get sentimental on me, big guy. You know how I hate that."

They passed an S and M shop, a cheery window of whips and harnesses and leather underwear. A female couple with Marine Corps haircuts held hands and admired the merchandise.

"To be young and in bondage," Bunko remarked.

"Don't start," Eamon warned.

"Listen, I got nothing against lesbians, except we're competing for a 'limited pool of donor resources.'"

"C'mon, Bunk. They got enough trouble without you making dumb comments."

"Yeah, you're right," Bunko said, shrugging. "Besides, I should know better. My own brother is gay. I probably never told you that. Yeah, only found out a year ago. I always had my suspicions, though."

"Does it change anything?"

"Not really. Frank is Frank, you know. That doesn't change. Oh, sometimes he'll talk about his life, about who he's seeing and all that, and I find I have a little problem there. For some reason I don't like to be confronted with it. Easier just not to deal with it. But then again that's not really fair to my brother. I tell him about my girlfriends and my experiences, so why shouldn't he be able to do the same?"

"Yeah, anyone who has to hear about your sordid love life should be able to get even."

"Ha, ha. Thanks a lot. I try to open up to you, try to confide my innermost, sacred feelings—and what do I get? A lot of insulting sarcasm, a lot of grief, that's what. Once again, Wearie, you've reminded me of how truly and bitterly alone we are on the planet. I think we better have a drink before I start feeling all miserable and everything."

The man was incorrigible. Eamon followed him into Michael's, a notoriously and flamboyantly gay club. They went from bright sunshine into a dark, velvety underworld. Pairs of earringed men slow danced to Sinatra's "Strangers in the Night."

"Great happy hour," Bunko said, unconcerned. "Twofers with a free buffet."

They made their way to the long faux-marble bar. A beautiful black transvestite came for their drink orders.

"I feel like something different today," Bunko said.

The he-she bartender with the fake breasts and silken legs said, "I make a fab lime daiquiri, darlings."

"Sweetheart, that sounds like just the ticket."

"Same for you too, my little Dove Bar?" the bartender said, searching Eamon's eyes.

"Yeah, I guess so," Eamon said. "We've come this far."

The bartender, who was in a low-cut, red satin dress with fishnet stockings, winked at him and then went to fix their drinks.

"How do I let you talk me into these things?" Eamon complained.

"You're easily led astray," Bunko said, watching the bartender pour Bacardi into a stainless-steel blender. "Still, she ain't bad for a guy. Christ, she's hotter than Franny."

"Oh, don't tell me you're going latent on me. I'll tell you right now, that's more than I can handle."

"We should probably check in with Kelsey," Bunko said, ignoring it.

"And Masterson. I want to tell him what Christy said about Ackerman."

"You don't really think he forced her into a life of pornography with a gun, do you?"

"I believe her," Eamon said shortly.

"Christ, you tell Masterson then. Because I'm sure he's going to want to know all about your little late-night phone calls with a teenage pro. Christ, you got some quarters?"

Bunko went off to make some calls. The bartender returned with two tall, frosty green drinks.

"I made them extra special," he-she said. "My secret is kiwi. Just a little dab will do you."

"I'm sure they're great. How much do I owe you?"

"You don't owe me a thing," the bartender said, winking again. "But your companion owes me three dollars. I know it's not any of my business, but I think you can do a whole lot better, really."

"Don't I know it," Eamon said glumly.

He sipped his daiquiri while watching the earringed men sway to Bobby Vinton's "Blue Velvet." It seemed to him, here, now, in the tainted light of a darkened lounge, in the strange, lost hours of a Friday afternoon, that all men suffered from a terrible, insatiable hunger and that it was all pretty much hopeless in the end.

"Who died?" Bunko said upon returning. "Cheer up, you just hit the goddamn jackpot."

"What are you talking about?"

"I'm talking about the date I arranged for you tonight."

Eamon said, "What now? Don't tell me you met somebody in the washroom, anything but that."

"You, my friend, are having after-dinner cocktails with one Detective Mary Seppala. You're on stakeout. At that Inner Harbor joint, Silk Stockings. The blonde last seen with Judge Draper showed up there the last two Fridays. You lucky, undeserving bastard."

"Things are definitely looking up," Eamon crowed happily. "Hey, not that I didn't want to spend Friday night *with you and the boys,* but—"

At that moment a muscular, leather-clad dude approached. Eamon braced himself for the inevitable —and was surprised when he directed his attentions toward Bunko.

"I know I haven't seen you in here before. It would be impossible to forget a face like yours. There's just so much character in it, so much honest living. My name's Rick. I don't want to be too forward, but I was hoping we might swing to a tune or two."

"I'm sorry, Rick," Bunko said to that expectant face. "It's just that my lover here gets so possessive with me. You know how it is. Someone just looks at me—"

"Oh, don't I know it," Rick said sympathetically. "Jealousy—that old green-eyed monster."

Eamon had had the time to go home and shower and shave again. He'd slicked his hair back and patted himself with Paco Rabanne. Then he'd chosen his clothes with unusual care, deliberating long and hard before arriving at the teal blue silk jacket and the impressionistic tie that was as beautiful as anything Monet ever painted.

He only had to keep reminding himself that he wasn't on a date.

Mary Seppala had no such problem. She ordered another Perrier with a twist. He did the same.

Eamon had been to Silk Stockings once before, a few months back on a restless, dateless night. It was on the top floor of one of the newer hotels, with floor-to-ceiling views of the harbor and its twinkle. It looked the same, lots of spruced-up yups and yupettes acting as indifferent as possible as they eyed each other with supreme horniness. A lucky few danced under the flashing, colored lights as a lonely wagon train of singles circled them and waited for that second glance from an impossible stranger. The music was an incessant Top-40 pounding, Madonna and the Stones, Janet Jackson and Boy George, one after the other, with no happy end in sight.

"I still don't understand the logic," Seppala said. "What's the motive for taking out Judge Draper and Molly Webster? What did they really do to earn the retribution of this chain letter?"

Before Eamon could answer, Seppala continued, "Do you remember the trial, really remember it? It was a sick little mess. You had that smug rich boy, Graham Cowel, who was obviously guilty as sin. Remember how those other women came forward with their own stories of attempted rape and worse?"

"Yes, but nothing was ever proved. I mean, those girls never went to the police with their charges or—"

"That's because the system doesn't work," Seppala issued forcefully. "And women know that. Who wants to have their name and reputation dragged through the mud? Defense attorneys are expert at taking apart a rape victim on the stand. In a few minutes they can transform a relatively virtuous young woman into the devil's whore—"

"I'm not going to disagree with you," Eamon said, "but I still don't see what this has to do with Draper and Webster."

"I don't know either," she said, coming up against it. "It's just that I understand the anger of the victim. Before I was shifted to homicide, I was with the sex crimes unit. So I had the unfortunate privilege of sitting through a dozen or so rape trials. And I remember Draper, I remember his scowling, ridiculing looks. The way he would look at these victims, with such unmitigated condescension. It was the same way at the Cowel trial."

"I still don't know what you're getting at."

48

He was practically annoyed with her, the way she kept going back to their grim workaday world. He wanted to converse with Mary, the beauty in the amber blouse and black mini with black stockings. Detective Seppala could wait for another day.

"Her name was Grace Sexton," she said. "No one was supposed to know who she was. But then one of the newspapers released her name—and that was all she wrote. Don't you remember? Through most of the trial, at least the televised trial, they covered her face with a black dot. Womanhood eradicated."

"So what are you saying? Are you saying this Grace Sexton had something to do with the killings?"

"I don't know," she said, getting herself worked up. "But every angle has to be pursued. We should check into Grace Sexton, and then maybe we should look into the matter of those other women who came out of the Graham Cowel woodwork."

"I don't know about you," Eamon said, moving on, "but I'm going to have a real drink now."

He called the bartender over and ordered a lime daiquiri. The tuxedoed lug made a face at the request, a blender special with a crowded, yammering bar.

He returned with said drink, slamming it down disdainfully. "That'll be five bucks, Lieutenant."

"Listen," Eamon said, "I need to know a few things more about this woman."

"Can't you see I'm busy?" he protested.

"I need a better description than what you've given. An attractive, short-haired blonde doesn't cut the mustard."

"Well, what do you want to know exactly?" he said, eyeing the clamoring throng.

"How old was she?"

"How should I know?"

"How old do you think?"

"Maybe forty, something like that."

"What was she wearing?"

"White pantsuit, silky kind of thing, expensive."

**49**

"Any jewelry?"

"Yeah, come to think of it, pearls. Ropes of pearls."

"Eye color?"

"Green, emerald green. Nice eyes, yeah."

"Glasses? Contacts?"

"I'm not sure. Maybe contacts. Hard to say."

"Was she smoking?"

"Yeah, come to think of it, she was. Merit Lights."

"How were her teeth?"

"Capped."

"Good. Any tattoos or scars?"

"Nah, nothing like that."

"Describe her haircut for me."

"Joan of Arc."

"Okay, how about her complexion? Blotchy, clear, what?"

"Some acne on the cheeks."

"How did she sound? Any inflections, a speech impediment, what?"

"Kind of like 'Cheers.'"

"What are you talking about?"

"You know, 'Cheers,' the TV show."

"Kind of a Boston accent, then?"

"Yeah, that's the ticket. Listen, I gotta get back to the mob."

As he disappeared into the clamoring sea, Seppala said, "I'm impressed. You have the instinct, Lieutenant."

"Let's change the subject," he said, taking the chance to look into her opaque eyes.

"Why, Lieutenant, we're on assignment," she said, laughing at his apparent ardor.

"Mary, talk to me," he said simply, directly.

"What do you want to know?" she asked, a bar stool away.

"Are you married?"

She laughed. "Boy, this doesn't sound like official business."

"Have you ever been?"

"No, I don't believe in making mistakes," she said forthrightly.

In that moment he realized that she was the whole package: smart, truthful, beautiful, sexy, as good as it gets. She was a keeper, all right.

"Don't look at me like that," she said.

"What do you mean?"

"Like the way you were looking at me at the courthouse yesterday. That way."

He was silent, confronted with the overwhelming evidence.

"We hardly know each other," she said quietly.

"Does it have to be that way?" he implored.

"Look, if you want to go out with me, you do like the other boys do. You call me up on the telephone and ask politely, and then I get to decide for myself."

"This is starting to look like a challenge," he said, smiling.

"Look," she said, unsmiling, "don't think of me in those terms. A mountain is a challenge, not a woman."

"I didn't mean it like that."

"Men are always doing that—looking at us like we're some kind of sporting event. It's always, 'How far did you go?' 'Did you score?' 'Did she put up any resistance?' There's something practically sick about it."

"I haven't said the right thing yet," he said, defeated.

"It's not about saying the right or the wrong thing. It's about being yourself. That's all I ask."

"Then you're asking for trouble," he joked. "The real me is no bargain."

She didn't crack a smile. "Incidentally, I liked your hair the way it was, without all the gook in it."

"At least you noticed," he said with all the mirth of a funeral.

"It doesn't look like our woman's going to show," she said, back on the case.

"Let's give it a little while longer," he said, still hoping to salvage what was left of the evening.

"Oh, all right," she said without an iota of enthusiasm.

To hell with what she said, he thought. This woman was one major-league challenge.

Bryan Ferry was crooning "Dance Away." Eamon stared out at the pulsating lights of the dance floor, at those energetic and temporary couplings. He looked as forlorn and alone as any other single there.

# *Six*

$\backsim\!\sim$

*H*e had made the Enoch Pratt Free Library—that giant, philanthropic monument on Cathedral—his first stop of the morning. He'd searched and clicked his way through the *Sun*'s coverage of the Sexton-Cowel trial, scanning thousands of column inches as quickly as humanly possible. With the assistance of a librarian he'd made copies from the microfilm of those stories he hoped might provide clues, but that he knew were just as likely to yield zilch. The librarian had said one thing that was slightly odd: "I'm getting tired of making copies of these same old clippings," she'd whined. In his hurry he had just let the remark fly by; it wasn't until a few hours later that it began to gnaw at him.

He had awoke that morning with only one thing on his mind.

Seppala's long, dark legs.

The Ultimate Challenge.

He'd blown the first impressions part of the test. Now it was time for the second part, the get back in her good graces part.

It was obvious that Detective Seppala liked nothing better than a snappy piece of detective work. Why, the only time she seemed to show any interest was when he'd extracted a physical description of their suspect —the last person to see Judge Draper alive—out of that tuxedoed lug of a bartender. They were looking for a forty-something, Merit Light–smoking, Boston-accented, bejeweled, apparently well-to-do, emerald-eyed blonde with a Joan of Arc haircut. Some acne on the cheeks, he almost forgot that.

Eamon Wearie, ace detective. Yeah, that was the ticket.

He was still thinking about violet eyes and ocher skin and silky dark legs when he arrived at the Command Post. It was just after ten in the morning, on a Saturday no less.

The place was practically deserted, a sore reminder of everyone else's lazy, barbecue-laden weekend plans. He himself should've been down at Nags Head, at his folks' ocean-front condo, lying on the beach and spying string bikinis. His vacation time was way past due.

The Command Post, with its leaden tones and metal furniture, never seemed more dreary. Or more warm. Because it was the weekend, the air was shut off, only adding to the noxiousness.

"Welcome to Club Med," Bunko said dejectedly, looking like a beached tourist in a Hawaiian shirt and Bermuda shorts. "Or should I say Club Dead."

"Ah, quit your bellyaching," Masterson admonished. "You should be grateful for a case like this. This is big time, the kind of thing that gets you noticed. Raises, promotions, newspaper stories. What's not to like?"

"I'd rather be losing my life's savings in Atlantic City," Bunko said.

Masterson paid no mind. "Our first order of business is to find out—and don't ask me how—if that chain letter has been sent to anyone else. Any suggestions?"

Eamon said, "Maybe we could plant a story in the paper."

Masterson shot it down. "How dumb can you get, Lieutenant? It's the one damn clue we have. The moment the press gets wind of it, it's all over."

"I was thinking of something a bit more subtle," Eamon said coolly. "I thought that we might get some little story in about, say, the problem of chain letters in general. Then what we do is quote directly from our little number. Plant a few lines and see if it rings any bells."

"And how, may I ask, are we going to get this story in the paper? Last time I checked we were postal inspectors and not reporters."

Bunko piped up, "Franny could get it in, no problem. At the end of it we post a police telephone number, advising the harassed and victimized to call. See what turns up. Worth a shot."

"I don't like it," Masterson said. "Who's ever behind the chain might see the story, too. We might just wind up scaring our bunny rabbit."

"I guess that's a chance we'll have to take," Bunko said.

"I'm with Bunko on this," Eamon said, providing backup.

"Of course you are," Masterson growled. "You two girls are always together. Makes me wonder sometimes. Because you two girls sure like each other an awful lot. I hate to say it, but it's almost unnatural."

Neither of them took the bait.

"Incidentally, Ryan, I love your costume. What are you supposed to be? A Hawaiian chieftain at a luau? You forget about the dress code? Or is this just another symptom on that growing list pointing to court-mandated institutionalization?"

"It's Saturday," Bunko reminded him. "Besides,

I'm on vacation. In fact, I'm not really here. I'm on the beach ordering another piña colada from the Swedish beach hostess. Uh-oh, Ulla wants to give me another Coppertone rubdown. And she won't take no for an answer. What shall I do?"

"Lard Ass, you're absolutely hopeless."

"Thank you for noticing, sir."

"All right, enough fun and games," Masterson announced. "Here's the way it's going to play: Plant the story and see that you don't fuck up."

"Your confidence is underwhelming," Bunko said. "We'll do our best to live down to it."

Masterson turned to Eamon and said, "I want you to call your little girlfriend and arrange for her to come back in. We need to formalize Baby Face's charges. Get it all on tape. That is, if the whore's telling the truth about Ackerman and the gun."

"She's telling the truth all right," Eamon said sharply. "And there's no need to refer to her as a whore."

"Take it easy, Lieutenant. I didn't mean to diss your little pudding pie. What you got goin' on? Is the little whore doing the pretty boy? Is that what it is?"

Eamon narrowed his eyes, but otherwise held his fire.

"All right then," a smiling Masterson said. "I'll be in my office if you fags need me."

When he was gone, Bunko said, "He's a sad case, really. The son of a bitch doesn't have a friend in the world."

"I don't know why not," Eamon said. "All that charm and good humor. You'd think the phone would never stop ringing."

"Believe me, he already regrets it. Right now the poor bastard is reaching back into his filing cabinet for the Wild Turkey. He spends most of his time trying to forget the things he says."

"Yeah, well so do I," Eamon said.

With that they returned to their desks to make calls.

Bunko punched up Franny, while Eamon phoned Christy Gertz.

"Oh," she squealed, delighted, "I just knew you'd call!"

"Christy, it's not what you think."

"You know what I want to do on our date? I just want to go out for a cheeseburger and a movie. Nothing fancy, you know. I just want to do what other girls my age do."

"Christy, we're not going on a date. That's not in the cards. Not ever."

"Do you know what I've been doin'? I've just been waitin' by the phone for you, good-lookin'. I don't even mind admittin' it."

"Christy, have you even heard a word I've said?"

"I keep playin' the same song over and over on the CD. It's this one by the Red Hot Chili Peppers called 'Under the Bridge.' You ever hear it?"

"Yeah, it's a good song, Christy."

"Well, I just keep playing it and thinkin' about you for some reason."

"Christy, you've got to stop thinking about me. You know that, don't you?"

"You can't tell me to stop thinking about you. You can't take that away. That's the only thing I got."

"Christy—"

"'Cause I know you got a good heart. And I need to be rescued by somebody. Can't you see that?"

"Christy, we need you to come back in and make another statement. About Lou Ackerman and your charge that he made you do things against your will with a gun."

There was silence on the other end.

"Christy? You there?"

"I'm not comin' in," she finally said.

"What are you talking about?"

"I want to put it behind me. I don't want to keep goin' through it. That part of my life is history."

"You don't want Lou Ackerman to get away with it, do you?"

"He'll get what's coming to him," she said adamantly. "Don't you worry."

"What do you mean?"

"He's a scumbag. And scumbags always die like scumbags."

The late afternoon found Eamon Wearie deep in the heart of Dead Letters, at the Unpublished Novelists' Hall of Fame. The desultory heat of the Command Post had driven him down into his favorite part of the netherworld, into the cool-as-a-grave Hall, which was where they shelved the thousands upon thousands of returned and rejected manuscripts. They were bruised and battered packages, showing all too clearly the outward scars of their struggle and fight upstream. Insufficient postage, the bane of authors everywhere, was usually behind their purgatorial detention.

The Hall was a comforting place, with its homey, stuffing-oozing armchair and reading lamp. In the old days, newly arrived and without friends, he had liked nothing better than killing his lunch hour in the musty timelessness of the Hall, thumbing through someone's idiosyncratic masterpiece. Oh, the books weren't much good—at least not if you were judging them on the predictable triumvirate of plot, characterization, and dialogue—not that they didn't offer their own sweetly held pleasures, since there was nothing quite like looking into the uncensored, ungrammatical, nonsensical soul.

But today Eamon sifted through the pages of a courtroom thriller—through the piecemeal newspaper history of the Sexton-Cowel trial. He kept coming back to the AP and UPI photos of Judge Draper and Assistant DA Molly Webster. Now that they were dead, it was easy to project added meaning into their blurry, out-of-focus faces. The twice-divorced Draper appeared to be your typical white-haired, black-robed institution, full of high-backed haughtiness and grim resolve. The thirty-five-year-old, Georgetown Law–educated Webster was pretty in a severe, professional way, the picture of eternal and singular unamusement. She had never married and had lived with her neutered cat, Bigsby, in a Federal Hill brownstone. Other than that, the stories were noticeably free of details from her personal life. Colleagues described her as "work devoted" and "brilliantly unemotional" and "trenchantly thorough." There was no sense that she had friends or hobbies or had in any way a life outside the courthouse.

Molly Webster proved to be Eamon Wearie's greatest headache. He couldn't at all fathom why the Committee—supposing that kiss-sealed missive had anything to do with it—would want to kill her. Why wouldn't the Committee, with all its extremist, anti-penile posturing, have taken out Graham Cowel instead? After all, wasn't he the smug, young, unconvicted rapist?

Eamon wondered again about the makeup of the Committee. Was it really a group of disenchanted, feminist vigilantes? Or was it more likely a committee of one? He couldn't help thinking of Grace Sexton, Cowel's accuser, the nineteen-year-old University of Maryland coed who'd been unlucky enough to appear in Draper's courtroom. Cowel's defense attorney painted her in predictable shades of scarlet, as he dipped his heavy-handed brush into her sexual past and colored her testimony with lurid suspicion. Although his searing cross-examination went a long way to discrediting Sexton in the eyes of the jury, he was not without help according to the reporters who covered the trial. Judge Draper offered his familiar raised eyebrows, that look of condescension and permanent disbelief of which Seppala had spoken. Eamon was surprised to learn that the judge who'd been known as "Hang 'Em High" Draper had, in fact, been notoriously lenient toward sexual offenders; in one celebrated incident, he'd given a convicted rapist a suspended sentence with this bit of irreverent advice: "I know you like the girls, son, but you have to learn to obey the laws."

While Eamon could see why the Committee might want to end the judicial career of Harold Draper, there was still the matter of Molly Webster. Reporters described her approach as one that mixed "icy detachment" with "prosecutorial zeal"; there was nothing in her manner that coddled the victim or lent emotional support to Grace Sexton's testimony.

Still.

Lack of warmth didn't seem like much of a reason to assassinate someone.

Eamon noted that Grace Sexton's father was a man of resources, the owner of a chain of supermarkets. After the trial, Grace had checked into a mental hospital for several months, suffering under the all-inclusive heading of "exhaustion." That was the last mention of her whereabouts.

He realized that they were going to have to look into the other rape trials Draper and Webster had worked together. Grace Sexton surely wasn't the only woman to have had a difficult time in Draper's *superior* court. And she probably wasn't the only one to have second-guessed Webster's chilly and unsympathetic method.

As usual there was too much to do. It made him tired just thinking about it. At least Dead Letters was quiet for once. Early on a Saturday evening the huge old sorting machines in Docket C 14 were working at half strength, more a distant rumble than the normal deafening roar. The only people about seemed to be the janitorial unit, a twenty-man division who took advantage of the lull by washing and waxing the dull, impenetrable flooring with their motorized mops.

The Unpublished Novelists' Hall of Fame smelled like chlorine and moldering paper, the schizophrenic flavoring of an antiseptic library. Just for the hell of it he decided to pick out one of those detained and

60

decaying manuscripts. He always got a kick out of it, the way his touch could bring those long-lost pages back to life.

His random choice had, fittingly enough, been sent to Random House on February 10, 1984. The Billings, Montana, postmark was still clear and true, but the Magic Marker return address had been smudged out of existence. The ten-year-old manuscript hadn't even got a cursory read. Someone, some intern most likely, had scrawled over the manila face, "RETURN TO SENDER/ NO UNSOLICITED MS."

The first thing he came across was a short cover letter. Eve Upton, the manuscript's author, had written simply:

> This here is a true story disguised as a novel. I've changed the names and everything, but that still don't mean it ain't true. Please do not be put off by its vulgarity and excessive sex scenes. It really happened the way I said it did.

The novel was called *What the Bastard Did to Me*. Underneath the title it said, "A true story of heartbreak and betrayal."

Eamon didn't need to read any more.

It was just the way his luck was running.

He couldn't sleep. The sealed-off feeling of air-conditioning always made him feel as if he were in some motel room. At around two in the morning he went outside on his porch to drink a beer and smoke a cigarette.

Even now it was warm and muggy as hell. All down the block he could hear the bedroom air-conditioning units humming away, doing their little drip-drip on the sidewalk. It was a relatively quiet, working-class neighborhood of bright red-brick row houses, solidly maintained and defended. But on a Saturday night in Fells Point that didn't mean much. There were so many bars and saloons in close proximity that you could hear the house rock bands and even the occasional drunk heaving or pissing in a nearby alleyway. And it wasn't all that faint.

Ah, what did it matter? he thought. It's what people did on a Saturday night, all through the land. Everyone got drunk and tried to forget about who they were. They danced to loud, amateur rantings and made passes at people they didn't know. It was all drink and try to get laid and piss all your troubles away into the giant, enamel urinal of life.

He understood it just fine. In truth, it made the most sense to him. What else was there? There was just pretty girls and cold beer and sometimes, if you were lucky, the two of them together. Anyone who told you different was a liar or a missionary.

He wanted Mary Seppala.

He wanted that.

She was a keeper, and he hadn't run into that in a long time. He was tired of the running around. He was tired of the lonely, air-conditioned nights. He didn't want to wind up like Pinkus, his tenant. He didn't want to go into the priesthood, or anywhere near it. And he didn't want to share his bedroom with two obese cats and a 15,000 megawatt air-conditioner. Pinkus's machine made about the same amount of noise as one of those supersonic jets.

He heard two guys getting into it a few blocks away. One of them said, "What's it to you, asshole?" The other said, "I saw her first." He didn't want to hear any more. He didn't want to be a part of it anymore. He'd done his fair share of drinking and staring and trying to pick up babes in the bar night. It wasn't worth it. Shit, it wasn't anywhere.

He lit up another Marlboro and took another long, unhealthy drag. In the blue darkness he thought of Seppala again. Her fragrant, raven hair. Those amethyst eyes. Her dark, Romanesque skin. Those legs that did forever.

# SEALED WITH A KISS

He needed something to believe in.

You see, it wasn't a question of wanting anymore.

Just like Christy Gertz he needed somebody to rescue him. His heart was no different from some fifteen-year-old girl's. It hungered just the same.

He would probably have smoked cigarettes and thought good things right until dawn if that phone hadn't started bleeping. He practically jumped at the sound. He knew nobody called that late unless something was terribly wrong.

It was Death's time of the morning.

# *Seven*

A uniformed patrolman directed traffic outside of Lou Ackerman's garishly lighted row house on Eden, which turned out to be only ten blocks away from Eamon's own place. Besides a gaggle of bathrobe-clad neighbors, there were two squad cars and an ambulance parked out front.

Inside it was organized confusion. There were just too many cops and detectives and forensic technicians. Eamon was surprised to find Mary Seppala directing traffic. She was in the entryway dismissing two blue uniforms; she gave them a photograph of Ackerman and asked them to canvass the immediate area.

"I found the snapshot on his bureau," she told Eamon. "Maybe someone remembers seeing him with somebody earlier in the evening."

"Who called it in?" he asked.

"Ackerman."

"He called in his own murder?"

"He needed an ambulance. Came in at one twenty-two this morning," she said matter-of-factly. "He was barely audible. I haven't listened to the tape yet but I've been told that he said something like, 'The bitch did me.' We assume he's referring to a female assailant. But we have no idea if he knew his killer."

Eamon couldn't help remembering Christy Gertz's prescient words: *He'll get what's coming to him. Don't you worry. He's a scumbag. And scumbags always die like scumbags.* He had a bad little feeling, but for some reason he didn't say anything about it to Seppala.

A police photographer, loaded down with cameras, pushed past them into the living room. He set up a floodlight and began filming with a videocamera. In fact, the whole house was bright with artificial light.

"Special Crime Scene Unit," Seppala explained. "They record everything. They've already dusted and checked for latents. I think they're almost through collecting and bagging the physical evidence. We usually do the mule work ourselves, but on the big cases we get the luxury of the SCSU."

"Impressive," he said, admiring their close attention to detail. "By the way, is Bunko here?"

"We tried to reach your partner, but had no luck."

"Oh, Bunk's probably out tying one on."

"Actually," she said, pausing to look him over, "I was surprised to find you home."

"I'm not sure how to take that," he said, doing his own pausing and looking. He was amazed at how well put together she was. Three in the morning and the makeup was applied and the hair perfectly set. "How the hell do you do it?"

"I'm used to late-night calls," she answered.

"Where did you find the chain letter?"

"You couldn't miss it, really. It was mailed right into his chest. Postmarked with a large kitchen knife."

"Wait a minute, I thought you said Ackerman called an ambulance. How could he do that with a knife in his chest?"

"We're not quite sure. I'm guessing that that came later. The killer might have been leaving when she

65

heard a badly wounded Ackerman making his call for help. She probably realized her mistake and came back to finish the job. Like I said, we're still piecing it together."

"So how was he wounded in the first place? With that same kitchen knife?"

"It looks like he was shot. We've found bullet casings. We won't know for sure until the medical examiner finishes with the body. He was stabbed so many times that it was impossible to notice a bullet's entry or exit."

"Sounds real pretty."

"Oh, it is. Whoever did this even took the trouble to remove Ackerman's eyes. How's your stomach, Lieutenant? You think you can handle it?"

"I don't know. I've been known to faint at the sight of blood."

"Then I guess I'll have to catch you."

"In that case, lead the way," he said.

She led him upstairs to Ackerman's crowded bedroom. Detective Kelsey was there. So was a pair of Emergency Medical Service workers, along with the medical examiner and someone from the district attorney's office. There was also a stiff, white-faced patrolman standing in a blood-soaked corner, as much out of the way as possible.

Eamon had never seen so much blood.

It was as if someone had poured a couple of cans of tomato juice into a topless blender and hit the spatter button.

It made no difference that the walls and carpeting had been an obscene lavender to begin with.

Ackerman's naked body was spread-eagled on the circular water bed, a giant hairy stain. That's what was left of him. It was just this eyeless, bearded, hirsute, matted thing. The ME was placing paper bags over its hands.

"To preserve the trace evidence," Seppala explained quietly. "Paper works better than plastic. Doesn't promote decomposition."

Ackerman's bedroom was a *pad*—a slick, air-brushed page out of the annals of Hugh Hefner, some primitive male notion of seduction and sixties cool, the last word in mirrored ceilings and track light-ing and remote-controlled excess. The lights were dimmed, the air was cooled, and the music swelled from a bedside panel.

Lou Ackerman had even shared Hugh Hefner's idea of art: a large, colorful LeRoy Neiman oil. It depicted a crowd scene at the old ballpark, thousands of dot-sized spectators in the throes of adulation.

That was part of it, after all.

The mirrors and the adoring crowds.

Eamon realized that that was how he'd got off. Sex, for him, had been a spectator sport, a see-and-be-seen virtual reality. And his killer seemed to know that. She hadn't left Ackerman that way by accident. No, she had wanted to make a point with that naked, empty-socketed thing.

Eamon had the sense of being on a movie set, the same ever-bright unrealness: cameras and floodlights; extras and crew mulling about a ketchup-splattered set; a polystyrene corpse that could have been left over from one of those *Nightmare on Elm Street* movies.

"Did you happen to notice the message on the mirror over his bed?" Seppala asked.

At first he thought it had been more blender spin-nings, but now he could make out the drippy red script:

*They just don't get it, do they?*

Seppala said, "We think it was done with his own blood. But we'll have to check that in the lab."

"Jesus, you'd think that the killer would've been drenched in the stuff. I mean, how could she get out of here without somebody noticing something?"

"The canvassing team is out there right now asking that very question."

"Where's the phone that Ackerman used to call nine-one-one?"

"Portable. Discovered on the bed."

"How long did it take for the EMS guys to get here after the call came in?"

"Seventeen minutes. Which is too long. But Saturday night is the busiest of the week. Ackerman was dead by the time they got here."

"When did the first uniformed officer arrive?"

"Five minutes later. The quiet one in the corner, Officer John Stoltz."

Eamon moved over to the young, stiff-backed officer. Seppala followed.

"John, I'm Lieutenant—"

"Lieutenant Eamon Wearie, sir," Officer Stoltz answered without making eye contact.

"How'd you know that?"

"It's my job, sir, to keep a running log of the crime-scene events, including all arrivals and departures."

"John," Eamon said, trying again to gain entry to his nervous, pale blue eyes, "this your first murder scene?"

"Yes sir."

"Mine too," Eamon said, trying to put him at ease.

"I've seen dead people before," the young man said, "but nothing like this. Usually old people who couldn't handle the heat, stuff like that. Always smells so bad, you know."

"This smell differently?"

"Actually, it did, sir. You could still smell the perfume. The EMS boys smelled it too. We finally decided it was that Ralph Lauren one. Only reason I know that is it's the one my gal likes. Alison made me get it for her last birthday. Called Ralph Lauren's Safari. Yes sir, I'm sure of it."

"That's real good, Stoltz," Eamon said.

"Yes it is," Seppala said, looking at Eamon.

Kelsey came over and tapped her on the shoulder. "Mary, the ME's ready to go, if you want to take one of your Kodak memories."

The EMS workers were lifting Ackerman's bulk onto a stretcher. Eamon watched as Seppala took out a minicamera and snapped a few flashes of Ackerman's backside and the spot where the body had been.

"She's very thorough," Kelsey said by way of explanation.

Eamon said, "I thought that Special Crime Scene Unit took care of all the pictures."

"They do. At least for the official court record. But Mary, she never goes anywhere without that thing. She says it helps to refresh her memory later."

The representative from the district attorney's office joined them. Arnold Bing was a short, balding, horn-rimmed nebbish in a madras jacket and white suede bucks. This was not to mention the tie, which was a full-blown aquatic disaster, full of laughing, splashing dolphins.

"Love the tie, Bing," Kelsey commented.

"Thanks. Big clearance sale at Brooks Brothers."

"I'll just bet."

You knew Bing was in trouble, Eamon thought, if Kelsey, not exactly a fashion plate himself, felt free to take potshots. The buzz-sawed redhead was dressed to confuse in a cranberry-colored shirt and black polyester pants. He had to be Bunko's long-lost twin.

"So what do you think, Kelse my man?" Bing said, trying to sound like one of the boys and failing miserably. "Are we talking about the same killing-machine bitch who aced my Molley McGee?"

"Bing, who the fuck knows at this point? You gotta remember those observant witnesses on Redwood couldn't even tell us if the trench coat who took out Webster was a boy or a girl. And then you got to throw into the slop the fact that a different gun was used on her than the one that took out the judge and that Mount Vernon barkeep. For all we know, her killing is unrelated to the others. It's impossible to say."

"Well, it's a terrible shame about Molly," Bing related in a newly reverent tone. "She was quite the lovely person. Not that I really knew her well. But I will tell you this, men: I had quite the soft spot for the Mollymeister. In fact, speaking in the strictest confidence, I was working up the old Bingster nerve to ask her out when this terrible tragedy struck."

"Bing, no way you were ever going to ask her out," Kelsey said scornfully. "It's a known fact you were scared shitless of her. Just like everybody else in your office."

"Well, let's face it," Bing said glibly, "the woman was a bit of a ball breaker."

"Well, there's a real nice thing to say about a dead colleague."

"Oh, c'mon, Kelse, they're all ball breakers. That's what makes them women of the nineties. I mean, have you gone out on a date lately?"

"No, my wife doesn't let me do that anymore."

"Believe me, my man, you are not missing anything. It is simply murder out there. Forget getting any nookie. Out of the question. No chance in hell with these nineties women. You just reach over and touch them and you're looking at aggravated assault and attempted rape charges. I'm not kidding. The way things are going I don't expect to get laid again in this century."

"Perhaps that's for the best," Kelsey said deadpan.

"Kelse, you can go ahead and joke all you want, but I'm telling you it's a serious situation out there. Just look what happened to this Ackerman fellow. He thought he was about to get lucky tonight—and what the heck happens? Some crazy *Basic Instinct* psychobitch is having PMS or something and—"

Eamon cut him off. "Is there any evidence that Ackerman had sex with his killer?"

"We don't know if he got anything," Kelsey said, "but I can tell you he was damn well expecting something. The autopsy will tell us more. We did find an unopened package of condoms next to the bed."

"Sounds like the same MO as Judge Draper. Both thought they were about to get lucky. Big time."

"Very good, Lieutenant. There may be hope for you postal guys yet."

"It's strange," Bing said, "that this Ackerman gets it just as the indictments come down."

"I think our killer has been paying close attention to the newspapers," Kelsey said.

"You don't suppose this Baby Face character has anything to do with this?" Bing threw out to them.

"No, of course not," Eamon answered too quickly. "She's just a fifteen-year-old kid, for Christ' sake."

"Hey, just asking," Bing said defensively.

"I didn't think it was such a bad question," Kelsey said, appraising Eamon with equanimity.

At that moment Seppala appeared.

"I think we're ready to close this scene," she said to Kelsey. "Stoltz will seal it off, okay?"

"Why not? That's quite enough fun and action for one evening."

"You said it, brother," Bing seconded.

Then there was a small, awkward silence.

Eamon decided to take a chance. He said to Seppala, "Maybe we could have a cup of coffee now? You know, talk over the case and all that."

She smiled benignly at him before delivering the mortal blow. "Lieutenant, I thought we'd discussed all that the other night."

Then she said her good-byes and walked away, long, dark legs and everything.

"What did I tell you about these nineties women?" Bing said.

# *Eight*

❦

*H*e decided on the coffee anyway.

That meant the Hollywood diner, a twenty-four-hour vinyl-and-Formica haven on Broadway, a beacon in the Fells Point night.

Depending on how you looked at it, it was either very late on a Saturday or very early on a Sunday. Either way, the Hollywood was busy at 4 A.M. Mostly it was full of ravenous, burger-craving drunks, beery-eyed zombies who functioned on some kind of automatic pilot.

On his way in he grabbed a *Sun* from the coin-operated cage. He took a seat at the counter and started separating sections from the Sunday heft. When Betsy said, "Hi, Eamon, the usual?" he didn't even bother to look up.

He sipped black coffee while he waited for the usual. That's just the way he was, a creature of sad and determined habit. He never needed to see a menu or hear the nightly specials. He always came in knowing exactly what he was looking for.

Maybe he was going about things all wrong.

Maybe he needed to change his MO. He was thinking about Seppala again. Hell, he wasn't used to having his advances rebuffed.

He opened to the sports and read about the pennant race—the Jays and Os and Yankees were in a virtual tie as they headed into August—with Seppala's dark, reproachful face superimposed over the standings.

He couldn't seem to get her out of his mind.

He didn't like that at all.

He scanned the hard news, and wondered who was going to be next. Who was going to be the next macho prick to say the wrong thing and wind up with a knife in the heart? He was starting to think that Lou Ackerman's biggest mistake might have been giving a newspaper interview; for all they knew, the Committee was just made up of irate readers. It was as good a guess as any.

If he was right, then Admiral Lerner was a dead man. His ill-advised comments about the U.S. Naval Academy scandal made the front page. While he "didn't condone the behavior" of the Navy midshipmen who had gang-raped a motel maid, he certainly "could understand how virile, healthy young men needed to sow their wild oats."

Jesus, it was never ending.

Flipping through the Living section he came across their plant, Franny's seemingly innocuous, written-to-order story about the dangers of chain mail. Besides quoting directly from the Committee's special rendition, they'd taken a chance and included the kiss-shaped seal in the accompanying artwork. It was a dangerous gamble, but then again what wasn't?

When his order arrived—eggs over easy with bacon and potatoes and whole wheat toast—he looked up to see that Betsy had a nasty shiner.

"What happened to you?"

"Oh, you know," she said.

"What, an accident?"

"No, nothing like that. You know how Frank gets when he's been drinking."

She said it like it was nothing, just the way of the world. She went off to tend to other customers. He shook salt and pepper on his eggs, everything as normal as could be.

It took Eamon twenty-five minutes to get to Christy's grandmother's house in Dundalk. He took the telephone number and used a cross-reference directory to come up with 467 Dewdrop Road.

It was another hot, soupy, inhumane day. Of course he hadn't bothered with the air-conditioning option. The Pontiac salesman would have included it for an extra three hundred dollars. But no, he was way too smart for that little ploy.

Jesus, just touching the dashboard meant risking third-degree burns.

Dewdrop was a dead-end street, a short, dusty, despairing stretch of warehouses and auto-body shops. Christy's grandmother's house was across the street from a no-name gas station. The red Coke machine stood out by sheer brightness.

The house was three stories of peeling yellow clapboard on a narrow lot. The front lawn was a brittle, dying brown. The windows were shuttered with lace curtains—and he imagined an interior of velvet-covered ottomans and slow-ticking grandfather clocks and tables set with yellowing doilies.

Fortunately he never got as far as the front door. He heard splashing out back.

He found her there, having a good time with a garden hose and an inflatable kiddie pool. The fifteen-year-old bombshell was falling out of an outrageous, neon thong bikini, something that would've looked just fine on the beaches of Rio de Janeiro but that was an uncommon sight in the backyards of Dundalk.

She couldn't have been more happy to see him.

"Oh, I just knew you'd come!"

She wrapped her wet arms around him and gave him a soul-searching kiss.

He took a moment too long to pull back.

"You liked that, didn't you?" Christy said. "Don't lie now."

He didn't say a word.

"You want me, don't you? But it's wrong, isn't it? You're not supposed to have these desires, are you?"

She tried to kiss him again. This time he had the good sense to push her away.

"Look," he said, "I'm human. But you know the way it has to play out. So let's not make it harder than it has to be."

"Just admit that you like me," she said from a foot away.

"Who wouldn't like you?" he said, looking her over. "Christ, I wish I was sixteen or something. But I'm not. And that's the way it is. So you know why I'm here, don't you?"

"Somebody killed Lou the Dog, right?"

"Yeah, that's it."

"Good," she said. "I hope he rots in hell, the sick little pervert."

"Did you have anything to do with it?"

"I wish I did," she said, meaning it.

"How did you know about it?"

"She called me."

"Who?"

"I don't know her name," Christy said. "And even if I did, I wouldn't tell you. 'Cause she did me a big favor."

"Tell me more about this woman."

"Not unless you kiss me."

"Christy, I can't do that. And you know it."

She came up to him again and put her mouth on his. He didn't stop it.

He finally pulled back, better late than never.

"Don't worry, I won't tell anyone," she said.

"So who was this woman?" he said, in complete denial.

"She didn't give her name. She just said she was my guardian angel. That she was going to protect me from the scum of the earth."

"Did she tell you that she was going to kill Ackerman?"

"Yeah, she promised me."

"What did you say to that?"

"I told her to make it hurt. I told her to hurt him the way he hurt me."

"Anything else?"

"No, nothing else, lover."

She was staring at him like that. Like a lover. Like she knew him in some dark and intimate way.

"I made a mistake," he conceded.

"Yeah, yeah you did," Christy said, unnerving him with a hard, inculpatory look.

# *Nine*

*Y*our problem is sex," Daniel P. Pinkus declared with a missionary zeal that was becoming far too typical for Eamon's liking. "Instead of giving you the pleasure and release that you so crave, it is tearing apart your very soul. Am I not right, sinner?"

He wasn't in the mood to argue with a Jesus look-alike in the middle of his overheated living room at the end of a thoroughly confusing and depressing Sunday. He was trying to put what happened with Christy Gertz—not that he was sure that anything really had—far behind him.

"Sex is not the tonic for what ails you, sinner. It is the very cause of your wretched, godforsaken pain. Can't you see that you are searching for redemption in all the wrong places? Sex, at least when it is practiced outside of the conjugal state, is the cause of misery and disease and—"

"Hey, Dan, lighten up. Just because you're not getting any doesn't mean the rest of us have to join the priesthood, too."

"Eamon Wearie, there is still time," he continued,

unabated. "Even your troubled and debauched soul can be saved. I urge you to find yourself a copy of Pope Paul VI's *Humanae Vitae*. Perhaps this brilliant and seminal work can provide you with some of the answers you so desperately seek."

"Dan, I'm not seeking anything, not a damn thing."

"If you want, I'll be happy to lend you mine. I think you will find yourself enthralled with Pope Paul VI's teachings on the evils of contraceptives and—"

The phone interrupted him.

Pinkus said, "Tell whoever it is to call back. That way we can continue with our most stimulating discussion."

Eamon didn't care who it was, he was so happy for the reprieve.

"Hello, Lieutenant," Seppala said, surprising the hell out of him. "I hope I haven't caught you at a bad moment."

"No, not at all. In fact, you couldn't have picked a better one."

"I don't know if you're free, but I thought you might be interested in a home-cooked meal tonight."

"I'd be absolutely thrilled. Should I get us a bottle of wine?"

"You'd do better if you picked up a six-pack. My father and brother like beer with their dinner."

"Oh," he said, the disappointment all too apparent.

The Seppalas lived up near Memorial Stadium, in a middle-class neighborhood of large, brick houses with small, immaculate squares of lawn. Sprinklers were going off all down the block. Kids pedaled by on their bicycles. Not too far away, an ice-cream truck tinkled its bells. The smell of barbecue wafted on the warm air. It was a golden dream of an evening, a memory of summer.

Seppala greeted him on the screened-in porch in a Tina Turner T-shirt—the "What's Love Got to Do With It?" Tour—and khaki shorts that showed off those impossible, brown legs. She actually gave him a little hug.

"Did you have any problem finding your way, Lieutenant?"

"C'mon, what's all this 'lieutenant' stuff?"

"I thought men liked being deferred to."

"Well, this man would just like to be called Eamon."

Her father was in the kitchen, laboring over a hot stove. It was a chef's paradise—a kitchen as elaborate as any restaurant's—with its majestic stainless-steel range and plenitude of hanging copper pots, and its overall sense of controlled chaos. Her father was a large, silver-haired man with some belly hanging over his trousers. He immediately reminded Eamon of his own dad—not just the way he looked, but how quickly he helped to put Eamon at ease.

"Brought some beer, did you?" he said good-naturedly. "That's what I like to see in a man. Listen, I hope you like pasta. Because that's what's on tonight's menu, son."

"Love it, sir," Eamon said.

"Why don't you grab a beer, then, and go out back with Mary. Dinner won't be too long."

The backyard was cramped but lush, just enough space for the redwood picnic table, a built-in grill, and a small garden ripe with tomatoes and zucchini.

"Nice," Eamon said, taking a slug of Rolling Rock.

"Dad's the cook and gardener," Mary said. "He takes great pride in his salads and his fresh herbs. Make sure you compliment the food. Otherwise he'll wind up holding it against you."

"What's the story? Where's your mom?"

"She died about seven years ago."

"Oh, I'm sorry," he said.

"Everything's so different now," she said, looking away. "I probably would've moved out and got my own place and everything, but I still worry about Dad. He's never really got over it."

"Seven years is a long time."

"It's a heartbeat," she said.

"Does he date or anything like that?"

"I wish. Mostly he just stays home and spends his time thumbing through cookbooks. Sometimes I even catch him watching 'Oprah' in the afternoon."

"I gather he's retired."

"Dad was on the force for thirty years."

"My dad was all blue, too."

"So then you know all about the problems of getting involved with one. The unpredictable hours, the insane stress."

"I'm willing to take my chances," Eamon said, grinning.

Her father came out with a heaping, steaming bowl of pasta. Her brother, a handsome, well-built Tom Selleck look-alike, followed close behind with the salad and bread. He and Eamon exchanged a terse hello, and then they all sat down at the picnic table.

The pasta was delicious, a spirited rendition of *rigatoni alla vodka* that was laced with prosciutto and crushed tomatoes and fresh basil leaves.

"Absolutely the best I've ever had," Eamon enthused.

"I don't stint, that's my secret," Mr. Seppala confided. "I just tripled what the recipe said. Must be a quart of Stoli in there."

Mary added, "Dad also makes a very good Bordeaux sauce. And a fine marsala. And a lovely cognac sauce."

"I'll bet you'll never guess what they all have in common," he said with a wide smile. "Hey, have you tried the salad yet? All the veggies are from the garden."

Eamon kept up a steady stream of superlatives while Mr. Seppala, for his part, explained the secrets of growing cherry tomatoes, Boston lettuce, and red peppers. Eamon noticed that Mary's brother stayed strangely silent throughout the table banter, preferring to concentrate his attention on his empty plate. After a short while he excused himself.

"Poor boy hasn't been the same since his wife filed for divorce," Mr. Seppala commented after he was gone. "All he does is lift weights now. Like he's preparing for some phantom fight."

"He needs help," Mary said. "That's what I think. He's got too much pent-up anger."

"Perhaps," Mr. Seppala said, appearing a tad uncomfortable. "But Dom's wife gave up on the boy way too easily. Didn't give him a second chance."

"That's because Dom beat her up," she charged in a hushed tone. "And you know that's the truth."

"I don't know anything of the kind," he said, his face suddenly going dark.

"Oh, all right, have it your way," she said through gritted teeth.

"So," he said, rapidly changing subjects, "how's that investigation coming? Any new leads?"

"I tell Dad everything," Mary explained.

"Very frustrating," Eamon admitted. "We're really not sure what we're dealing with at all."

"The first thing I'd do," Mr. Seppala instructed, "is check out every rape victim in the state who's got a gun permit."

"Dad, don't you think we're already doing that?"

"What about the possibility that there are a bunch of different killers? You know, that some of these chain letter recipients are taking it seriously and doing exactly what it says?"

"I don't buy it," Eamon said. "I just don't see all these ordinary people just suddenly becoming homicidal maniacs. No, I think what the average person does is go to the police or just simply ignore it."

"Probably right," he conceded, looking as frustrated as they were.

"Dad, why don't you take Eamon inside and show him your pool table while I clean up around here."

"It's a deal," he declared happily. "I'd love to show

the boy some of the finer points of the game of pocket billiards."

As it turned out, Eamon showed Mr. Seppala those finer points.

"Where did you learn to play like that?" he asked, exasperated that Eamon had won his sixth or seventh game of eight ball in a row.

"A misspent youth," Eamon replied. "Actually, we had a table in our basement."

"Jesus, it shows," Mr. Seppala said in a tone approximating awe.

The stunted barroom table, with its ruined, drink-stained felt and telltale coin slots, had once seen action in Mr. Seppala's favorite tavern. Now it was just another personal trophy in his pine-paneled rec room.

"They were just going to throw it out, can you believe it?" he was saying. "Part of history, my history, at least. I used to go down to O'Leary's every time I had a fight with the missus. Which happened often enough, I'm ashamed to admit. Was crazy about her and yet we could go at it like cats and dogs. I could never admit I was wrong, that was my problem. I thought because I was the man and brought home the bacon that she should just shut up and do whatever I told her to do. It was all about power, but I was such a stupid ox that I couldn't even see it. Men and women —who can figure?"

"Tell me about it," Eamon said.

"Well, I'll tell you one thing: I wouldn't mind finding me someone like Sophia again. But they just don't make 'em like that anymore. A real old-fashioned girl that's what she was. For all my complaints, she treated me with absolute total respect. I always had the final say."

Eamon was quiet as he considered the merits of old-fashioned girls. He wasn't sure he always wanted that final say. He remembered Heather, his last girlfriend. The way she was always kowtowing to him. Boy, he thought, that could get boring in a hurry.

"So you know what they turned my beloved O'Leary's into? Something called the Artist's Cafe, if you can believe it. Some pishy place with a juice bar and live poetry readings. I can't tell you how much that pleased me. Can't even get a cold glass of draft at the corner tavern anymore. And then the Orioles deserted us for Camden Yards. At least in the old days I could always walk to a ball game. But now Memorial Stadium's just this great big empty tomb. Sometimes I go by it and I feel that the whole world has passed me by."

Eamon was smart enough to keep his mouth shut. He wasn't about to tell Mr. Seppala that the new ballpark offered a superior viewing experience. In a way he felt for him, for his vanishing breed and all their vanishing times.

They kept shooting eight ball and drinking beer, and every so often Mary would look in on them. She kept trying to drop hints to her dad that she wanted a little time alone with Eamon, but he seemed oblivious. Finally she told him quite plainly that it was her turn to play with the pool shark.

Eamon was glad for that. He didn't want to spend the whole night with her old man, no matter how good a guy he was. He just didn't want to be the parentally approved boyfriend. It was the kiss of death, and it was indeed classic.

"What do you want to hear?" she asked, flipping through the CDs that were racked over the stereo system. "How do you feel about U2? Or how about some Springsteen?"

"Bruce is always good," he said, admiring those long, brown legs all over again.

He leaned on the pool table, holding a long-neck bottle of Rolling Rock and a boldly salacious gaze. He didn't feel like they were in the Seppala family room;

he felt like they'd been left in some bar after closing time.

God, he wanted to kiss her something awful.

"Thunder Road" was the first one out of the box.

She came to him, without any need for instructions. Then just like that they were dancing slow, taking those first funny little steps.

The mighty Springsteen had been reduced to mere background noise; the music that they heard was all their own.

Her eyes finally met his. It seemed he would get to kiss her at last.

Except the phone started to ring in the unrealness.

Mary's father yelled from another room that it was Kelsey. Something important. She excused herself.

She was gone awhile, long enough for Eamon to begin to sober up. The strangeness of the past two days was catching up with him. He realized he hadn't even gone to sleep last night. He had gone right from the bright lights of the homicide scene to the Hollywood diner, to Lolita's kiddie pool, to slow dancing with Detective Mary Seppala.

It's what happened at the kiddie pool that didn't sit right.

He kept playing it back in his mind, the part where Christy Thong Bikini kissed him and he didn't let go until it was too late for excuses. It was just an extra second or two, but it counted all the same. There was some hard-to-swallow truth there, something he was doing his damnedest to ignore.

This was the bad stuff preying on him when Mary reentered the room. It was clear that she had sobered up also.

"Another one," she said. "Another chain letter victim."

He nodded solemnly.

"Down in Annapolis," she said. "At the Naval Academy. An Admiral Lerner."

"I should've known," he said.

She looked at him funny, but otherwise didn't skip a beat. "He was all over the papers today. He'd defended those cadets who'd raped that motel maid. Said something along the lines of boys will be boys. Not too bright, really."

"Not in retrospect," he said.

"Well," she said, signaling the end of their evening together.

"Of course," he said, understanding perfectly.

"I have to be up bright and early. Kelsey and I are going down there. See what we can come up with."

Even so, he tried to look into her eyes again. Like from before, when they had been only millimeters away from a kiss.

But she wasn't having any of it. She promptly led the way to the front door.

He had missed his opportunity, and now he only hoped it wouldn't be his last.

# Ten

*T*he two very dejected-looking postal inspectors sat on a bench on the freshly cut grounds of the U.S. Naval Academy on another warm and soiled day. At least they had a good view. They were at the spot where the Spa Creek pours into the Severn River, all of which washed into the great panorama of the Chesapeake. The watched as a racing shell, urged on by its coxswain, cut through the placid gray murk.

"I wish they'd get it over with," Bunko said.

"You said it," Eamon agreed, bringing the beauteous Mary Seppala into his field of vision again.

She was with the others, who were mulling their concerns under a large, ancient weeping willow not thirty feet from them. A red-faced Detective Kelsey was gesticulating to the two representatives from the Annapolis Police Department. The FBI investigators, in their Ray-Bans and dark wool suits, shuffled uneasily in the background. While the Navy's own starchy best, these unsmiling crew cuts in dress uniform, remained rigidly in place.

The whole joint was overrun by top guns.

Bunko and Eamon knew they were about to be cut out. No one had to tell them. They had seen it happen too many times before. Postal was always getting outranked.

Eamon kept looking over at Mary. Occasionally she would glance his way. But it was a look of cool reserve, of unaccountable distance and formality, not nearly the look of secret and barely contained longing that he would've wished for.

"This thing's out of hand," Bunko said. "Somebody's getting aced almost every other day now. I don't see how one person can be responsible for all of it. Maybe there is some goddamn Committee after all."

"Who knows," Eamon said, stealing another look at Mary.

"You're right on top of this, Wearie. A regular goddamn Pinkerton man."

He kept it fixed on her. She was dressed coolly and simply in jeans and a ribbed, sleeveless turtleneck—the season's most fashionable ensemble—which was complimented by a subtle assortment of turquoise and silver jewelry. In the sunshine, under the willow tree, with the white brick and terra-cotta dormitory buildings behind her, in the French Renaissance style, so much like the campus of some Ivy League college, Mary looked nothing so much as like a lovely, self-effacing coed.

Except he noticed the high definition in her upper arms, the tautness that came from working out regularly. For this was a coed who lifted weights and knew karate and could flip bad guys upside down.

He was totally smitten.

"Enough with the goo-goo eyes already," Bunko said, waving a hand across his hypnotized face.

"That's the girl I'm going to marry," Eamon said quietly.

"Oh, Jesus," the thrice-divorced Bunko muttered. "Didn't I tell you never to use the M-word around me?"

"She's the one," he said again.

"Yeah, she's the one this week," Bunko said with utter contempt. "You're always falling in love. You just see a pretty girl walking down the street and you're ready to declare your undying devotion. For Christ' sake, a waitress just happens to smile at you and a minute later you're asking her to bear your children."

"Don't you think you're exaggerating a little?"

"Not a bit," Bunko said seriously. "How long have I known you now? What is it, close to ten years, right? And how many women have you gone through in that time? Give me a number, a nice, round ballpark figure."

"Hey, c'mon, give me a break. That's not a fair question."

"It might not be fair, but it's a relatively simple question. At least for most people. I mean, look at me. In those ten years I've been involved in what, four or five serious relationships? Something like that."

"Does that include the Queen Elizabeth blow-up doll and that unfortunate incident in the sheep pasture?"

Bunko shook his head grimly. "Joke all you want, Wearie, but you're still avoiding the real issue."

"And what's that?" Eamon asked, sounding a defensive note. "How many women I've gone out with?"

"Well, you gotta admit you're fairly promiscuous."

"What the hell are you talking about?"

"I'm talking about the fact that you have all the morals of a German shepherd."

"You're . . . you're out of your mind," he stammered, not comprehending this assault on him.

"Just look at the last few months. There was Heather. Before that, that dental hygienist whose name I forget. Not that I think you'd remember it either—"

"Debra," Eamon noted sullenly.

"Right, Debra. Then there was that Justine wack-job. Another one you were crazy about and were sure you wanted to marry. Remember that? And how long did that last? A weekend?"

"It went slightly longer than that," Eamon replied, the fight going out of him.

"Do you see what I'm getting at, kid? That's not to mention all your one-night stands and two-day love affairs."

Eamon was silent, pondering it on the moody, gray waters of the Severn. There was something to what Bunko was saying, even if he didn't like it much. He thought about it some more and thought maybe his problem was believing that *she*—the she of adolescent dreams and grown-up disappointments—was out there in the first place. Because if you didn't believe, you just settled. But if you were one of the faithful, you kept searching and moving on, always certain of those greener pastures.

He took in Mary again, who was still under the cascading willow with the others, in a golden splash of sunshine that made her appear practically celestial. She was an untouchable vision of haloed loveliness, and he doubted that he would ever forget her as she was now, an impressionistic dappling of a pretty girl on a summer's day—all she needed was a frilly white parasol—crystallized and eternal.

"She's the one," he told Bunko again. "This one's different from the others."

"How do you know?"

"I just know. It's a feeling I've had since the first moment I laid eyes on her. It was meant to be."

"Yeah, right," Bunko said, unconvinced.

They watched as the top guns began to disperse. Seppala and Kelsey came over to where they were sitting.

Kelsey was his usual mottled self, looking wet and splotchy and vastly uncomfortable. He said, "Looks like we're going to be here awhile. The government boys want a thorough briefing on this chain letter business. So far they're having some trouble believing it. Their first instinct is to go after all known terrorists. They've got it in their thick skulls that it's some kind of Iraqi plot."

Bunko said, "I wish it were. At least that would leave us out."

"Well, I'm glad you brought that up," Kelsey said, grinning.

Eamon and Mary stayed quiet as their two partners conducted business. Kelsey was telling Bunko that it was getting mighty crowded in Annapolis, and Bunko was assuring Kelsey that he understood perfectly. Eamon tried to make eye contact with her, with no success whatsoever. He wondered what she was thinking, why she was ignoring him so.

"Okay, we'll get out of town," Bunko assured Kelsey. "But what can you tell us? Off the record, that is."

"I can tell you that Admiral Lerner was killed at around eight-thirty last night. He'd just come out of the White Horse Tavern on Pinkney. Sprayed with nine-millimeter action. Most of it aimed at his groin. Nobody saw anything, but everybody heard it."

"Iraqi assassins don't usually go for the groin area," Bunko remarked.

"Speaking of which, we had confirmation today that Lou Ackerman was shot with the same Glock 19 that did in Judge Draper and Eddie Dooley. I'm now of the opinion that we have a professionally trained killer on our hands. One single, solitary hit woman who's made it her business to know the ins and outs of her craft. I'm wondering if we're dealing with a former cop or something. Because her technique and disposition aren't anything close to being amateur."

Bunko said, "Still hard to believe one broad could cause all this havoc. Then again it's nothing one of my former wives wouldn't be capable of. So where'd they find that chain letter anyway?"

"In the breast pocket of his jacket. Lerner had gotten it only the day before. He thought it was pretty hilarious and had been carrying it around to show people."

"Christ, I don't get it. Why him? What did he really do anyway? Hell, what did any of them really do for that matter?"

"Well, not enough to warrant the death penalty, that's for sure. But Lerner had been doin' a lot of mouthin' off to the newspapers ever since that motel maid was raped by those midshipmen. Or should I say allegedly raped. Because those boys claim it was consensual sex."

"Yeah, right," Bunko said disgustedly. "That was her idea of a good time—taking on six guys in sailor uniforms at once."

"Yeah, every woman's dream," Kelsey said with equal disgust.

Then they exchanged grunts—no need for fussy good-byes in their line of work—and went their separate ways. The inspectors headed for the main gate while Seppala and Kelsey hurried to join the other top guns in a formal briefing.

"Go back to Dead Letters?" Eamon asked, watching Mary disappear from view.

"That's how much you know," Bunko said cryptically.

Eamon followed his partner down the narrow, picturesque streets of Annapolis, which still hearkened back to colonial times with their terribly quaint brick sidewalks and oil-burning lanterns and tiny, tightly fitted, eighteenth-century frame buildings. Pinkney Street was only a couple of blocks from the Maryland State House, the impressive cypress-domed capital, which appeared like a radiant beacon over the three-story rooftops.

A TV crew was setting up outside the White Horse, circling like vultures around the chalked-off, blood-stained outline of Admiral Lerner. A female hairdo began to speak in the breathless, psuedo-dramatic way of television news.

"Speculation abounds today as to who is responsible for the assassination of Admiral Guy Lerner, the much-decorated Navy commander who has been so much in the news recently with his controversial comments on everything from gays in the military to the Tailhook embarrassment, to the still-erupting Anchor Motel scandal. So far three Islamic fundamentalist groups have come forward to claim credit for the attack. . . ."

They slipped behind the hairdo—briefly appearing in the frame before being shooed away in angry pantomime by the beefy camera operator—and escaped into the dark, woody interior of the White Horse.

The pub was stale, dank, and charmless. It suffered from a bad case of split personality. Tiffany windows reflecting off Budweiser mirrors; soft, gas-lit sconces competing with the streaky, garish light of pinball machines; imposing, Tudor-style booths that were planted among the plastic ferns and palms. Except for the insistent, buoyant sounds of the Beach Boys surfing in from the juke, it was a slackly quiet, practically mournful Monday afternoon. Two clean-cut young men shared a pitcher of beer in one corner of the small mahogany bar.

The chesty bartender didn't seem all that thrilled with the idea of two more customers. "Yeah?" she said with a jigger of suspicion.

Bunko ordered a double Johnnie Red on the rocks while Eamon opted for a low-key tap beer. She brought the drinks back with palpable disdain, carelessly slapping them down. Eamon didn't like her or the place at all. Bunko, on the other hand, was more curious about this woman with the world-weary, battered attitude.

"So what the hell are we doing here?" Eamon demanded, tired of the way the day was going. "You know Kelsey wants us out of town."

"Since when have we started listening to what people tell us?"

"I thought we might try a new policy."

"Following orders is for losers," Bunko said before downing the entire amber drink in one death-defying gulp.

He called the bartender over for another. He liked her hair, a wicked, spurious blond that was overgrown with dark, telltale roots.

"That was fast," she said, taking a moment to judge his sobriety among other things. "You must have been awfully thirsty."

"I've got a wooden leg," Bunko quipped.

"I've heard that one," she said with perceptible boredom.

"I've bet you've heard them all," Bunko felt compelled to tell the fortyish blonde with the cynical green eyes and tawdry blue mascara.

"When you've been in this business as long as I have there aren't any more surprises left. Believe me."

"Even a dead admiral on your doorstep?"

"Hey, life goes on," she said without sanctimony.

"Not for Admiral Lerner it doesn't," Bunko said.

"Hey, the guy was a battleship-size prick. The world's better off as far as I'm concerned."

She poured him another double, and Bunko found himself admiring her tough-as-nails, seen-it-all attitude and her been-through-the-mill, seen-better-days body. She was zircon hard—even her amply displayed bosom seemed unwelcoming—yet sympathetic in the way of anyone challenging the world to ante up a good reason not to be that way.

Much to Eamon's dismay, Bunko asked for menus.

"C'mon, Bunk," he said, close to pleading, "we really should be going."

"How many times I gotta tell ya, kid? We're on an endless, all-expenses-paid vacation."

"I'm sure Masterson will be delighted to hear that."

Bunko ordered the thirty-two-ounce, marinated porterhouse. Blood rare. French fries, screw the baked potato. Creamy blue cheese on his salad.

"Comes with a vegetable," she said, taking it down on a pad.

"Better not chance it," Bunko said. "Hate to overdo it, ya know."

She smiled just a little at that, starting to like him.

"I'm Alice," she said, holding back just the tiniest bit, still sizing him up, as if no man could really be trusted, no matter how nice he seemed.

"Alice, what do they marinate that steak in anyway?"

"It's a secret recipe. I'm not supposed to tell."

"Alice, if we're to be friends, then you're going to have to put your full and unconditional faith in me," Bunko told her with all the smoky smoothness of fine aged whisky.

Oh, God, Eamon thought, watching his partner at work. He had seen the man operate too many times before to miss the subtleties of his well-honed technique.

She hesitated, her face momentarily shaded with mistrust.

"Soy sauce and Jack Daniel's," she finally dispensed, as if she were revealing a great and terrible secret of the heart.

"I'll take it to the grave," Bunko swore.

She reluctantly turned her attention to Eamon. "Have you made up your mind yet?"

"How're the crab cakes?"

"As good as anything, I suppose."

He should've known better, just by her bedraggled,

uncaring tone, but he proceeded ahead nonetheless, on a culinary collision course.

She bought the next round, and brought her solicitous gaze back to Bunko. The Beach Boys harmonized about California girls while Eamon thought dark, unprintable thoughts.

"So," Alice said, "what brings you boys to the White Horse today?"

"Actually, honey, we're helping with the investigation into Lerner's murder."

"Cops?"

"Something like that."

"He was such a hypocritical prick," she said, unrestrained. "Always pretending to be the big family man even though he spent most of his time downing martinis and checking out the nubile young flesh."

"I gather he came in here a lot."

"All the time. He was like every other guy—just interested in the one thing. Had a totally bogus marriage, but what else is new?"

"Were you involved with him at one point?"

"Something like that," she said with a dirty little smile. "So are you married? Or seeing a special someone right now?"

"I'm as free as the wind," Bunko lied.

Franny would just kill him, Eamon thought.

"A nice-looking guy like yourself?" she pressed.

"Bizarre, isn't it?"

The food arrived much too quickly for Eamon's liking; he pictured the Popeye-armed cook sweating over a microwave, and unfortunately the crab cakes tasted it. Instead of the desired tender flakiness, they had all the consistency and subtlety of canned tuna fish. Bunko was pleased with his steak, though, a mammoth, blackened T-bone that was juicy and red in the center. Eamon, who could make only halfhearted jabs at his own plate, was an envious bystander to Bunko's greedy, lip-smacking carnivorism.

"Let's finish lunch and get the hell out of here," he said to Bunko when Alice went to pay some attention to her other two customers.

"What's your hurry? I'm rather enjoying myself."

"I can see that. And you should be glad that Franny can't see the *way* you're enjoying yourself."

"Give me a break, kid. A man has got to be free to live life on his own terms. It's our natural instinct to roam and wander, to search out fresh, new possibilities, as it were. See, that's where men and women are different. We're not big on the domestic front, on taking care of the house and children and doing all that nurturing junk. Oh, sure, we play along to keep the broads happy and society functioning, but in the end it's not really what we're born to do."

"Fascinating," Eamon said, arching his eyebrows.

"I'm glad you agree," Bunko, the social anthropologist, continued. "Because, unfortunately, women don't always understand these fundamental differences. See, men are hunters and warriors and sex machines. Basically what we like to do is beat each other up and make love to big-breasted women. To put it another way, we're on a constant babe alert. It's a goddamn genetic trait, coded right into our DNA. I kid you not. It's the screw around and have a good time before you die gene."

"You kill me," Eamon said, flabbergasted. "A couple hours ago you're giving me a whole big hard time about my so-called promiscuity. Do you remember any of that? Or is a convenient memory imprinted into your screwed-up DNA too?"

"Kid, I was just trying to be helpful. Just trying to share that vast wealth of knowledge that I've been so lucky to inherit from my Maker."

"You want to be helpful, let's get cracking on this case. Let's see if we can find a killer before she or they or whoever it is decides to strike again."

"Listen, J. Edgar Hoover," Bunko said, "there's not

much more we can do today, so let's give it a rest already. We'll turn back into crimebusters bright and early tomorrow morning. But tonight I say we kick back in Annapolis and let the chips fall where they may."

"I'm glad you're in such a hurry to solve this. It really instills public confidence."

"What's with you, Wearie? Christ, I can remember a time when you were actually fun to be around."

"Cherish those memories," Eamon said glumly.

"Why, just think of some of the advantageous possibilities that an evening like this might offer up to a couple of good-lookin' bachelors like ourselves."

Bunko was staring at Alice's backside as he spoke, his eyes somewhere between love and lechery.

"Besides," he said, picking up a copy of the *Sun* off the bar, "it's all random anyway. Just look at the goddamn front page. Because, I'm telling you, that's just what our clever little killer is doing right now. And what the hell do you see?"

Eamon shook his head doubtfully, not quite sure what his partner was after.

"Here's one for you," Bunko said, delighting in such a quick and appropriate find. "Story about a top official of the DEA being accused of sexual harassment by an underling. The guy was always pestering her for oral sex, it says. He never let up, and she finally had to quit. Do you see what I'm getting at, kid?

"No? How about this one then? Article about the rap artist Dr. Big One, about how some human rights group called Right the Wrong has been 'taking to the streets to protest against the misogynous nature of his lyrics.'

"See, one after the other. The newspaper, like the very world we live in, is just filled with stories of harassment and sexism and woman hatred. So what are you going to do? I mean, how are we going to protect all the moronic pricks out there? What, are we going to put around-the-clock guards on that DEA guy and Dr. Big One?—just on the off chance that they're next on our killer's mailing list?"

Eamon was respectfully quiet; for once the big guy was making some sense.

"Look, here's another, a follow-up on those midshipmen who raped that motel maid. Of course they're all pleading innocent to the charges. It's their story that the maid *got them drunk and forced herself on them.* Pretty nifty turn of events, huh?"

It was at that moment that one of the clean-cut young men at the other end of the bar jumped into their discussion.

"Hell, I believe them over that stupid lyin' bitch, I'll tell you that."

He was three sheets to the wind, ugly with the drink and his own filthy ignorance.

"You know she loved every minute of it, the whore."

Which prompted his friend to life.

"They're all like that. They say they don't want it, but, hey, they want it just like we do. Except they all gotta pretend to be good little girls. Like they're all prissy little virgins or somethin'. So sometimes you gotta force the issue, know what I mean? Believe me, them bitches are secretly glad for it. Maybe they won't tell you that, but you can be sure you done 'em a favor, all right."

They were upright-looking, all-American boys with short, neatly combed, sandy hair and the sort of bland, airbrushed features that are routinely found in catalogs for menswear. They were memorable in precisely the way that they were so unmemorable; they were models of deception, Eamon thought.

"Yeah, I was out last week with this college bitch," one of the Eagle Scouts was recounting, "and I knew she wanted it bad, but she was giving me all this 'No, I'm not ready' and 'I hardly know you' shit. Like I haven't heard that crap before. Like I'm going to wait for some fuckin' green light to go off or somethin'. Man, she kept sayin' 'No, no, no,' but I knew she really meant 'Go, go, go!' Believe me, fellas, the bitch loved it, couldn't get enough of it."

The other guy practically applauded. "Yeah, good show, dude!" he exclaimed. "Girl met her match for sure, dude."

Eamon didn't feel so good. He told Bunko that he needed some air and that he would be back later.

# *Eleven*

⌒⌒

*I*t turned out to be a lovely dusk, a stunning convergence of purples and pinks that seemed much too good for the likes of the Anchor Motel, which was twenty rooms of cinder-block sadness on the Spa Creek. Its dyslexic neon sign—missing too many letters to make sense—blinked like a red warning light.

Eamon Wearie pulled the Pontiac up alongside the manager's office. A white-haired narcoleptic emerged to yawn out, "Hourly, or nightly?" Eamon flipped open his blue and gold shield, but before he could ask his question, the old man said, "Joanie's in Room Twelve. I suppose that's who you're here for. Two over from the Reef." He said it all with a sorrowful emptiness.

Eamon parked it in front of the motel lounge, the Drifter's Reef, a hellish crossing that reverberated with drunken shrieks of laughter and the ghostly soul-wrecks of too many foggy, forlorn nights.

He knocked on her door, feeling the uneasiness that always came with the unknown.

"Yes?" a tiny, broken voice said.

He held his shield up to the peephole.

"Lieutenant Eamon Wearie," he barked officiously.

The door opened to expose a ponytailed girl who couldn't have been more than nineteen and who might even have been pretty if it weren't for two black eyes, stitches across one cheek, and a broken arm. He heard a baby cry in the background.

"I'm sorry to intrude on you," he said.

"It doesn't matter," she said flatly. "Nothin' matters now, mister."

She didn't bother to invite him in; they stood awkwardly in the open. The baby let out a long, sustained wail.

"She's cranky, hasn't had her feeding yet," she said with some hill-country twang. "It's tough with them broken ribs. That's the thing that bothers most. They can't even wrap them or do nothin'. I just keep poppin' them Percodans for the hurt."

It was hard even looking at her, to see that swollen, blue face and know just the starkest outline of what happened.

"So are you working with Sergeant Holmes on my case?"

"I'm with federal law enforcement," he said, not wanting to get into a long, drawn-out explanation of the Postal Inspection Service and what its role might be in any of this.

"I guess I believe you," she said dubiously.

"What do you mean?"

"You know, they'll try anything, them TV people."

He dutifully displayed his badge again and handed over his official card.

"You just don't know what it's been like," she said, partially relieved. "Reporters have just been houndin' me. I'm just worried they'll use them pictures."

"What pictures?"

"Practically every time I stick my head out they're hiding somewhere with them big bazooka cameras.

**101**

I'm surprised they're not around now. Even been threatenin' to give out my name if I don't cooperate with them. Good God, that's the last thing in this world I need, for my kin back home in West Virginia to get wind of this."

"Maybe they could help," Eamon suggested softly.

"Oh, yeah, right. You don't know them. All they'd do is blame me, just like everybody else. They'd say I was awfully stupid to be in some bar by my lonesome with six shitfaced sailors."

"Perhaps you're underestimating your folks."

"I seriously doubt it, mister. Where I come from it ain't proper for a lady to go into no bar by herself. That's a privilege reserved for men, plain and simple. Just like a lot of other things in this life, you can be sure."

It was turning dark outside, twilight's last gleaming.

"I'm sorry for your troubles," he said, not quite knowing the right thing to say.

"You don't know what sorry is," she said with all the bitterness and hatred due her. "You don't know anything about it. Those sons-of-a-bitch bastards are going to pay for what they did done to me. You wait and see. One by one by one. . . ."

"That's why I'm here," Eamon pronounced, taking his shot. "She spoke to you, didn't she?"

The small, broken-boned, puffy-blue girl went silent. The baby began to cry again from the television-radiated darkness of the motel room.

"She told you all about her plans for the admiral, didn't she, Joanie?"

Joanie wasn't about to say a damn thing. But it registered in her anguished, comprehending face nonetheless. Their one-member Committee had reached her with the news about Admiral Lerner's death sentence. Just as Christy Gertz had got advance word about Lou Ackerman's bloody fate.

"What did she tell you, Joanie? Are there going to

be any other executions? Anything else we should know about?"

She was a picture of dark, silent resolve.

"Oh, that's just great," Eamon sneered, trying to get a rise out of her. "We'll just kill everybody. Why even bother with a criminal justice system anymore?"

"A lot you know," she suddenly spouted. "Them boys will probably never do jail time. That's what the DA told me. Said we didn't have much of a case, if you can believe that horseshit. They break into my room after I've gone to bed and break every bone in my body and rape me in front of my little baby, and that don't seem to be good enough to get no conviction. Because the DA said I'd been drinking, and I was an unwed mother, and that I was dressed *provocatively* besides. I was in some old pair of jeans and an ugly old sweatshirt, for the love of Jesus. But the DA says that's not the problem. You know what the problem is? The panties I had on that night. DA says they were too sexy for my own good and that no jury will believe I wasn't some slut out lookin' for a good time."

Now it was Eamon's turn to be quiet.

"Yeah, see how it plays now," she said.

"I can't believe that these men will get away with it. All the jury has to do is take one look at you to know what really happened."

"Maybe there won't be no need for a trial," she said ominously.

"Don't tell me you're not going to go through with it?"

She went darkly silent again.

And he filled with realization. "Oh, I get it, she's made you a promise, hasn't she? She's going to kill each and every one of them, is that it?"

"She's going to protect me," Joanie said like a zombie. "She's my protector."

"What's her name? Who is she? What else can you tell me about her?"

"I'm not telling you anything. You're just like all the rest. You don't know what we been through."

"Has your protector been raped, too?"

"We've all been raped, you can be sure of that."

"What are you talking about, Joanie?"

"There ain't no justice," she said. "Only the justice you take into your own hands."

Eamon thought it sounded rehearsed, as if the words weren't her own but those of her vengeful protector.

"That's the only way the world's going to pay attention," she continued, "if we first pay attention to ourselves. That's the law of the jungle."

She didn't give him a chance to pursue it further. She simply turned her back on him and returned to the cries of her child and the confines of their TV-radiated motel room.

Eamon walked across the gravelly parking lot to a phone booth—ghostly fluorescent in the wasteland—and punched up Masterson.

"Del, we have a little problem."

"What is it now, Pretty Boy?"

"You know those six midshipmen accused of rape? Well, they're going to need protection. They're next on the hit parade. Admiral Lerner was only the beginning."

"How do you know that?"

"Seems the rape victim had a little chat with our killer."

"You're kidding me. What else you find out?"

"Not much. Although I'd bet the farm that our killer is a rape victim herself. Too many wild deuces to ignore."

"You saying only one bitch is behind all this?"

"Maybe. I don't know. Look, it's hard to say."

"Jesus," Masterson said in a more reproachful tone, "you can't get more definitive than that."

"It's too early to make the call."

"No, it's too fuckin' late, you stupid fuck,"

Masterson replied, the nastiness and Wild Turkey flashing at once. "Speaking of fat fucks, I want to talk to that good-for-nothing partner of yours."

"Uh, Bunko's checking out another angle in town," Eamon said, trying to think on his feet.

"You mean he's in some bar getting drunk, don't you?"

"No, that's not it at all—"

"Save it, Pretty Boy. I'm not interested in your bullshit. I got some new marching orders for you two clowns. I want you to check out a Brook Ellsworth on the Eastern Shore. Town of St. Michaels. The lady saw our little plant in the newspaper. Says she recognizes that wax seal on the chain letter, the one included in the artwork."

"You think it's really worth the trip? How unusual do you think that lip-shaped seal is? I mean, maybe she saw something similar somewhere. What's the big deal?"

"The big deal, Pretty Boy, is that Brook Ellsworth's husband was murdered in June. It's an unsolved case—and, to top the whole sloppy mess off, this Mrs. Ellsworth says she found that kissy seal on some of her husband's private correspondence. Some kind of weird love letters or something. Who the fuck knows? That's why I'm asking you and Lard Ass to check it out."

"Enough with the Pretty Boy and Lard Ass already."

"Oh, jeeze, I forgot how sensitive you girls were."

"Later, Del," he said, not bothering to part amicably.

He stepped out of the ghostly booth, shaking off Del's ugliness. It was another steamy, enervated evening, making him wonder if this weather was ever going to break. He didn't think he could take much more of it.

* * *

The difference at the White Horse was the difference between day and night: As dismal and melancholy as the afternoon had been, the early evening proved to be a full-wattage display of wet, lit-up faces and boozy, temporal pulsations.

Eamon found himself in the juke's eerie light, flush on Jack Daniel's, with two indistinct girls in their early twenties. He had his arm around one of them, a trashy blonde in a miniskirt and fishnet stockings. She was telling him, over the opening chords of Dire Straits's "Walk of Life," that she had some beer and wine back at her apartment.

That he was even considering it showed just how far gone he was.

"You know, somebody got shot outside here last night," the other girl said.

"Yeah, good idea," he said. "Let's do some shots."

Bunko was sitting at the crowded bar with Alice, whose shift was over, with one paw on her thigh and only one idea on his mind.

So it was that the postal inspectors were not exactly covering themselves in glory when Brian Kelsey and Mary Seppala arrived on the scene. Kelsey shook his head in good-natured dismay, clearly amused at catching the inspectors with their pants down. Mary, not nearly so amused, shot Eamon a look of murderous disbelief before following her partner to the bar.

Eamon let go of the trashy blonde as quickly as it took for the first sober thought to race to his pickled brain.

"I do something wrong, baby?" she asked into the din, fading away from him like any other song on the juke.

Eamon watched as one of the locals approached Mary and bought her a beer. He was a big, scruffy animal in a tank top, and his eyes roamed over Mary as if she were a succulent piece of prime rib.

Eamon had seen enough.

"Hey," he said, pushing between them, "I'd like a word with my girlfriend, if you don't mind."

"Your girlfriend?" the beast said, perturbed. "I seen you over by the jukebox. You already got more than your share."

"Those are my friends," Eamon explained.

"Lookin' awfully cozy, if you don't mind my sayin' so, amigo."

"I mind."

"All I'm sayin' is that you gotta be careful when you have a girl that looks like this one does."

"Lissen, pal," Eamon slurred, "it's not like I'm not grayful for the advice, but why don't you go fuck yourself."

"Why, you . . ."

The guy took a swing at Eamon, but didn't come close to landing it. Mary Seppala stopped it with the palm of her hand, and before he could say uncle she'd used another nifty kung fu move to get his arm twisted behind his back.

"Ow, ow, ow," the oaf groaned.

"Now that's enough," she commanded.

He nodded his big, scruffy head up and down before she let go. Some in the crowd hooted and applauded the humiliation.

"And let that be a lesson to you," Eamon said, head wagging, as the interloper backed off.

Mary said, "You're drunk."

"Thanks for noticing. I like that in a woman."

"Do you spend all your time in bars?"

Eamon said, "No, sometimes I have to go to work, too. Drinking's expensive."

"Were you like this when you were married? Didn't your wife get tired of your behavior?"

"What, Trish? Hell, we met in a bar."

"How romantic," Mary said, making a face.

"Okay," he admitted, "maybe it wasn't the best."

He tried to gain entrance to her amazing purple

eyes, but she was having none of it. He wished he weren't so wasted, that he could somehow tell her how he really felt. About all the crazy stuff inside him. How he knew she was the one, how sure he was. That his life, at least the part that had come before her, hadn't really counted. That he could make it work with her, that it wasn't too late for him to change. All these things and more that had been lost hours ago in the incoherence of a shot glass.

"I didn't have a reason before," he said in the unsteady haze.

"I don't understand."

"I just didn't have a reason to be straight."

"Let me get this right, you need a reason to be sane and sober?"

Eamon nodded, his lids half closed.

"What about those girls by the jukebox? Is that just sport?"

"They're nobody," he protested, "nobody important."

"That's where I have to disagree," Mary said.

"Just babes, tha's all," he said, tottering.

"God, what a horrible thing to say."

"What? What I say?"

"You better be careful, Eamon Wearie," she warned. "Or else you might find yourself on the receiving end of one of those chain letters."

# Twelve

❧

The stately mansion was perched on several sweeping acres of dewy, impossible lawn overlooking the Miles River. With its freshly painted white brick, graceful window awnings, and imposing portico, it could have easily been mistaken for a first-class hotel or a sanitarium for the discriminating.

They pulled up a circular drive lined with jockey lanterns and magnolia. A uniformed maid greeted them at the brass-knockered front door and led them through an airy and elegant house littered with Persian rugs and Ming vases and enormous, gilt-framed portraits of sea captains and racehorses. Brook Ellsworth was waiting for them in one of the living rooms; the inspectors couldn't be sure if it was the third or fourth one that they'd seen.

"Why, gentlemen, you look tired," Mrs. Ellsworth said with artful concern.

Hung over is more like it, Eamon thought.

She was an ash blonde in her late forties who was sporting crisp tennis whites and blue-blood varicose veins.

"Sarah, dear," she said, addressing the maid with more of her patrician airs, "why don't you fetch us a pitcher of lemonade."

Lemonade seemed an appropriate choice for the high-ceilinged room, which was a tall, cool, yellow drink in its own right. French doors, which opened to a view of the rolling lawn and the river, were festooned with gold damask. An eclectic collection of richly brocaded armchairs in the most lovely saffrons and citrines were perfectly placed around a marble coffee table holding a crystal vase of black-eyed Susans. As if that were not enough, Cézanne's burnished apples—looking every bit like the real McCoy —glowed from above the mantel of the walk-in fireplace.

It was a splendid, unimaginable slice of life that made the inspectors feel uncouth and just plain dirty. They settled into the regal armchairs anyway.

"I've always adored the Yellow Room," Mrs. Ellsworth was saying. "There are thirty-two rooms in the Adams-Talbot House, all of them delightful and curious in their own way, but this is where I like to sip my Earl Grey and reflect on happier times."

Only the rich do that, Bunko thought harshly. Name their rooms and houses and reflect on happier times.

"Well, I certainly hope this will prove worthwhile," she said, still exercising propriety. "I'd hate to think that I was wasting the taxpayers' money with some wild goose chase."

"If you don't mind, we'd like a look at those letters," Bunko asserted.

"Of course, Inspector. But I thought we'd have our lemonade first."

She was a model of refinement, of sanguine comportment, but there was something fragile and birdlike about her nonetheless, something that was only hinted at in her pursed, colorless lips and the crow's-feet stamped in the corners of her pale, practically lifeless blue eyes.

"Tourists," she said, breaking the unfortunate silence, pointing in the direction of the French doors to a slow-moving river ferry that was a bright flash of cameras and sun hats. "Heaven knows, we get our share."

Finally, to the relief of all, Sarah arrived with the drinks.

Bunko, not one for the small amenities, guzzled his. Mrs. Ellsworth did her best to appear unruffled—even as he wiped his mouth with a shirt sleeve.

"Now what can you tell us about your husband?" he said, starting to sense that his manners were on trial.

"Whit was a proper gentleman," she said, sipping daintily. "The last of his kind, I suppose. A man of breeding and *exquisite* manners."

"Right, gotcha," Bunko said, feeling less and less comfortable on Planet Yellow. "So what line of work was he in?"

"Whit *owned* newspapers," she said, correcting him. "Didn't the chief of police fill you in on any of this?"

"'Fraid not, Mrs. Ellsworth. We're coming in blind."

"Well, Whit was a transplanted Boston Brahmin. The scion of a family that traces its arrival on these shores to the *Mayflower* and—"

"What we need to know," Bunko said, interrupting her patronizing tones, "is how your husband was killed."

"Whit was shot. They found him in St. Michaels. At the office he kept at the *Lantern,* which is one of our twenty-five weeklies on the Eastern Shore."

"Ma'am, can you tell us what kind of gun was used to kill your husband?"

"You'll have to talk to Chief Proxmire about that. Some sort of German pistol, I believe."

"Have there been any leads?"

"Nothing promising. I can tell you that the chief seems to think that it has something to do with the Mafia, of all things. I don't believe it for a minute. Whit would have nothing to do with that sort. Perhaps now is a good time to let you examine the letters. To see if there is any point in continuing with this conversation. As you might imagine, this is all very unpleasant, the reliving of it all."

They followed the brittle, ashen blonde to her late husband's private study, which was a dark haven of books and ancient maritime maps and brass navigational compasses. She paused in front of the somber, seafaring Ahab that sat in judgment above the fireplace—as if debating whether she could really trust them—before removing the painting to reveal a hidden wall safe. She dialed the combination most surreptitiously.

"Is this where you discovered the letters in the first place?" Bunko asked.

"Yes, that was a bit strange," she answered, obviously bothered by the question. "Because Whit and I weren't ones to keep secrets. We had such a lovely marriage, really. One founded on mutual trust and respect. So I can only speculate that he didn't want to concern me."

"I beg your pardon," Bunko said, the explanation lost on him.

"Well, it's all so simple," she said, still looking awfully strained. "Whit was obviously being bothered by some kook—some insane woman who probably just saw his name in the newspaper or something—and he just didn't want me to worry. My Lord, the people who are out there. As if I had to tell you two gentlemen."

"But why didn't he just throw the letters out? Why was he saving them?"

"Questions, questions," she snapped, removing the small bundle from the safe. "Don't you think I've wondered the same? But I knew Whit, and hanky-panky was the last thing on his mind."

"Excuse me—"

"They're love letters, just the most crazy things. Why, it's absolutely absurd. Whit was a loyal, faithful husband. Just some madwoman, believe me. The things she writes—why, it's all nonsense, the concoction of a twisted mind, you can be sure."

"Jesus," Eamon exclaimed, catching sight of one of the envelopes. There was no mistaking those ruby-melted lips, the same ones kissing their chain letter.

"We'll need these," Bunko said, snatching them from her grip.

"It's absurd," she repeated numbly. "Just some crazy woman, believe me."

The inspectors noted right away the absence of return addresses and that the letters were all postmarked Provincetown, Massachusetts. They skimmed them—perusal would have to come later—for a signature, a name, anything into which they could sink their teeth. Their cursory expedition yielded only the initials *L.C.*, which were lodged at the bottom of each handwritten note.

"And you have no idea who L.C. is?" Bunko demanded.

"Of course not," she said, bristling.

"What about Provincetown? Did your husband know anyone up there?"

"Well, of course. We bought a house in Wellfleet not two years ago. Whit was expanding his reach to the Cape, well on his way to creating another successful newspaper. In fact, that's one of the reasons Chief Proxmire suspects organized crime. He theorizes that a contract was put on Whit's life because he was encroaching on older, more established publishing concerns and decimating their businesses. The chief has even sent investigators up there. But so far they haven't turned up anything of value."

"Why did your husband target Cape Cod for his newest venture?"

"The obvious reasons. He had roots there; his people have always maintained a summer place in Hyannis Port. And he felt the Cape offered the same kind of opportunistic and moneyed terrain that the Eastern Shore had provided him."

"Did you always accompany Whit on his trips to the Cape?"

"I'm not sure what you're implying, Inspector."

"Just wondering," he said, trying to sound merely curious.

"Well, you have some nerve," she erupted. "I know *exactly* what you're trying to imply. But just because we often went our separate ways does not mean that our marriage was not strong and resilient. It was not merely a thing of convenience and show, you can be sure."

Eamon felt sorry for the frayed, prickly, all-too-sheltered woman before them. The more she protested, and the more defensive she became about her marriage, the less believable that cherished union seemed.

"Oh, you just didn't know Whit. A man of principles. A correct and proper gentleman. The notion that he would carry on in such a sordid manner is unthinkable. The woman behind these letters is suffering some sort of paranoid delusion. I will not be surprised to find out that this lunatic is also behind my husband's murder. It's so outrageous, the absurdity of it all."

Her patience had been tried, and now it was time to lead them back out through the sweeping elegance of the Adams-Talbot House, passing the lovely pastel rooms with their serene floral arrangements, admiring the museum-quality paintings and marble busts. Such a perfectly self-contained world! Glittering chandeliers and hushed grand pianos, courtly tapestries and

Louis XIV writing desks. A hermetically sealed world that tried hard to keep out the dust and dirt along with so many other little unpleasantries.

They stopped for lunch in St. Michaels, a trendy, touristy port on the Chesapeake, a Waspy refuge for seersucker jackets and gingham shirts and madras shorts. It was not by any means a utilitarian town, not the sort of place where you might easily find a pharmacy or a hardware store, or even a supermarket. But if you wanted to park your yacht and browse expensive, artsy-craftsy shops for duck decoys and precious bottle-encased clipper ships, then this was indeed the pearl in your oyster.

They sat outside under a Perrier umbrella at one of the waterfront restaurants and ordered soft-shell crab sandwiches and a pitcher of beer. It was warm and breezeless, the way it seemed it would always be, and the bay was sad with dozens of powerless, bereft spinnakers.

Bunko took out the letters. "We'll go through them chronologically. There's only four of them and they were mailed out within a two-week period in May. Just before Whit got aced."

"Maybe we should have bagged them," Eamon said, nervous about their sloppiness. "Had 'em checked for prints."

"Give me a break," Bunko said, "there's nothing to be lifted off these. All you'll find are Mrs. Ellsworth's, believe me. Look how worn and mangled they are, like they've been squeezed to death. Believe me, these babies have gone through the wringer."

"Poor Mrs. Ellsworth," Eamon remarked with a note of sympathy.

"Christ, are you kidding me? The lady's a damn ostrich. Got her stupid head in the sand, for crying out loud."

"Maybe that was the only way," Eamon said. "May-

**115**

be shutting things out was the only way she could hold her marriage together. The only way she could keep her fragile world from coming apart."

"Christ, give me a break already," Bunko shot back disgustedly. "Just for that—for your ill-advised attempt at psychobabble—you get to take first crack at the letters."

Eamon was once again struck by that waxen seal, which was starting to look like molten blood to his eyes. The envelopes had all been addressed to Whit Ellsworth's place of business—c/o the *Lantern*—in a likely attempt to circumvent Mrs. Ellsworth. Before reading a word, Eamon studied the handwriting, noting the tiny, yet determined script—a pervading sense of forcefulness—with its unusual, backward-leaning slant, as if the letter writer were being pulled inexorably into the past.

May 14

W.,

I miss you already. I long for your ready-made strength and your strong, facile way of seeing the world. I long for your easy explanations and easy ways. And, yes, I even long for your grunting, beastly body on top of mine. You are right, after all. For all my protestations to the contrary, I still want to do the evil, dirty deed with you. I need to go back through the years with you, crossing over that unspeakable divide.

It is wrong of course, but like so many other things that are wrong it offers up such a cheap and unnerving thrill. Oh, don't mistake me, you are a bastard, a truly selfish and inconsiderate bastard, just like the rest of your penis-driven kind. You just want to stick it into me, don't you, darling? I am faceless to you, just boobs and orifices, just some wide and gaping hole that you find so necessary for your own needy and perverse pleasures. Don't you think I know that, darling? Just the thought of you using me that way excites me; the way you dirty me with your foul-smelling seed, the way I take it.

It's all so degenerative, so lacking in the fundamentals like love and tenderness and even foreplay. Oh, I long for you right now, for your brutal, hard touch. Fill me, fill me up with your filthiness. Oh, darling, is this not exciting?

Absolutely wet at the thought,

L.C.

May 19

W.,

You really should call, darling. I've left messages, oodles of them. Didn't you get my deliriously wicked note?

I think next time you're up here we should take your Mercedes out one night into the lonely back country and do the absolutely unthinkable. What do you say to that, about howling in the moonlight all over again? Let's go back to that dead and gone time and place, to that treacherous, ruinous turn in the road, where it all began. I'll even wear a tartan skirt for you and knee-length socks and saddle shoes, the whole warped fantasy. Oh, doesn't that turn you on, darling? Or don't you like talking about it?

You must wonder now if it was indeed a coincidence running into me again after so many years. It seemed all too amazing, didn't it? Well, I guess you'll never know for sure. Because I'm certainly not telling. I've come too far for that, for petty truths and insincere lies.

Oh, you must call me, darling. We have so much more to talk about, so much more to clear up. If you're a smart, good little boy you'll do as I ask.

Still waiting,

L.C.

May 25

W.,

My patience is running very thin. You've made promises to me, darling, and I expect you to keep them this time. I will not go through that again, not ever, trust me. And this time I won't act like some weak, namby-pamby, eighteen-year-old frosh. No, that poor little innocent girl is gone forever, thanks to you.

We both belong to that cold, rushing river of time, and, believe me, her strong, aching current threatens to pull us under. You know we will always be driving your spanking-new Olds 88—a present from your rich and beloved daddy—up those dark and lonely roads. Do you remember that big and terrifying car? For a long time I wouldn't allow myself to remember, but now I can never forget that unholy front seat with its smell of Chesterfields and bourbon and lime cologne and new vinyl. You drove recklessly, darling, swigging from a pint of Old Grand-Dad (yes, I recall even that unremarkable detail) while I fiddled with the radio dial. That was the year of the folkies and of the Beatles' "Yesterday." I remember arguing with you over the merits of Dylan; I really loved his "The Times They Are a-Changin'," but you thought it was just a bunch of coffeehouse nonsense.

We couldn't seem to agree on anything that night—not civil rights, not Vietnam, not even the space program. We even tried to talk literature and wound up having another dumb row. You loved Norman Mailer and that big, dumb, penile book of his—I can't think of the title now; some ridiculous claptrap about a man murdering his wife so that he could feel alive again—and became angry with me for not sharing your wholly misguided opinion. That was the autumn that I carried around *Miss MacIntosh, My Darling,* the season's big book for women, poetic tripe about a girl in search of herself. Oh, I hauled it with me everywhere, down to Lake Waban and up to Clapp Library, just hoping that the others would notice that I was reading the right stuff.

Oh, darling, it was such a different world back then, such a good time to be alive. Those vanished days were so delicious and thrilling, fraught with possibilities and American can-do. Do you remember those lost, glowing days? The space race was on, and *Life* and *Look* were full of pictures of heroic astronauts and Gemini capsules. The highways glinted with Detroit's finest, with sporty new Mustangs and Corvairs and T-Birds. The streets of Boston bustled with fresh, lemony Breck girls and all those handsome, frisky, Jack Lemmon junior executives. And everyone, it seemed, was lighting up Lucky Strikes and sipping Scotch on the rocks, as if that were the epitome of continental sophistication. There was, for just a fleeting moment, a marvelous, almost divine, sense of togetherness, as if we were all rushing forward together. At least that's how I remember it.

Oh, darling, you stole so much from me, took so much that wasn't yours to take. I said, "Why are we pulling over? Something wrong with the car?" And you didn't have the decency to answer me or even to look me in the eyes. I didn't even know what you were doing at first; I was absolutely uncomprehending throughout the entire episode. After it was over, you just zipped up your fly, like nothing had happened, and started the car again. And then we were driving away from that terrible crime scene, and you were saying something unfathomable like, "Now aren't you a delightful girl."

We had only met a few hours before at the harvest moon mixer, you bastard.

Mister Suave Harvard Senior. Lettering in tennis, fencing, and ingenuous virgins.

You seemed too good to be true.

You were so charming and good-looking, with an easy laugh and cocksure way. You looked like a young Peter Lawford, in your burgundy turtleneck and hound's-tooth tweeds.

You certainly didn't look like a rapist, at least not like any I could imagine.

But that's what you did to me in your daddy's car.

If only it could have ended there.

If only that thing hadn't started to grow inside of me. Like some evil pod creature.

Then all those delicious and thrilling days were over for me. Then I began to notice the decay, the stench of life. It's everywhere, have you noticed, darling?

Call me, if you know what's good for you.

L.C.

May 29

W.,

You are a bloodless beast.

So you've done it to me again, have you?

Does it make you feel powerful? Is it the only way you can get off? Does your manhood throb with the sweet obscenity of it all?

The worst part is that it's my own damn fault. I should have known better. But I wanted to confront you again, to somehow make sense of that terrible moonlit night and all the terrible wasted years that followed.

Believe me, Whit, it was no accident running into me again. It was nothing of the sort. Now doesn't that scare you just a smidge?

Well, it should, darling.

You never even took the trouble to learn more about me. Weren't you even the least bit curious about what I'd been up to during the last thirty years?

No, you just wanted to start right up where we

left off. You couldn't wait to get into my pants again.

Just like any other married man.

I wonder what would have happened if I hadn't had the abortion and had married you instead.

Do you know that I'd even gone so far as to pick out a name for our unborn child? That's how sick and frightened I was; I thought that I could still take that terrible wrong and turn it into something less wrong. I'll marry him, I thought. Marry the rapist! Lord, have you ever heard of something so insane?

But what was I to do? Go to the police, tell my parents? Can you even begin to imagine the shame?

But then you paid that doctor and everything was supposed to go away.

Well, at least you went away for a while. And of course the baby went away.

But where was I going to go?

Did you ever think of that? In all those long years did you ever once think about me?

Believe me, I brooded over you.

About all the things I wanted to say to you. Never mind all the things I wanted to do to you. And all the things I still may do.

L.C.

After he'd finished, Eamon wasted no time reaching for the pitcher of beer. He downed a glassful, then another. And once again. Then he sat back and waited for it to take effect.

Bunko watched with interest. "Mighty thirsty, ain't we?"

"No, not thirsty," Eamon answered strangely. "Not anything like it."

"What, something in them letters?"

"I don't even know where to begin."

"Well, for starters, you think it's the same person behind the chain letter?"

"I don't think there's much doubt," Eamon said, staring out at the anemic harbor.

Bunko took out his cigarettes. He extended the pack to Eamon, who accepted, before taking one for himself. For a while they just sat quietly, contemplating the drifting, dissipating smoke.

"So," Bunko said, breaking it, "are we in possession of what the French like to call *les billets-doux?* That's love letters, for the unwashed and unsophisticated like yourself."

Eamon was tempted to laugh. The same man who used "ain't" a moment ago was now peppering his speech with precocious foreign phrases. But then again, that was the beauty of the man.

"What is that, something you remembered from high-school French?"

"What? *Billets-doux?* No, that's something I remembered from a girl named Annette."

"I don't recall you ever going out with a French babe."

"It happened a long time ago, long before I ever met you, kid."

"Were you in love?"

"Who ever really knows for sure? But I'll tell you this, I was crazy about Annette. I guess that was the problem. It was one of those crazy kind of love things. No rhyme or reason to it. I just wanted her—and what she was doing with me, I'll never know."

"Love's never logical," Eamon said, taking another thoughtful drag.

"That's very fuckin' deep, kid."

"Best I could come up with on such short notice."

"So what about the *billets-doux?"* Bunko pressed. "Love letters, or what?"

"I don't know."

"What do you mean, you don't know?"

"It's a damn grab bag, a little of everything. You've

122

got sex and hate. You've got rape and revenge. You've even got something on the extreme, far-off borders of love. Hell, you've got all sorts of human strangeness in those letters."

"You've got to be joking," Bunko said.

"Actually, that's the only thing we don't have here."

# *Thirteen*

❦

*E*amon had arrived at the Command Post to find that someone had messed with his desk, plastering it with porno magazine cutouts of Christy Gertz. He didn't have to be told who the culprit was; Masterson's ugly prints were all over this one.

At one point Masterson had even stopped by, clearly intent on seeing the results of his handiwork. "Oh," he said, snickering, "I see you pasted down some pictures of your girlfriend. What a nice, homey touch."

But for all his juvenile delinquency, Del Masterson was, for once, in an astonishingly good mood. The new leads had brought a gloating, anticipatory smile to his hammy face. He wanted this one, badly. Eamon knew this was the opportunity Masterson had long been waiting for, the chance to turn the tables on his former taskmasters, to take a small measure of revenge on the Bureau for shipping him off to Postal Siberia, which was his quaint way of referring to Dead Letters.

It was all about hard feelings. And that's why Del

wasn't going to share their new leads with the FBI, or even with Seppala and Kelsey. Eamon didn't like it one bit. It wasn't that he was such a team player himself. But, hell, he knew enough to play ball when you had dead judges and dead admirals.

Eamon and Bunko had spent most of the day working the phones, dialing up the clues that were scattered throughout L.C.'s letters to Whit Ellsworth like so many dropped crumbs. They started with plain old geography. The letters were mailed out of Provincetown, Massachusetts. She mentioned Boston and Harvard and Lake Waban. They had no trouble finding out that Lake Waban was located twenty-five miles outside Boston, that it in fact bordered the Wellesley campus, a women's liberal arts college of some distinction. They also learned that Wellesley included the Margaret Clapp Library, which was just another of L.C.'s discarded crumbs.

It stood to reason then that L.C. was an eighteen-year-old (an age she herself had so kindly provided) Wellesley freshman when she met Harvard senior Whit Ellsworth at the harvest moon mixer.

Ascertaining the year was only a bit trickier. But by making use of the *Encyclopaedia Britannica*'s Book of the Year reference series they were able to arrive at 1965.

According to *Britannica,* 1965 was the year that the Beatles released "Yesterday" and that Bob Dylan strummed "The Times They Are a-Changin'." It was also the same year that Joan Baez sang "We Shall Overcome" and that a kid named Donovan broke through with "Catch the Wind."

Marguerite Young published *Miss MacIntosh, My Darling.* And Norman Mailer's *An American Dream* also came out in 1965, which *Britannica* described as a "bizarre, violent story."

There were more than enough matches to satisfy the two postal inspectors.

Eamon found himself caught up in time's passing,

in that web of barely remembered miscellany. Sandy Koufax went 26 and 8 in 1965, and the Dodgers beat the Twins in the seventh game of the World Series. UCLA was on its way to becoming a college basketball dynasty. Lyndon Johnson was beginning his first elected term in office, while Robert McNamara was in his fifth year as secretary of defense. The war in Vietnam was no longer a footnote. The big movies that year were *The Great Race,* starring Tony Curtis and Jack Lemmon, and *The Sound of Music.*

Eamon wasn't at all sure why any of this was important. But he couldn't seem to get around the feeling that indeed it was, that the key to solving L.C.'s identity lay in the flotsam and jetsam of the past.

Armed with the information that L.C. was a member of Wellesley's class of 1969, Eamon had contacted the alumnae association. He'd been put through to their president, Virginia Smite, who turned out to be most obliging on the matter of requisitioning old yearbooks and current alumnae listings.

"Do you mean to tell me," Virginia had said most excitedly, "that one of *our* girls is up to no good? How frightfully delicious."

As it turned out, there were only three girls in the class of 1969 with the initials L.C. And Laurie Calhoun was dead, three years ago with breast cancer. And Linda Carey was a botanist on the island of Fiji, which pretty much counted her out. And Luella Coonts, though alive and well and living in New York City, was a rather well-known society woman whose comings and goings were easily accounted for.

It was fair to guess then that L.C. had most likely changed her surname through marriage. At least that's what they were betting. Unfortunately, by Virginia Smite's compilations, there were at least twenty-eight women from the class of '69 who could have at one time or another—through either marriage or remarriage—gone by the initials *L.C.*, seventeen of whom were residents of the state of Massachusetts. Linda was by far the most common first name, closely followed by Lauren and Lois. Actually, until now, the inspectors hadn't quite realized just how many women's first names began with the letter *L;* and what a long parade it was, of Lydias and Leslies, of Lilians and Louises, of Lucys and Lenores, of so many names that seemed to cry out from the nurseries of yesteryear.

They began with the Massachusetts Seventeen.

And by late afternoon they were still counting down. They relied on cold calling, on lavish deceit. It was Bunko's idea. He knew they couldn't just identify themselves as postal inspectors and ask each woman outright if she were some murdering loon. It was imperative that they not scare the quarry. So, with that in mind, they pretended to be conducting a national survey for Citizens Speak Up, ostensibly a polling organization. This gave them the opportunity to ask telling questions about handgun control, women's rights, gay rights, and even date rape. The content of the answers was not the only thing interesting them. They were also taking measure of reactions, checking for volatility and any unusual amount of rancor. Unfortunately, a few would not take part in their poll, and there were also quite a few answering machines with which to contend.

Eamon's desk was still burdened with Masterson's smut—attempts to remove it had resulted in a bizarre montage of disembodied sexual parts—which just added to the overall strangeness. As he questioned the Wellesley alumnae about their attitudes toward rape and punishment—"Is castration something that society should consider? Is execution a just and fair solution?"—he couldn't help notice Christy's glossy, distorted flesh.

Christy, in fact, had left several messages for him.

But that was the last thing Eamon wanted to deal with right now. He had his own problems, his own screwed-up love life. Mary Seppala wasn't taking his calls. He'd already tried four or five times, but no dice. At a quarter to five he decided to give it one last toss. Once again the desk sergeant told him she'd stepped out. But this time Eamon asked to leave an urgent message, explaining that a new lead had opened up in the case they were working. Before Eamon could hang up, the sergeant said, "Hey, hold on a sec, wilya?"

A few seconds later Mary got on and said, "This better be good, Lieutenant."

"I just need to see you," he said, pleading. "Can't you understand that?"

"I'm sorry, Lieutenant, I just don't think this is going to work out between us." Then she took the opportunity to add, "Incidentally, don't ever use that ploy again with the desk sergeant. You do remember the story about the boy who cried wolf, don't you?"

"Yeah, as I recall it didn't have a very happy ending."

"If you turn up something on the case, I'd appreciate it if you'd go through Kelsey from now on."

End of conversation. And the end of any budding romance. Damn, he should never have got drunk in that bar in Annapolis.

"Why the long face, kid?" asked Bunko from his gunmetal corner of the world.

"Women," Eamon lamented.

"Unquestionably the source of all the world's misery," Bunko readily agreed.

"Bunk, tell me what the hell were we doing in Annapolis? At the White Horse, getting wasted and hitting on strangers?"

"Kid, we were acting out an ancient male drama. A ritual of chromosomal stupidity that's been played out for a good ten thousand years. So at least we're in good company."

128

"Mary's not even talking to me."

"Well, Christ, join the club. Franny's not talking to me either."

"I don't see why not," Eamon said. "She wasn't down there. She didn't see anything. She didn't know what you were up to with that barmaid."

"It seems she doesn't need evidence of the visual kind. Somehow, and don't ask me how, she just knows. The woman's a born detective. Nothing goes by her. I come home last night and Franny just says, 'Who the hell is she?' Damn, there must be something in their chromosomes, too."

At that moment Masterson showed up, looking none too pleased. But what else was new?

"Looks like you girls fucked up again," he said, his fuse already lit with the Wild Turkey. "One of them TV news bimbos recognized you down in Annapolis, in front of that saloon where Admiral Lerner got his. Seems you girls passed right in front of the camera while they were filming some post mortem glop. The bimbo also remembers seeing both of you at the Baltimore courthouse in connection with Judge Draper and that Webster broad. It gets worse. She's heard rumors from her police informants about the chain letter. So naturally she wants to know all about Postal's involvement."

"Who's the newswoman?" Bunko asked.

"Another girlfriend of Pretty Boy's, it looks like."

Eamon said, "What on earth are you talking about?" He felt himself already tensing, as if bracing for some unknown assault.

"Diana Hunter, Channel Six."

"Real dishy blonde," Bunko added. "Always wearing them low-cut blouses. A former beauty queen or something."

"Well, the bimbo queen specifically asked for Pretty Boy."

"Del, I happen to know her *professionally,*" Eamon

explained defensively. "Don't you remember that stalker who sent her threatening letters about a year ago?"

Masterson said, "You fuck her, too?"

"Of course not," Eamon said, bristling.

"Oh, I thought you fucked all your clients," Masterson said, positively jolly at the thought. "That's what I heard, anyway."

"Mind telling me what the hell you're getting at, Del?"

"Well, I happened to have had the most extraordinary chat about you and your little girlfriend today. It seems Baby Face's mommy is most concerned about your very special relationship with her fifteen-year-old daughter."

Masterson paused to relish the inroads he was making. Cruel, unmistakable delight colored his face.

"Mrs. Gertz seems to think you've made some improper advances on little Christy. And I hate to say it, but I myself have sensed a certain unhealthy attraction between you two young people. As much as it pains me, I might even have to bring it to the attention of the Sexual Harassment Review Board. Why, just the appearance of impropriety is a blot on the Service's fine reputation. What a shame, too. Just as Pretty Boy's career was getting into high gear."

"What an absolute load of manure!" Bunko thundered, rushing to Eamon's defense. "You know as well as I do, Del, that he hasn't done a damn thing to that girl. Bunch of crazy lies. Nothing there, believe me, you stinking son of a bitch. So don't you go threatening him or me or anybody else with your goddamn review board."

"Easy there, Lard Ass. I'm just making inquiries. You seem to forget that's my job."

Masterson was still smiling, still delighting in his small, petty, evil triumph.

"So, Pretty Boy, did you pork our little porn princess?"

"Not a chance."

"Was it an oral agreement? Like, does the number sixty-nine mean anything to you, Pretty Boy?"

"We did nothing of the sort," Eamon said, trying hard to remain calm.

"You expect me to believe that? That nothing happened between you and that hotsy-totsy piece of junior-high ass?"

Eamon kept his mouth shut about that kiss at the kiddie pool. That short-lived little disaster. Even if he had finally done the right thing by getting the hell out of there.

"Well?" Masterson persisted. "Is there something you want to tell me? Something you want to get off your conscience? Maybe some little blow job you forgot about?"

Eamon rejoined, "I think you're way out of line, Del. That's what I think."

"Yeah," Bunko said, jumping in, "if you ask me, that harassment committee should be investigating you."

"Well," Masterson said, just slightly more contrite, "I'm not doing anything for the moment. Look, there'll be no suspensions until I'm in possession of a few more facts—"

"Few more brains is more like it," Bunko said.

"Did you even talk to Christy yet?" Eamon asked.

"No, I haven't," Masterson admitted. "The mother doesn't think that's such a good idea at the moment. Besides, the little slut would probably just lie anyway. To protect her postal stud muffin."

"Del, you do know, of course, that Christy lives with her grandmother and not her mother. In fact, I don't even believe Christy talks to her mom anymore."

"That's not the way I heard it."

Eamon said, "Are you even sure you were talking to Christy's mother?"

"Hey, what do you take me for? Some kind of

fuckhead like yourself? Now let's move on to other more pressing matters. Like that TV bimbo, for one thing. Pretty Boy, you've got a date with her tonight."

"Del, I think I'm missing something here."

"Not a date exactly. Drinks at P. J. Rascal's. To discuss the case. Says she trusts you. I've promised her an exclusive if she'll just hold back on the story."

Bunko said, "But we've already promised Franny an exclusive."

Masterson ignored him. "Now, Pretty Boy, you be real charming and nice to this Diana bimbo. Just dole out the absolute minimum, you understand?"

"I'm not so sure this is such a good idea," Eamon said.

"Oh, one more thing," Masterson said, as another cruel smile began to take shape, "you have my permission to pork this one. She's old enough to know better."

# *Fourteen*

❦

*P.* J. Rascal's, a single's bar-restaurant on the Inner Harbor, was not Eamon's kind of terrain at all. But it was the sudsy, generic beerscape of choice for smartly attired professional women and their wolfish, pin-striped counterparts. Generic might have seemed like an odd description for any joint that housed seemingly one-of-a-kind collections of B-movie posters, mounted antlers, ornamental steins, old-time baseball caps, college pennants, and antique license plates. Then again, there were four other P. J. Rascal's, and they were, for all sensorial purposes, interchangeable. Although designed to conjure up an atmosphere of collegial fun and games—all the more conducive for instant camaraderie among strangers—Eamon thought that these giant saloon warehouses summoned up instead a potpourri of unctuous pickup lines and lonely, longing glances.

Actually, what Eamon really disliked about P. J. Rascal's was that there were no buybacks; expressionless, humorless bartenders never poured one on the house, no matter how long you sat there, or how large your tab got. Of course, with so many clamoring suits, there was no need for small courtesies.

But Diana Hunter, sad to say, looked at home here, among the attractive, ambitious Philistines. She was a staggeringly sexual presence who smelled wildly of expensive, musky secretions and who never thought to stop flirting with her expert green eyes. She was dressed to provoke in a cleavage-inviting silk blouse and a dangerous black mini that startled with sheer, transparent motive. There was just one thing wrong with the picture. Eamon was not responding.

"Are you sure I can't talk you into a martini?" the blond newswoman asked again. "I so hate to drink alone."

"No, thanks," he said, "just some coffee."

He was getting tired of beautiful, sexy women. If such a thing were possible. Well, he'd certainly had enough of them for one day. Mary Seppala, the keeper, the real thing, wouldn't even take his calls anymore. And then there was Christy Gertz, a black cloud hanging over everything.

"Eamon," Diana said familiarly, placing her hand over his, "don't be such a spoilsport."

"Miss Hunter, what do you want to know?" he asked, getting down to business.

"Why are you being like this?"

"Like what?" he said indignantly.

"You know," she said, fluttering her false eyelashes and implying so much more. "You just acted so differently the last time we met."

Almost a year ago. Lunch at the Stouffer Hotel. Ostensibly to talk about her case. That creep who'd been sending her poison-pen letters. Two bottles of wine later and they were playing touchy-feely under the table. Nothing ever came of it—and he wondered why. The woman had it all: looks, brains, and a cushy job. She'd called a few times, but for some unremembered reason he'd cooled to the idea.

"Is there someone special in your life now?" she asked. "Is that what it is?"

"Yeah, that's it," he said, trying to settle the issue for her.

She eyed him suspiciously. "Well, you're not married, are you? And you're not living with anyone? So then. I don't see any problem. I mean, not with me, anyway."

To illustrate this problem-free arrangement, she moved extra close to him and began to stroke his leg.

"We could have some fun together," she said.

He removed her hand without saying a word.

"Don't you find me attractive?" she persisted.

"That's not the problem," he said.

"What is then? What's with you?"

It came out harshly, all too accusing; quite obviously, this was not a woman who was used to having her advances rebuffed.

"Oh, don't tell me you're gay or something?"

"That's right," he said coldly. "I'm gay. Now let's get to the interview part. You know, the part where you ask me questions that are job related."

"Okay, have it your way," she said. Only she said it like, Okay, you asked for it and now I'm going to make you sorry that you were ever born.

He was annoyed. Put off by her pawing and groping, the way she was all over him without a second thought. Why, they hardly knew each other. And she didn't seem all that interested in knowing anything about him except whether he was willing and able. Eamon Wearie understood that a kind of role reversal had taken place: He had been granted a sudden, momentary glimpse into a woman's world, that unvarying nightmare of oily, pushy men only after the one thing. For one all-too-brief moment he found himself disgusted with himself and his gender; how often had he done the very same thing, how often had he pursued his quarry with the same salacious intent, and how often had he muttered to himself, "Damn lesbian," when his advances were spurned.

Diana said, "I'd like to see that chain letter now, if you don't have any objections."

"I'm afraid I can't do that."

"Then what are you good for, Lieutenant? Not much, it seems."

She had all the warmth now of that chilled martini in front of her.

"I can only give you a bare-bones outline," responded Eamon with dreary officialism. "Those are my orders."

"Okay, who's sending it?"

"We don't know. Something or somebody called the Committee."

"What demands does the letter make?"

"I'm not sure I should reveal that."

"You can trust me," she said with effortless guile. "Remember, I've given my word to wait on it."

"There are three demands," Eamon said, knowing he was relenting too easily. "The Committee tells the recipient to: one, relinquish all their worldly goods; two, make some kind of public statement to acknowledge their wrongdoings; and three, send the letter on to some other person of their own choosing."

"And what happens if you fail to do these things?"

Eamon was silent.

"So that's what happened to Judge Draper and that woman DA?" she asked excitedly.

"We're not quite sure," Eamon said, backing off. "Perhaps it's all a hoax."

"But you don't think so?" she pressed, the realization that this was the mother lode shining in her eager, greedy face. "And Admiral Lerner? Is that connected to this, too? Oh, God, this is just huge."

Eamon wasn't about to say anything more. And he sure as hell wasn't going to mention the other names on their killer's mailing list. Or those German guns. The Glock19, which had taken the lives of Eddie

Dooley, Judge Harold Draper, Lou Ackerman, and—as was confirmed today by Chief Proxmire in St. Michaels—Whit Ellsworth. Then there was that Sig Sauer P226, which had sprayed its hate into the bodies of Assistant DA Molly Webster and Admiral Guy Lerner.

"Is there anything else you can tell me, Lieutenant?"

"I think I've said enough already."

She didn't bother with a good-bye; it was clear she had no more use for him. She gulped back her martini and made her way to the door. As he watched her shimmy through the boisterous P. J. Rascal's throng, he couldn't help but feel that he was going to pay dearly for rebuffing her highly practiced advances.

Inserting the key into the door of his house, Eamon heard long, low rumblings of thunder in the distance. Good, he thought, perhaps this miserable humid weather will finally break.

Daniel P. Pinkus and the two cats were on the living room couch watching the news. Pope John Paul II spoke before the multitudinous faithful in some huge arena. Pinkus's irradiated face was awash in tears.

Eamon, too exhausted for words, just plopped down in his easy chair. The pontiff appeared in flowing white robes, a small, wizened figure in a sea of colorful thousands.

"I appeal especially to young people," he droned softly, "to rediscover the wealth of wisdom, the integrity of conscience, and the deep interior joy which flow from respect for human sexuality understood as a great gift from God and lived according to the truth of the body's nuptial meaning."

Pinkus punctuated these remarks with amens and heartfelt sobs.

"America needs much prayer," the pope concluded, "lest it lose its soul."

Then Peter Jennings said somberly that they'd return in a moment. Pinkus muted the sound.

"Have you learned anything?" Pinkus said, wiping at his eyes. "Have you not taken anything away from this . . . this divine experience?"

Eamon said, "Did His Holiness happen to mention how the Orioles did this afternoon?"

"Oh, you are beyond hope!" Pinkus cried out. "A barbaric heathen who cares only about beer and sex-crazed women."

"Jesus, you even got the order in which I like them right."

"Which reminds me, some woman keeps calling for you. She must've tried six or seven times in the last couple of hours."

"Did she leave her name?" Eamon couldn't help hoping that it was Mary, that she'd had a change of heart.

"No, she did not," Pinkus said, sounding quite disgusted with these nameless calls. "In fact, she was most rude to my inquiries."

*"Inquiries?"*

"Yes, *inquiries.* I think it best that I start screening your personal calls. You're just not a very good judge of character. Why, just look at some of the strays you've brought home in the past."

*"Strays?"*

"Such horrid, awful girls. One wonders if they even take the trouble to read the Scriptures. Or even bathe, for that matter."

"Daniel," Eamon said tightly, on the very verge of exploding, "I don't think it's your place to—"

"You should give up sex. Look how it controls you. You're like some horrid junkie who can only think about his next fix. Oh, if you would only give Christ's teachings a chance."

"And if only you would shut up, for the love of Christ!"

"Giving up sex is not as hard as you think," Pinkus

continued, unperturbed. "I can tell you quite truthfully that it hasn't bothered me in the least."

"That's because you haven't been laid in years anyway."

"I'm not saying that didn't make it a little bit easier on me. But still you should heed the pope's warning. Why, only today, he was saying how sex only led to disease, violence, pornography, drug abuse, and all sorts of other horrid things. There's even talk that the pope is thinking about issuing a new encyclical, his own updating of the *Humanae Vitae.*"

"Oh, Daniel, I hope it's not just talk. Because I, for one, could hardly stand the disappointment."

"I guess we're all excited at the prospect," Pinkus said, oblivious to sarcasm. "There's even speculation that he wants to outlaw sex altogether. Even between married people. I think it's about time, myself."

"Dan, I don't believe you've taken the trouble to think this through properly. Because how in the hell could the human race survive without sex?"

"Oh, but think what a nicer world it would be."

Eamon had had enough. He left Pinkus for the merciful privacy of his own bedroom. The windows flickered with blue, and he could still hear those low, ominous rumblings. He wished for downpours, for a thorough drenching. Then maybe some cool air would be allowed to blow in, giving them a fresh, renewed world in the morning. In the meantime he turned on the air-conditioner, that deafening, energy-inefficient relic. He settled back with Elmore Leonard's latest, which was another good, fast read about low-life scum scamming their way through the Florida Keys. He hadn't got ten pages into it when the phone began to bleep.

"You really ought to be more careful," some woman said. "She's just a child, even if she does look all grown-up."

"Who is this? Do I know you?"

"Christy's very upset with you," the woman said.

"You've hurt her deeply. She thought you would be different from the others. But you're just like all the rest of your sick, penile kind."

He knew now. Her choice of words. That Bostonian quiver.

Their Committee of one.

"I want to help," he said evenly.

"More lies from you and your kind. Don't you think I've heard it all before. I should say so. All those doctors. Such self-righteous pricks. Freudians cloaked in the Great White Male Penis Myth. Doctors, they're the worst, I tell you. Those little, somber, tweedy, bearded bastards. Pretending to listen. Pretending to care. But in the end, they're just like every other penis person. Little jerk offs who spend their esteemed time pondering that imponderable mystery of what's between your legs. Dawkins was by far the worst. To think that I put my faith in him. But I suppose we don't have to worry about that penis person anymore."

Eamon forced the name to memory. Dawkins, Dawkins, Dawkins. Most likely her former psychiatrist. And most likely dead.

He said, "Why did you call me?"

"I like toying with my prey," she replied matter-of-factly. "I find it quite exciting, almost sexually so. The power is mine now, to do with as I please. Although I must admit to a certain hesitancy in your case. As you know, Christy's grown quite fond of you, Eamon Wearie."

"You called my boss today, didn't you? Pretending to be Christy's mom, pretending a lot of things. Mind telling me what that was all about?"

"You need to take responsibility for your actions, Mister Wearie."

"The same could be said of you, I suppose."

"Responsibility is everything to me," she said firmly. "I am conscience itself, final arbiter in the Court of

Wayward Souls. I have been chosen for this role by God, by She Herself."

"I don't doubt your convictions," Eamon said, continuing in his efforts to keep her on the line and to learn as much as possible about her. "I doubt, though, that God would approve of your methods."

"Not only does She approve, She has called upon me to make this ultimate sacrifice. She has visited me in my dreams. She has spoken to me about millennium-old wrongs that must be righted; of lying, thieving, old men who claim to have written the holy truth, but who've instead hoodwinked a hundred generations. God has spoken to me and She has told me in no uncertain terms that evil must be eradicated by any means necessary. We must fight the Devil's fire with a hellfire of our own. We must burn it all down now so that God and all Her infinite love can one day reign supreme. So that what happened to me shall never again happen to another."

"What happened to you? It must have been very terrible to make you feel this way."

"It is beyond you and your kind, Mister Wearie."

"No, it's not," he said, taking his chance now. "You were just a kid, your first year in college. How were you to know? It's just this nice, innocent harvest moon mixer. And there's this handsome, charming Harvard boy. You're talking and laughing, getting along just great. So when he asks if you want to take a ride in his new car, you say, 'Sure thing,' not thinking much about it, except what a fine, moonlit night it is for a drive. How were you supposed to know that your fate was sealed the moment you got into Whit Ellsworth's Olds 88?"

He used the details sparingly and purposefully, trying hard to force her hand. It was high-stakes poker, all or nothing, and he was betting everything that she wouldn't see his raise. He wanted her to fold her cards right now—to just admit everything, including who the hell she was. The bluff was that he already knew her identity.

"Listen," he said, pressing his final advantage, "Wellesley and 1965 happened a long time ago. Whit's dead now. And so are a bunch of other people. You've had your little revenge, and now it's time to let go. Look, we're closing in anyway. We know everything about you at this point. There's truly no way out."

Silence. Just the static of a bad telephone connection. He sensed, nonetheless, her lurking intelligence, the dark outer edges of her desperation.

"You don't fool me for a minute," she finally said. "You don't know anything."

He should've known better; he'd underestimated his opponent and, in the process, misplayed his hand.

"But I know everything about you, Mister Wearie," she asserted, startling him with the menace in her voice. "By the way, I very much liked the suit you were wearing today. Its color was most lovely, sort of a teal blue, wouldn't you say?"

The hairs on the back of his neck went electric.

"But I found P. J. Rascal's most disappointing. Nothing but an overpriced meat market. And that plastic woman you were with. Nothing but a little cock teaser, don't you think?"

Now it was his turn to be silent.

Not only was she seeing his bet, she was raising him back.

"My, you were driving most absentmindedly today. Much more than usual. You kept neglecting to use your blinker, and you even went through a red light on Pratt. You just seemed so preoccupied behind the wheel of your Grand Am. What a nice, sporty car that is."

His mind raced through possibilities, as if he were shuffling through a deck of marked cards. He sorted and sifted through the day's faces and events, trying in vain to locate the wicked queen of hearts.

"I so enjoyed our time together," she purred. "It's a shame it has to end so soon. Toodle-oo."

It was a rigged game—and he was clearly in over his head. Unfortunately, the hand had to be played out, whether he liked it or not.

He burrowed into his underwear drawer for his Smith & Wesson .38. The next thing he did was check every window and door in the house to make sure they were bolted shut.

He debated calling Masterson or Bunko. But there wasn't much they could do right now anyway. He decided he'd be okay until morning. After all, he had his own gun and the training to go along with it.

He tried to get back into his Elmore Leonard, but he was too edgy for words and all the patience they required. He paced in front of the flickering blue windows, checking the familiar, quiet street below for strange cars and strange women. He spotted nothing of the kind. Just the usual, a barking dog, a toppled garbage can, a profound sense of the ordinary.

It took a little while, but he began to calm down. He'd been threatened before on the phone. Lots of times. Anonymous calls that weren't so anonymous. Always some gruff male voice. Always some turd they were closing in on. Mail fraud, dealing in child porn, something. But the gruff voice always said the same damn thing: "You're dead, Wearie." It was unvarying, really.

In his career he must've received several dozen calls like that.

And the thing was, not a one of them had ever backed it up.

Idle threats.

Made by idle minds.

Outside the thunder grew closer, louder. He turned on the TV. Marlins and Mets, ESPN Game of the Week. Battle of the cellar dwellers. He went down to the kitchen and returned with a couple of Old Bohs and a bag of chips. He settled back to an endless, sloppy, error-prone affair. He drifted in and out of sleep, in and out of the baseball game.

By eleven-thirty he was snoring in the nocturnal glow of the television.

Sometime later the rain began to fall in thundering torrents.

Even this did not wake him.

*Kaboom! Kaboom!*

He was all gone to the world, lost in the comfort of his dreams. He and his dad cruised out to sea on a big new Hatteras with twin Mercs. The ocean was a turquoise jewel. The sky, an unblemished blue. Beers were unsnapped, laughter abounded. They didn't even care about the fishing part. They talked, really talked for once. It seemed like the good times would never end. And then his dad said seriously:

"Son, I want to tell you something. I guess it won't come as any great surprise to know that I was unfaithful to your mother. Lots of times. Too many to count, I suppose. You see, Son, I was always looking for something. Something that probably ain't even out there. Sometimes I looked for it in a bottle of Jimmy Beam. Other times in the company of strange women. The shame of it was, I hurt your ma, a good, proud woman who deserved better. And I want to tell you not to waste your life looking, like I did."

All of a sudden storm clouds began to gather. Suddenly a great black mass covered that bluest of horizons and dreams. . . .

*Kaboom! Kaboom!*

It was hard to say whether it was the titanic thunder. Or the racket from that ancient air-conditioner. Or those TV voices.

Or maybe it was Pinkus's hysterical screams.

Or the smatterings of automatic gunfire from within his own house.

Eamon sprang to life, grabbing the Smith & Wesson on the nightstand beside him.

He slid out of his bedroom, into the nighmarish

darkness at the top of the stairs. The intruder was at the bottom, discharging her weapon with apparent randomness. Suddenly she appeared in a great flash of blue lightning, in the open doorway of his house.

A blond Joan of Arc in a yellow rain slicker.

Dripping wet and spraying bullets from a semiautomatic.

An avenging angel of death.

Eamon didn't bother to announce his presence. He just began firing back at that apparition in the doorway.

The tiny house blazed with gunfire and God's lightning.

In no time Eamon had emptied the chamber of his gun. But it didn't matter. She was already gone. He ran after her, out into the street and the deluge, but there was no sign of her. There was just the rain, just the sobering rain.

Then he remembered Pinkus.

He ran back in, turning the lights on, seeing the wild, deranged clusters of bullet holes in the walls and doors.

He heard Pinkus's soft moans coming from his downstairs bedroom.

Pinkus was lying on the floor, sobbing that he was going to die.

Just a flesh wound it looked like. Eamon called nine-one-one, for the ambulance and the police.

Then he tried to comfort Pinkus. "It's going to be all right, Dan. Don't you worry. They'll have you fixed up in no time."

Pinkus cried out hysterically for a priest, for last rites.

"No, you're going to be fine," Eamon assured him.

"Oh, God, I'm going to die," Pinkus sobbed again.

"Not a chance."

"Who was it? Who would want to do this to us?"

"I have no idea," Eamon said.

Maybe it was the way he said it. Or maybe Pinkus

was just a pretty good lie detector. Whatever the reason, he wasn't buying it. "You're lying," Pinkus said, dead certain. "You do know. Now tell me. You owe me that much."

"I really can't—"

"Oh, my God!" Pinkus cried, his face filling with realization. "Not another one of your crazy girlfriends!"

# *Fifteen*

"Lieutenant, I need a detailed physical description," a coldly impersonal Detective Seppala said over the phone. "In fact, I think you should come down here and spend some time with one of our sketch artists."

"I'm not going to do a damn thing," Eamon replied, "until you stop addressing me as 'Lieutenant.'"

"I've already told you that it's over. Not that we really had anything going anyway."

Eamon got a quick image in his head of the two of them dancing to Springsteen's "Thunder Road" in the Seppala family rec room. The way they were holding each other close, the way they were looking into each other's eyes. It seemed like a long time ago now, from the doleful perspective of his gunmetal desk in the raw-lit Command Post.

He said, "Meet me at Camden Yards tonight. Seven o'clock. O's and Blue Jays. The battle for first place."

"I don't think you understood me, Lieutenant. I'm not going anywhere with you. Especially not to some ball game. We have a lot to do here. These killings are priority number one. And we still have plenty of unanswered questions. I need to know a lot more, like why did our killer come after you? What's your connection with her? What's—"

"It's a long story, Mary. I need some time to tell it. You show up at Gate 38 tonight and I promise that all your questions will be answered. It's up to you."

He didn't let her get another word in; he placed the receiver back down, gently but firmly.

It occurred to him that he was somehow going to have to get Bunko to relinquish his ticket to tonight's big game; the big guy was not likely to be too thrilled about that. Oh well, he'd deal with that later.

He went back to work, back to examining mug shots. Well, not exactly mug shots, but DMV photos off the computer. In the old days they would have had to write to the Department of Motor Vehicles—waste valuable time in bureaucratic limbo—but these days they had no trouble entering into state license registration records. It was referred to as Breaking and Entering, even if it was all legal. Methodically, Eamon went about the chore of tapping their Wellesley alumnae with the initials *L.C.* into the Massachusetts program, which was a computerized filing cabinet holding over four million individual driving licenses.

The full-color licenses, including their original application forms, appeared almost instantaneously. And he was able to discard most of them with the same instantaneity. He'd got a good look at the killer last night, in that flashbulb of blue lightning. He would never forget the way those green eyes had blazed red, the absolute, unbelievable madness in that strange, boyish face. A tall, bony creature with a high forehead, thin lips, WASP nose, and ghoulish complexion. All of this in a crackling instant, from the top of the stairs, no less. Still, he knew what he saw, and he was ready to testify to that effect.

He kept punching in the names and kept watching as those names materialized into faces. He was lost in cyberspace, in that soul-less space between keyboard and illuminated screen.

Lila Cooper gave him pause.

She had mousy brown, shoulder-length hair and prescription glasses. Still, there was something about this one. He noted that her eye color was green. He further noted that she was five foot nine, 122 pounds. And that she was born on March 13, 1947. Her address was listed as a P.O. box in Belmont, Massachusetts. The license had been issued three years earlier and was due for renewal on her next birthday.

Lila Cooper continued to hover before him.

He tried to visualize her with blond hair. Dyed bright and cut short and severe.

Maybe. Just maybe.

On the back of her license she had filled out organ donor information. She had made an "anatomical gift, to be effective upon my death" of "any needed organ parts." Under "limitations," Lila Cooper had specified:

*"I only want my parts to go to a woman. No people with penises."*

Jesus Christ, Eamon thought, it has to be her.

And that handwriting, that tiny, determined script. He called up the application forms for a larger sample, just to be sure. No, there was no doubt about that backward-leaning slant. No doubt at all.

Lila Cooper was their man.

"Bingo!" he crowed. "I've got her! America's Most Wanted!"

Bunko and Masterson hurried over. They hunched over the IBM, examining Lila Cooper's driver's license photo.

"Put out the all-points bulletin," Eamon exhorted.

"Are you positive?" Masterson said, more than a little dubious.

Bunko wasn't convinced either. "She don't look anything like what you said."

"It's her, I tell you," Eamon said. "Just look at the handwriting sample, for Christ' sake."

"What's she driving?" Masterson demanded.

"I don't know," Eamon said, quickly tapping into the car registration records. "Nothing's showing up."

"What else do we know about her?"

"According to the Wellesley info, she's divorced. From Jared Cooper, an attorney. She has two daughters. Hard to believe she's a mom. I gather Jared has custody. The alumnae association gives another Belmont address. On Concord Avenue."

"Okay, okay," Masterson said, trying to think. "I want you to get in touch with this Jared guy. See what you can find out about his ex-wife. On the q.t. We don't want to set off any alarm bells, know what I mean."

"I can look into her credit history," Bunko volunteered. "Get her plastic. Maybe track her with her Visa cards. Who knows? Any luck, she's using them for gas and motel."

"Good, good," Masterson said, as a look of unvarnished pleasure came over that cruel, bulldog face.

"I'll see what I can do about getting a better picture of her," Eamon said. "It might even be possible to do a computer enhancement."

"Beautiful, beautiful," Masterson said, just beaming. "You boys are all over this baby. We've put those overrated cocksuckers at the Bureau to shame. In fact, that's a call I'm going to make right now. No sense in delaying. After all, we're going to need all the help we can get in catching this bitch, now that we know who she is. Excellent work, all the way around. I'm damn proud of you boys."

Masterson returned to his office, whistling "When the Saints Come Marching In."

"Christ, I've never seen him so happy," Bunko said. "It's a little scary. Like Hitler in a good mood."

"Well, better than Hitler in a bad mood," said Eamon.

"Which was just what kind of mood he was in this morning. Worst ever. The man wanted your hide, kid. Lucky thing you just hit the lottery."

"What are you talking about?"

"I'm talking about Diana Hunter not sitting on the story. Our chain letter led off the eleven o'clock news last night. You'll be pleased to know you were even referred to by name."

"God no," Eamon said, disbelieving.

"Oh, yes. Accused you of stonewalling the investigation. Topped it off by saying you were rude and inconsiderate and that your behavior bordered on professional incompetence. I take it your little date for drinks went real well."

"Just super. Another satisfied customer."

"Well, kid, Masterson was not pleased. And last night's shooting didn't help matters. Christ, how stupid can you get, not calling in this psycho job's threat. If we'd had your place staked out, we would've nabbed her right then and there. Saving a lot of trouble, believe me."

"Ah, but then I would've missed out on all that fun. It's not often I get to use my gun and shoot at bad guys. Especially in the privacy of my own home."

"Anyway, how's your tenant doing? That Pinko guy."

"Physically, he's fine. Mentally, he's the same old fruitcake. Bullet just grazed his shoulder. He didn't even have to stay overnight at the hospital."

"Glad to hear it. Now let's get cracking. Because with any luck we may just get to take our summer vacations, after all."

They went back to their respective phones and computer screens, back into cyberspace.

Eamon reached Jared Cooper at his Cambridge law firm. Eamon identified himself as a process server who had a subpoena for Jared's ex-wife.

"What's she done this time?" Jared asked.

"I'm not at liberty to say, sir."

"Well, I wish I could help you, but I haven't had contact with her in over two years. It took a damn restraining order, but, by God, that finally did the trick. And for that I count my blessings."

"Didn't she leave some kind of forwarding address? Isn't there someone who might know where she is? A family member, a close friend?"

"Look," Jared said sharply, "she didn't have any friends. And I've done my damnedest to wipe her from my mind. So if you'll excuse me I have to get back to work now. Good day."

The very next thing Eamon did was make a call to the Belmont Police Department, to see whether they had any record of Jared Cooper's restraining order. This time he identified himself as a federal postal inspector working in conjunction with the FBI. That put him right through to Chief Connor O'Brian.

"It was a bizarre case, all right," O'Brian said. "Had the mother there, this Mrs. Cooper, a real loon, and she was harassing not only Hubby, but the two daughters as well. It was a regular goddamn TV movie of the week. You know, one of those 'based on a true and shocking story' deals.

"You see, to begin with, this Mrs. Cooper was a real pain in the ass, a continuing nuisance. Even though Mr. Cooper had got the restraining order for him and the girls, it didn't stop this Mrs. Cooper from bothering them. Spent most of her time following the oldest daughter, for some insane reason. Don't get me wrong, she kept her distance, the whole 250 feet mandated by the court, but she just wouldn't leave Meggy alone. Following the poor girl to school. And then standing outside, just watching through the classroom windows, spooking everyone with her presence. I guess it was just a matter of time, really."

"What are you talking about?"

"One night Mrs. Cooper follows Meggy home from a date. Anyways, the daughter and the boyfriend are doing some heavy petting on the living room sofa when this Mrs. Cooper bursts into the house and tries to dismember the boy with a pair of scissors. Real pretty, let me tell you."

"How bad was it?"

"Cut off one of his testicles, the poor bastard. Kid underwent eleven hours of microsurgery. Pulled through all right, but it was enough to get this Cooper lady shipped off to the funny farm. Which was the best thing that could've happened, all the way around. The saddest part, if you ask me, is that this Mrs. Cooper really loved her family. It was like she was protecting them, like she didn't want any harm to come to them. I could just never figure out what she was protecting them from."

"Do you remember where they committed her? Which mental hospital?"

"That big state farm down in Bedford. Used to be called the New Bedford Hospital for the Criminally Insane. Now it's been changed to something a bit more politically correct. You know, something like the New Bedford Hospital for the Mentally Challenged."

Eamon suddenly remembered that doctor, the one Lila Cooper had named on the phone and the one he'd tried putting to memory: Dawkins, Dawkins, Dawkins.

There was a chance Dawkins was at Bedford.

That is, if he was still alive.

Before thanking Chief O'Brian for his time, Eamon told him it might not be such a bad idea to keep a man posted at the Cooper house.

"You're not telling me that crazy lady is back out there?"

"Consider her very armed and very dangerous," Eamon said.

"What the hell she do this time?"

"She's killing this time," Eamon said. "I gather she finds it very therapeutic."

His next call was to New Bedford, the state hospital. Helpful they were not. All they could, or would, tell him was that, yes, Lila Cooper had been a patient there for two years and that she'd been released this past March.

It was no use asking about her diagnosis, her prognosis, or even what medication she might be on. He was told to write for this information, that it had to clear official waivers.

He asked to speak to Dr. Dawkins.

There was a pause. A moment of official indecision.

"I'm afraid he's no longer at this hospital," the unhelpful administrator finally said.

"Where might I find him, then?"

"I don't think you understand. Dr. Dawkins is no longer with us. He died not long ago."

"How? How did he die?"

"It was ruled a suicide," the faceless administrator said. "That's all I know. And that's all I have to say."

They drove through the subterranean gloom of Dead Letters, through a preternatural world that had all the eeriness of a moonscape. Bunko was at the wheel of the Bob Hope Special, driving with his usual reckless abandon.

"Found out she declared bankruptcy four years ago. Listed no assets or income except for alimony. Owed a fortune on the plastic. And it doesn't look like she ever took out any new cards after that."

"I don't see how she does it," Eamon said. "I mean, stalking people takes bucks. I know she has a car because she followed me in one. Then there's meals and motel rooms. Not to mention those expensive guns. And she sure as hell doesn't have a regular nine-to-five job somewhere. So where is she getting the money from?"

"Beats me, kid."

"And where in the hell did she learn how to be an assassin? Who taught her how to handle a semiautomatic?"

"Maybe Gloria Steinem opened up a shooting range," Bunko cracked.

Eamon didn't even smile. "You might be on to something at that. And where might that shooting range be?"

"Maybe Provincetown," Bunko answered. "The letters to Whit Ellsworth were all postmarked there."

"That's my guess, too. It's also my guess that it's home base, that Provincetown is where Lila Cooper hangs her hat. But I've already checked and there's no listing for her in the Cape Cod telephone directory."

"Doesn't prove a thing."

Bunko slowed the golf cart as they approached Procurements and Seizures, as they left behind the cardboard mountains of the Holding Station for those acres of confiscated merchandise for which the federal government couldn't seem to find any other place. Procurements and Seizures was a glittering showcase of IRS and DEA trophies; a vast warehousing of classic cars and Learjets and phallic speed boats.

They passed one of Willie Nelson's old touring buses, a huge, refurbished Greyhound that managed, nonetheless, to look small and insignificant in the bowels of the nation's largest warehouse.

"Here's to Willie," Bunko said, having pulled a flask from his sport coat. "Here's to all the girls we've loved before."

He passed it to Eamon, who felt obliged to say, "Jesus, we're on duty," before taking a slug himself.

"Yeah, I guess I just forgot again," Bunko said, taking another hit of the bourbon. "There's just so many rules to keep track of. And you know how easily confused I can get."

"It's amazing you function at all."

"So everyone tells me."

"Okay," Eamon said, his tone suddenly serious, "so what's our next move?"

"Christ, I don't know. We did our job. Coming up

with Lila Cooper. Now it's up to the feds and cops to do their job, which means apprehending her."

"And what are the odds of that happening?"

"Christ, what do I look like? A goddamn bookie?" Bunko snapped. "What're you worried about? They'll get her. That's what the prima donnas get paid for. We're due some serious vacation time. And, as far as I'm concerned, that's our next move."

"My next move is New Bedford," Eamon said flatly. "I'm going up to the hospital tomorrow morning. You do what you like, but I want to find out what happened to Dawkins and see if I can't find out some more about Cooper's stay there."

"I'm getting a sinking feeling. This is just like you, Wearie. Just like you to ruin my vacation plans. It's the middle of August already. Christ, another summer without a vacation. Another year passing me by—"

"From New Bedford," Eamon continued, like a travel agent reeling off an itinerary, "we'll proceed to Belmont to interview Cooper's husband. There's no telling what this Jared fellow could tell us about his ex-wife. Her habits, acquaintances, places she used to haunt—"

"Christ, why are we doing all of this?"

"Look, Bunk, it's better than just sitting around waiting for her to hit again."

"Oh, how many times do I gotta tell ya? It's all random; she's making it up as she goes along. These are the PMS Killings, for Christ' sake. She's experiencing bloating and migraines and taking it out on the rest of the world."

"She was raped," Eamon said quietly.

"Maybe, maybe not," Bunko said, unconvinced. "That's what they all say now. This whole date rape thing, bunch of crap, that's what I think."

"I really don't know how you can say that," Eamon said, disbelieving. "Happens all the time. Even a Neanderthal like yourself should realize that."

Bunko slammed the brakes of the Bob Hope Special, right in front of the DeLoreans, that row of sleek stainless steel that had somehow come to be garaged at Dead Letters in 1984. There must have been a dozen of the glinting silver cars.

"But why does it happen all the time? Can you answer me that? Well, I'll tell ya why: It's because women are always giving off mixed signals. On the one hand, they have the same desires as we do, but on the other they're taught to suppress those same desires. Why? Because there's a clear and obvious double standard at work in our society. Women are not allowed to be full, willing, sexual beings. Because that would make them whores and sluts. So what to do? Well, women are taught early on to say no, to act the part of good little girls. That's why men are so often the initiators of sex. Don't you see? Why, for example, do you think that rape is such a prevalent female fantasy? Very same reason. Because it allows the woman to have sex without the moral responsibility of making that choice for herself."

"But, Bunk, there's a huge difference between what a woman fantasizes about and the horrible reality of something like rape. I mean, we all have fantasies that we probably would never want to see acted out. Men and women, both."

"Don't get me wrong, kid. But my point is, who really knows what happened to this Lila Cooper fruitcake? Maybe she and this Whit Ellsworth guy were making out like crazy that night all them years ago. You know, maybe they were doing everything but the one thing."

"Yeah, so what's your point? He still raped her in the end."

"Bullshit. There's a point of no return, know what I'm saying. There's a point where a woman loses the right to say no. Like with that Mike Tyson. Girl shows up in his hotel room at, like, two in the morning. Give me a break. Mike's lying on his bed, half-undressed. Christ, you telling me the girl doesn't know the score?"

"I'm telling you that you can't force a woman to have sex against her will. That's the law. That's the way it should be in any civilized country."

"Oh, easy for you to say," Bunko sneered, "you still have your looks."

"God, you're hopeless, beyond redemption."

"You do go on. But enough about me. Let's change the subject to something happy and pleasant. Like tonight's showdown for first place in the American League's eastern division."

"In fact, I'm glad you brought that up—"

"Christ, you can't believe how much I've been looking forward to this game. O's and Jays. Battle of the birds. For all the feathers. A reason to live right there. Am I right, kid?"

"Well—"

"You know, the game's a total sellout. Boy, were we smart to get tickets for this one all the way back in April. Think of all the sad fucks who're going to have to be relegated to watching this make-or-break game at home on TV. While we, on the other hand, are sitting behind the third base dugout, in the most primo spot in the whole damn house."

"Yeah, like I said, I've been wanting to talk to you about that. . . ."

158

# Sixteen

❧

Somehow he doubted she would show.

Still, Eamon stood sentry outside Gate 38, waiting for Mary Seppala, as waves of white short sleeves and pastel dresses washed past him.

Oriole Park was festive with the cries of hawkers and scalpers, with the giddy anticipation of a big ball game on an otherwise languid August evening. Utah Street was alive with revelers and tailgaters, with cookouts and precelebratory drinking.

Even though it had rained yesterday, the warm, sticky weather had already returned, covering the world with its ethereal, pink gauziness. He wished he could have taken his jacket off, but he was packing tonight, taking no chances. In fact, driving to the ballpark he had kept careful vigilance, constantly checking the rearview to make sure that he wasn't being followed. The FBI had his house staked out—just in case Lila Cooper got any ideas about finishing the job—and Daniel P. Pinkus was staying elsewhere until the whole thing blew over.

Mary Seppala showed up after all, just as the "Star-Spangled Banner" began to play.

"I'm glad you made it," Eamon said, ushering her through the turnstile. "It's going to be a great game."

"I didn't come here for baseball," she said shortly.

"You want anything to eat or drink?" he asked as they passed the refreshment stands inside the stadium.

"Let's just get this over with, all right?" she said.

They came out of the tunnel, into the great roar of the crowd. Ben McDonald had just thrown the first pitch, a called strike. It was always a thrill, Eamon felt, to come out of that tomblike darkness into the bright floodlights, to see the surreal greenness of the field, to be so close up to one's gloved heroes.

An old, red-jacketed usher led them to their seats, to a piece of prime real estate behind the third base dugout.

"Not bad," Mary said, softening just a little. "What did you have to do to get these?"

"I only had to break my partner's heart," Eamon said. "But don't worry, disappointment is a way of life for Bunko. He'd be the first one to tell you that."

"I feel just terrible," she said. "He was probably really looking forward to this game."

"Actually, I think that's understating it. I believe this game was intricately tied to his will to live."

"God, how could you do that to him then?"

That didn't strike him as such a difficult question. Not when he saw that dark, exquisite, Romanesque face. Not when he looked into those rare amethyst eyes, startling him all over again with their clarity and sense of purpose. This was not to mention the brown legs that went on forever, or any of several other physical attributes that he was doing his best not to moon over.

He called out for two beers, not waiting for her consent. He passed her one and said, "Looks like

McDonald's got his good stuff. Blew away the side on eleven pitches."

"Look, Lieutenant, like I've told you, the game isn't my main concern."

"Aren't you a fan?"

"The biggest. I grew up just blocks from Memorial Stadium, remember? But I've got other things on my mind tonight. . . ."

She stopped talking, noticing that his attention was elsewhere. He was scanning the crowd, rifling through faces in an impossible attempt at security.

"I don't blame you," she said. "Not after what happened last night."

"You can't be too careful."

"Don't worry," she said soothingly, "I don't even think Lila Cooper could get a ticket for this one."

"What do you think her next move is going to be?"

She took a moment to consider. "My best guess is that she's going to get out of town. Start all over somewhere else. There's just too much heat around here now. And it's just going to get hotter, now that we know who she is. Every beat cop in the state is on the lookout for her. Her photo has been faxed to practically every department down the Eastern Seaboard. The FBI alone has practically three dozen agents combing the Baltimore area."

"Teamwork and shared information make everyone look good."

"Explain to me then why we weren't told about those letters to Whit Ellsworth," she said with steeliness.

"Look, that wasn't my idea. Masterson, my boss, wanted it all for himself. Del doesn't like to share, and he doesn't like to play nice with the other children."

"Maybe it doesn't even matter. You did nice work coming up with Cooper's name as quickly as you did."

"I don't know how much it's going to help us,

really," Eamon said resignedly. "She's probably using another name entirely. And along with everything else, she's a master of disguise."

Brady Anderson went downtown, hitting a blast in the direction of the B&O warehouse, that solid wall of brick that fortified right field. The crowd rose to its feet as Brady rounded the bases. Eamon and Mary remained seated, continued talking.

"You know, I came here tonight more out of curiosity than anything else," Mary said. "I still don't understand why Lila Cooper made a house call on you. I mean, you're definitely another boorish example of your gender, but that hardly explains why she'd want you dead."

Eamon gulped back the rest of his beer, needing courage. He started his story at the beginning, started with fifteen-year-old Christy Gertz. The voluptuous porn star who looked a lot older than her years but who was just a mixed-up kid nonetheless. He told Mary about the phone calls, the ones that came late at night and left him feeling sorry for her. Christy needed a friend, just someone to talk to. He knew that some invisible line was being crossed, that their relationship was becoming less official and less and less clear. It wasn't like he ever wanted anything to happen between the two of them. He made sure to emphasize this to Mary, to make her understand that he damn well knew the difference between right and wrong.

He stopped his story to call out for more beer, more courage. It was strange confiding to Mary in the middle of Oriole Park, in the presence of thousands, amid the ever-constant murmur of anticipation. It was a confession punctuated by cheers and boos, but he was hardly aware of the game in progress or of the disembodied voices that floated around him; it was just the two of them, somehow safe in the womb of all that discordant humanity.

So he told her. About going out to Christy's grandmother's, about finding her out back in that neon thong bikini. About the kiss that followed. How he took a moment too long to pull away. Telling Mary that he didn't know how he'd let it happen, how he was just as bad as all the rest. Then he got to the part about the phone call from Lila Cooper and the bullets that followed.

Through all of this, Mary stayed very quiet, not interrupting him, not seeming to pass judgment. All the same, Eamon felt it probably just confirmed her worst opinion of him.

Except she surprised him, doing the unimaginable. She looked into his eyes with more feeling than he could ever recount and began to stroke his hair with more unaccountable tenderness. Then she brought his face to hers and kissed him, with more real feeling. He never wanted to pull back, never wanted to wake up.

They kissed in that sea of rising and falling voices, in the rough swells. They kissed gently and lovingly, even if the smells were of hot dogs, peanuts, and beer.

When he could stand his exultant happiness no longer, he pulled back and said hoarsely, "I've wanted this from the beginning."

"I know," she said levelly.

"I don't get it. Why now?"

"Because you were finally honest with me. That's what I've wanted from the beginning, that kind of trust. Because, as I get older, I'm not willing to settle for anything less. I'm just at a point where I don't want to play games anymore."

"I wasn't sure you even liked me."

"Eamon, I always liked you. I mean, there was always something about you, something that I couldn't quite get out of my mind."

"I knew right away with you—that you were the keeper, the real thing."

She smiled, a warm, delicious blush of a smile.

He kissed her again, just because.

And then he pulled back again. Maybe because he

wasn't used to things feeling so right. He said, "What about what I told you, about Christy?"

"I don't really think you've done anything so wrong," she said squarely. "I think what you've got is the Catholic's fine-tuned sense of guilt."

"Still, it wasn't my finest hour."

"People make mistakes. Look, you didn't sleep with her. You didn't do anything like it."

"I feel bad for Christy," Eamon admitted. "Who's ever going to do right by that young girl? Who's ever going to care enough to help turn it around for her?"

Mary said, "Maybe I could talk to her, possibly help. You forget I used to work sex crimes. I've worked with abused children, rape victims. I'm a veteran of these wars. You wouldn't believe what goes on out there. . . ."

He didn't want to believe. The world Mary described was nothing less than grotesque, full of conscienceless predators and their terrible, enraging, all-too-defining acts. In a single minute whole lives could be shattered, rendered mute.

"I saw it all the time. One moment a woman's walking home from work and thinking about what to make for dinner—and the next she's a catatonic being wheeled into the hospital. Then the long, hard recovery time, not just for the victim, but for everyone else around her. I'm telling you, rape is America's terrible secret. The numbers are staggering. It's like some undeclared war going on out there. I don't think men have a clue."

"That's not fair—"

"No, what's not fair is to be a woman. To live in fear. Men have no idea what that's like; you're free to come and go as you please. Women must always gauge their personal safety. We always have to think about which streets we can walk without undue concern and which places we can enter without having to think twice about it. Every time we meet someone we make a decision regarding our own personal safety. Can you really understand that?"

"Well, you don't have to worry," Eamon made the mistake of saying. "You've been trained in the art of self-defense."

"You're missing the whole point," she said, annoyed now. "It's not about me personally. It's about being a woman. It's about being a second-class citizen."

"But you've got to admit things are changing for the better," he pronounced with a touch of timidity.

"As slowly and surely as a glacier," she said darkly.

"What I mean is, there's not the same kind of discrimination against women that there was just twenty years ago, for example. Women continue to make strides in practically every way imaginable. Look at education, at the fact that just as many women go to college as men. The gains in the workforce, how many more women have good-paying jobs—"

"I have to stop you right there," she said, shaking her head. "What you're saying sounds good on paper, but the reality is far different. First of all, women aren't even close to having equal pay for equal work. Second of all, it's much more complicated than that. Because your equation doesn't take into account the absolute, pervading reality of sexual harassment in the workplace and everywhere else, for that matter. And, believe me, this is something I know more than a little about. I didn't become a detective-sergeant in the homicide division without experiencing my fair share of hard knocks.

"My superiors made it twice as hard. It wasn't that I had to be as good as the men I was competing against, so much as I had to be even better. And so I was. I scored highest on the aptitude tests. I was rated A-1 in marksmanship, the highest possible ranking. I left nothing to chance. And still they doubted me. This is not to mention the leering and the rude comments I was made to endure. Or the men who wouldn't take no for an answer. It never stopped. There was one son of a bitch that never stopped calling, never stopped leaving me little love notes. How many times do you have to tell someone no before they get it through their thick skulls?"

Eamon said, "I think you're asking the wrong guy. Look how I've been pestering you. Look how I never stopped coming on to you."

"That's different. I *liked* you. I didn't want you to give up."

"How's a guy to know that? I mean, you gave out the same signals, the same frost warnings to both this jerk and myself."

"Believe me, it's *different*," she said resolutely. "There was *nothing* with this other guy. I never looked twice at him. I never flirted with him. In fact, just the opposite was true. If anything, I scowled at him, I went out of my way to ignore him. There was no way he could get the wrong idea. Believe me, we never danced close in my family rec room, never shared a moment like that."

She smiled at him again, acknowledging what was true and clear from the beginning, that they liked each other.

She said, "Eamon, you would never try to do what this other guy tried to do. Not ever. Not in a million years. This bastard comes up to me in the locker room after martial arts training and he just grabs me and tries to stick his fucking tongue down my throat. I threw him to the ground before he ever knew what hit him. And, let me tell you, that creep never bothered me again. Which just goes to show you, I guess."

"Shows you what?"

"That women will not be equal until two things happen: until they have the physical strength to put down any threat, and until they have the good sense to pay their own way in this world."

"I don't follow."

"It's all about power and money," she said, as if nothing else made sense. "We have to teach our little girls to defend themselves. All the mommies out there should just enroll their daughters in karate classes or jujitsu, or whatever. That would be a good first step; that would change the equation right there. Because a good defense is the best offense."

Eamon said, "But what about the money? Where does that fit in?"

"Where *doesn't* it fit in? Men use money as sexual power. That's why they buy us drinks. That's why they like to pick up the check at dinner, and it's the same reason they like to buy us jewelry. But we're just as bad. Because not only do we allow them to buy us all these things, we *expect* it, we *demand* it, in fact. And that's what makes us damn fools. We should know better than that, that there's no such thing as a free lunch or a free ride. And until we learn any better, I don't think we're going to change the status quo."

"Well, you can buy me dinner anytime you like," Eamon said, grinning. "I'm easy."

"I don't doubt it," she said, still looking serious.

"Look," he said, wiping the grin from his face, "I didn't mean to diminish in any way what you were saying. Quite the contrary. I think you're on to something here."

"I know, I know," she said, acknowledging her own seriousness, "I get carried away. But it's hard for me to ignore the implications. Women have just got to learn to be stronger. I don't believe in the current policy of victimization—blaming men all the time for everything. Give me a break. When are we going to stop becoming victims? What's it going to take?"

"Maybe it takes a Lila Cooper," he said gravely.

"I think you're closer to the truth than you might imagine. I mean, there's a part of me that really understands our vigilante. Fight fire with fire. It seems like the only thing that works, the only way of getting through to the Bob Packwoods and Clarence Thomases of the world."

"You'll have to forgive me if I'm not as enthusiastic about the woman who tried to murder me last night."

She went quiet for a moment as Eamon turned his attention back to the ball game. They had got so caught up in their conversation that they'd missed a good part of the game; it was already the bottom of the seventh inning. At least the O's were ahead 5-0.

"Oh, no!" Eamon gasped, as it suddenly dawned on him.

"What? What is it?"

"Look at the scoreboard," he said, pointing in the direction of center field.

"What?" she said, still uncomprehending. "We're ahead, doing great."

"Look at all those electronic goose eggs up there," he said, still pointing. "McDonald's throwing a no-hitter, of all things."

"Wow, that's incredible. I've never seen a no-no."

"That's just it. It's one of those rare, once-in-a-lifetime events, the kind of thing most people never get to experience in person."

"I know, it's just phenomenal. I don't understand why you look so upset."

"Bunko," he said morosely. "He'll never forgive me."

"Well," she said, trying to cheer him up, "McDonald still needs six more outs. And the last six are always the toughest."

"Right," he said, rallying, "and the Jays are a good hitting team. Yeah, they'll get a hit, sure. Nothing to worry about."

Eamon must've been the only one in the entire ballpark rooting for the Jays to break up McDonald's no-hitter. He screamed encouragement to the opposing players—"C'mon, Alomar, line it right up the middle! You can do it!"—remaining oblivious to the angry, beery-eyed faces around him, looking so much like a newly formed lynch mob.

It came down to the last out in the ninth inning, the way these things usually do. Paul Molitar had worked the count full, each pitch an excruciating minidrama, as hopes and dreams rose and fell on the effectiveness of McDonald's fast ball.

Strike three, swinging. Hoiles, the catcher, rushed the mound, lifting Ben McDonald heavenward. Fans began swarming onto the field. Everyone else, including Mary, was jumping up and down, rocking the stadium in an earthquake of jubilation.

"My dumb luck," Eamon muttered gloomily.

It was not, he thought, unfamiliar territory.

Even the feelings it engendered were familiar.

It was like being back in high school or something. Sitting there, on the living room couch, with his arm around her, the rest of the household asleep. Late at night, that warm and cozy feeling. The way they kept making out, kissing with sophomoric concentration, hot and heavy. Just like high school. Not to mention the horny, adolescent thoughts he was experiencing.

Except in high school the girl usually didn't take out the cognac from her father's liquor cabinet.

And you'd be hard-pressed to find one that looked like Mary Seppala.

She poured some more Courvoisier into their snifters.

"This feels so right," she cooed.

"You're so beautiful," he murmured right back.

"I've been waiting a long time for a man like you. In fact, I have a confession to make." She paused to fortify herself with cognac. "I haven't been out with someone in a long, long time. I'd practically given up hope of ever finding Mister Right."

"I never gave up. I knew you were out there somewhere. Oh God, Mary, I think I really love you."

"This is happening so fast."

Eamon fell back into her eyes, into those eternal, violet pools, and she did nothing to prevent him from swimming there.

He was under her spell, suspended from the here and now, seduced by powerful witchcraft. Then he was nibbling at her ears, kissing her throat, all over her. Her womanly perfume was nothing less than a magical potion, intoxicating him, pushing him on.

"I don't know about this," she managed to get out.

He kept at it, determined. He unbuttoned her blouse, took liberties. Another hand began to caress one of her silken legs, began to glide up her panty hose, such black magic.

"No," she cried, as he continued with hands and mouth.

It didn't do her any good; her plaintive cries hardly registered.

"No," she uttered again, "I'm not ready."

Finally she just slapped him hard across the face.

*"No means no,"* she issued forcefully, thereby breaking the wicked spell.

# *Seventeen*

❦

*E*amon was getting a little tired of hearing it.

Bunko had started right in from the moment Eamon had arrived at his house to pick him up for the airport. At first Eamon could hardly begrudge him; after all, the big guy had a point, even if he was jabbing it in relentlessly.

Eamon didn't begin to lose his patience until they were airborne. With Bunko's continued carping, the hour-long flight seemed as onerous as a transatlantic crossing.

By the time they'd landed in Providence, Rhode Island, Eamon was not even making an effort to acknowledge Bunko's incessant barbs.

Eamon fared no better with the car ride; Bunko would just not give it a rest. Mercifully, it took no more than thirty minutes to cross over into Massachusetts and make the short dip into New Bedford. The state hospital, located inland from the bleak, seen-better-times seaport, was a drab grouping of institutional brick set back on a sea of green tranquility.

As they approached the main gate, Bunko was still

hammering away at the injustice of it all. "A freakin' no-hitter, for crying out loud. I've been going to ball games for close to fifty years and have yet to see a no-hitter. My God, it'll probably be another half century before I get a chance again. All because I'm stupid enough to listen to you. 'Oh, Bunk, I just want this one teeny-weeny little favor. Thanks for the ticket, thanks a mill. I owe ya.' Oh, why do I ever listen to you? The road to ruin runs right through Wearieville—"

"Bunk, I hope to God you never get to see a no-hitter. Not only that, I hope the next time I go without you I see a perfect game and Ripkin hits seven home runs. That's how much I give a damn. You've been harping on this since early this morning. Just give me a break already."

As they passed through security clearance, leaving behind the gatehouse and electrified fencing, Eamon was struck by the absence of people. He'd half-expected dysfunctional herds of the drooling and lobotomized, that whole straitjacketed set from *One Flew Over the Cuckoo's Nest.* But he didn't glimpse a single patient or, for that matter, any other soul about on the peaceful, practically catatonic grounds. Not even a gardener, which might've explained the acres of overgrown lawn, the palpable sense that it was being allowed to go to seed.

They came up a long, leafy drive lined with maples, to the main administration building, which was at the center of a sepia-toned universe, a dying sun to myriad, desolate, and seemingly forsaken planets. So many of the brown brick edifices, five and six stories high, were clearly deserted, ghostly reminders of a small, harrowing city of misery. Eamon thought of that Edvard Munch painting, *The Scream;* there was just something about all those silent, darkened windows, some sad, terrifying trace that would never go away and that remained even on a sunny, blue-skied, summer's day.

Inside the administration building they were told by the lone receptionist that they could find Dr. Leon Slavitt in his office on the fifth floor. They climbed the stairs, hearing only the harsh echo of their own footsteps. Before coming upon Dr. Slavitt, they passed huge, empty dormitory rooms, more institutional sadness; paint-peeling arenas that still held dozens of metal bed frames and an inescapable sense of mass, chaotic anguish; that reeked of the ancient but still overpowering duality of urine and antiseptic.

Dr. Slavitt, looking so much the part, was a small, owlish man in horn-rims with thinning, silver hair and a thick Freudian beard. He was even in a well-worn, hound's-tooth tweed jacket, no matter that the temperature had to be in the eighties.

"Gentlemen, what can I do for you today?" the good doctor said, greeting them most genially.

"Lila Cooper," was all that Eamon had to say.

"Righto," he said, the syllables clipped and British sounding. "Those federal investigators we've been expecting. Yes, of course."

He steered them to the two rudimentary metal chairs that faced his own gray, nuts-and-bolts desk and swivel. It was an ugly little office, painted canary yellow—surely in the hopes of cheering depressives and schizophrenics—and managing, nonetheless, to depress by sheer, intolerable brightness. The paint job and the streaming sunlight only managed to expose the room's glaring deficiencies, its fundamental lack of character and warmth, no artwork or calming plants, no homey touches whatsoever, not even a decorous bookshelf, just cold metal, filing cabinets and bare essentials, nothing that would stop the potential suicide from thinking twice.

"Yes, not exactly posh, is it?" Dr. Slavitt said by way of apology.

"Feels just like home," Bunko said.

"I don't understand what's going on around here," Eamon said. "Where the hell is everybody?"

"The Bedford era is coming to a close. One of the last of the state psychiatric dinosaurs, you see. In its heyday this institution housed over eight thousand inmates. Been steadily downsizing since the Reagan eighties. Federal government stopped with the largess —and of course this, in turn, led the state of Massachusetts to do its own paring down. In fact, much of this penuriousness has resulted in the burgeoning homeless populations of New Bedford and Boston and so many other urban centers. In truth, a good portion of these indigent street people are actually patients that we've released in the all-too-recent past, people in dire need of counseling and, more to the point, effective drugs.

"Of course, the closing of Bedford is not only the result of federal shortsightedness. The psychiatric community has also seen the wisdom of disbanding these huge institutional curiosities. Smaller is better, in fact. Outpatient care and hospices . . ."

Dr. Slavitt trailed off, not above realizing that he was trying the inspectors' patience.

"Ah yes," he said moving on to the thick manila folder before him. "Lila Cooper. Quite an extraordinary case. But who isn't, of course. But this one—"

"What was she suffering from?" Eamon asked, anxious to get down to brass tacks.

"I don't rightly know, to be perfectly frank."

"You must be kidding. She was here for two years. Don't you have some kind of clue? A guess, for God's sake?"

"Well, I wasn't her main doctor, so to speak. Of course I saw her regularly. But that was in a group therapy session I conducted. Unfortunately, Dr. Dawkins, my late and esteemed colleague, was Lila's personal physician, as it were. He met with her every day. He knew much better than I what ailed her."

"First of all, what happened to Dawkins?"

"All rather tragic. A first-rate mind. Terrible."

Eamon said, "We understand he killed himself. Do you know the circumstances?"

"Rather shabby, I'm afraid. Found in his office, quite a shock. Wasn't a suicide, though. Quite accidental, I'm sure."

They sat back and waited for Slavitt to continue, for the uncomfortable silence to prompt a reply.

"Autoerotism," Dr. Slavitt finally dispensed. "Found him in a most uncompromising position. Hanging from a duct in the ceiling. His pants unzipped. An open pornography magazine."

"So let me get this straight," Eamon said. "Dawkins was masturbating with a noose around his neck, and something went wrong?"

"To put it so bluntly, yes—"

"Can you tell me anything else about the way he was found? Was there anything, for example, that could've pointed to foul play?"

"The police ruled that out. But there was one priapic oddity. To do with that pornographic magazine, which was homosexual in nature, and its prurient display."

Bunko said, "I'm afraid you're going to have to talk English, pal. Wearie and me have about the equivalent of a ninth-grade education."

"Yes, of course," Dr. Slavitt said, taking Bunko at his word. "Well, what I'm getting at is that Dr. Dawkins apparently had quite a preoccupation with the phallus. He had gone through that magazine and taken the trouble to cut out all the male equipment, as it were. These priapic photos were scattered throughout his office."

"So what you're saying," Eamon said, translating again, "is that these were photos of penises?"

"Exactly."

Eamon and Bunko exchanged a look that wasn't about to discount the involvement of one Lila Cooper.

"How would you describe Dawkins's relationship with Lila Cooper?" Eamon asked. "Was it purely professional?"

Dr. Slavitt leaned back in his chair and combed his fingers through his salt-and-pepper beard. His owlish face was racked with uneasiness.

"It's a nasty element of our profession," he finally managed, still rubbing his beard. "Let me just say that I think Dr. Dawkins may have been too involved with the patient. Enough said."

Bunko wanted some answers, some straight answers, and he wanted them now. "Did he or didn't he sleep with her? No ifs, buts, or enough saids."

"I don't rightly know. But I will tell you that there were whispers. There were always whispers about Dawkins."

"Jesus Christ," Bunko muttered.

"It's just that I don't want to sully a dead man's reputation, especially when it's so difficult to judge the veracity of these most persistent rumors. But let me just say that it wouldn't surprise me in the least if I were to learn that Dawkins had been sleeping—as you so quaintly put it—with Lila. There's just too much of this sort of thing. I read some study somewhere that a good seventy percent of my profession has at one time or another slept with a patient. Absolutely appalling. We must pass laws to make it illegal for psychologists and psychiatrists to have sex with patients. Suspending their licenses doesn't go far enough. When people seek medical help of this nature they are particularly vulnerable and susceptible."

"Yeah," Bunko said cynically, "and while we're at it why don't we pass some more laws to make it illegal to have sex with your lawyer and your family physician, and how about even your friendly neighborhood cop on the beat? I mean, after all, when we seek help from these people we're particularly vulnerable and susceptible, too."

"That's quite an illuminating point—"

"Bullshit, hear me?" Bunko said, his voice rising several decibels. "I'm sick and tired of this kind of reasoning. People have got to start taking responsibility for their own behavior. Otherwise, where does it ever stop? I mean, if a professional baseball player making a million dollars a year makes a pass at the average broad, he's going to have an unfair advantage, wouldn't you say? I mean, how many babes are going to refuse him? Now what do you do? Make it illegal for rich guys and professional athletes to come on to—"

"You're completely twisting my words around. There's a vast difference between what you're saying and professional misconduct. I am talking about the trust that has to be implicit in the doctor–patient relationship and—"

"Look," Eamon interrupted, "why don't you guys settle this on the next episode of Sally Jessy Raphael. Let's get back to Lila Cooper. There's a lot more that we need to cover here. Such as Whit Ellsworth. Did that name ever come up, Doctor?"

"You know about that?" he said, looking surprised.

"Yes, we have some reason to believe that Lila Cooper was raped by Whit Ellsworth almost thirty years ago. And that this might go a long way to explaining her problems."

"I have my doubts, gentlemen," Dr. Slavitt said portentiously. "I suspect that this may be just another cruel hoax on all of us, including poor sad Lila Cooper. Dr. Dawkins was quite an advocate of repressed-memory therapy. And it is my considered opinion that Dawkins, through suggestion or hypnosis, helped to plant the seeds of this false memory."

"Slow down," Bunko commanded. "Ninth-grade educations, remember?"

"Well, as you may or may not know, repressed-memory therapy is probably the single most hotly debated topic in the psychotherapy field. Many of my fellow professionals believe that a significant number of adults—most of whom are women, I dare say—who are suffering from such symptoms as long-term depression, eating disorders, sexual maladies, et cetera, may, in fact, be really suffering from early traumatic sexual abuse. And that this sexual abuse, be it rape or incest or what have you, has been buried deep in the subconscious, that is, it is not something readily remembered.

"Repressed-memory therapy is about recovering these painful and traumatic memories. With the hope of burrowing to the root cause of an individual patient's dilemma. So instead of treating the symptoms of the abuse, you treat the abuse itself."

"Well, that sounds sensible," Bunko said.

"Except there is a growing number of mental-health practitioners who are equally convinced that this is all a lot of hooey. Some question the very idea that so many people could be walking around not remembering that they have been sexually abused. The thinking goes that it's not possible for a person to be repeatedly molested or raped over many years and not have some surface memory of it. In fact, there are whole organizations, like the False Memory Syndrome Foundation, that are devoted to refuting the claims of the recovered-memory minions."

Eamon said, "I gather you're not a believer either."

"No, I have no doubt that people are capable of great denials, great blocking outs, as it were. For example, Professor Linda Williams did a rather compelling study at the University of New Hampshire that checked up on one hundred sexually abused children seventeen years after the fact. Now, you must remember, these were documented cases of abuse, children who had been treated at hospitals. Williams found that thirty-eight percent of these children as adults had absolutely no memory of the abuse. I find that makes a rather convincing case for repressed memories."

"Then what about Lila Cooper? Why don't you believe her about Whit Ellsworth?"

"It's not that I don't believe her, precisely. I believe she thinks Whit Ellsworth raped her all those years ago. I just don't believe that it actually happened."

"Listen," Eamon said, "I believe her. We came across some letters she wrote not so long ago to Whit Ellsworth, confronting him with what happened. And I've got to tell you that they were filled with remarkable details about that night, not the kind of stuff one could easily make up."

Dr. Slavitt took a moment to rifle through the file in front of him. "Ah, yes," he said, pulling a sheet from the folder, "the evil that happened in Whit Ellsworth's Olds 88. He was drinking Old Grand-Dad that demonic, moonlit night, and smoking Chesterfields and driving recklessly and—"

"See, she told you. How could she make all that up?"

"She didn't."

"But you just said—"

"My dear boy," Dr. Slavitt said, somewhat condescendingly, "all of that probably did happen. I just don't think this Ellsworth chap raped her."

"How can you be so sure?"

"I'm not. Except that wasn't Lila Cooper's first recovered memory with Dr. Dawkins."

"Come again?"

"Her first recovered memories, and just as vivid and excruciating, mind you, detailed how her father had molested her until she was fifteen years old, right under her mother's watchful eye, no less. Later, she recanted this tale, saying only that she'd been mistaken."

"Unbelievable," Eamon said.

"Precisely," Dr. Slavitt said. "And I don't blame

Lila at all. I blame Dawkins with his overly aggressive techniques. He was just so convinced that the root cause of almost every one of his female patients' problems was sexual abuse. Through his manipulations he virtually extracted these false memories out of them."

"Isn't it possible that both things happened to Lila Cooper? That her father molested her *and* Whit Ellsworth raped her?"

"Anything's possible, my dear boy. But I think what's more likely is that she's gifted with an active imagination. In fact, she always wanted to be a fiction writer, a novelist, as it were. Did you boys know that?"

"Then what the hell happened to her?" Eamon said, growing increasingly frustrated with Slavitt's mental gymnastics.

"Hard to say. My best guess is that some sort of transference is at work here. That is to say, that something did indeed happen to Lila Cooper, and that she is blocking it out and transferring the pain to these other false and manufactured memories. So, in the final analysis, it is my expert opinion that we'll probably never get to the bottom of Lila's trauma."

"Oh, great," Bunko said. "And for this you get two hundred dollars an hour?"

"I should also tell you," Dr. Slavitt continued, choosing to ignore the remark, "that my colleague, Dr. Dawkins, was convinced that Lila Cooper was more than just another case of post-traumatic stress disorder. He believed, most strongly, that she was also suffering from multiple-personality disorder."

"You mean like that book *Sybil?*" Eamon said, incredulous. "Talking in all sorts of crazy voices, that kind of thing?"

"Well, I must tell you that I never saw any indication of it. And I should also point out that this disorder was exceedingly rare up to just a few years ago. So rare, in fact, that there had only been several dozen documented cases in this country. Now there are thousands of them. So either the entire country is going bonkers all at once—as it sometimes seems, if you've ever watched Oprah or Donahue—or this disorder has always been prevalent, and for some inescapable reason we just weren't able to verify it in the past."

"What made Dawkins believe that Lila was a multiple?"

"Well, mind you I'm going by his notes now, but Lila evidenced signs of a fractured personality in hypnosis sessions. She seems to have lashed out at Dr. Dawkins during the memory-recovery process in an unknown voice or voices. She definitely seemed to exhibit a darker half, a part of herself more given over to destructive and violent forces. Dr. Dawkins felt that it was a classic good-girl, bad-girl split. That these two very pronounced sides of her were unable to merge. He points to her sexuality as proof of this."

There was no doubt that Dr. Slavitt was the master of the pregnant pause. Once again the inspectors chose to wait him out.

"Well, ah yes, it seems that Lila was quite confused on this point. Seems she suffered from an all-too-common fear of intimacy. Quite normal, really, in its own perverted, stilted way. Beyond that, Dr. Dawkins notes that Lila was quite undetermined on the matter of sexual preference. She doesn't seem to be all that crazy about men, but on the other hand she doesn't seem all that enamored of the fairer sex either."

"Jesus Christ!" Bunko exclaimed in frustration. "Can't you just forget all this mumbo jumbo for once and just give it to us straight?"

"Well, as you know," Dr. Slavitt said, "psychoanalysis is not exactly rocket science. Penetrating the mysteries of the human mind, whose very opacity is more than daunting, requires a certain amount of, shall we say, *speculation.* So often it is left for us professionals to make the educated guess, to read between the lines. I think even you gentlemen can appreciate that. So bearing that in mind, I shall go out on a most precarious limb: I believe that Lila's problems led to the husband. I don't know how, I don't know why. It's just a gut feeling, a hunch, as it were."

"Well, thanks a lot," Bunko said, getting up. "For muddling everything up that much more. Christ Almighty."

Dr. Slavitt remained unfailingly polite. He smiled and extended his hand to them. Told them to feel free to call on him anytime.

They could hardly wait to get out of there. Not to hear another word about the mind's gift for opacity, of psychobabble. To leave that miserable, reeking, haunted tomb of a building. To walk back out into the summer sunshine and the land of the real.

At the car Bunko suggested that they go into town and have some lunch. "Christ, I'm starving. Get a bowl of New England clam chowder, the real McCoy. Whatayasay?"

"Sounds good. I'm pretty hungry myself. Should be some good seafood in New Bedford. Wasn't it once some big whaling port?"

"I don't know about that, kid. I only remember hearing about Bedford because of that big rape trial a few years back. Remember that story? About that girl who was gang-raped by six or seven guys in that bar? They even made a movie about it, remember? Starring that *Silence of the Lambs* actress—"

"Jodie Foster. *The Accused.* I remember the movie."

"Right, whatever. Yeah, just terrible, though, what happened to this Bedford girl. I read somewhere, I forget where now, that she died down in Florida not so long ago. She'd gone down there to try to start a new life and all that, but I guess she just couldn't ever get over what happened to her. Became this lonely, notorious alcoholic. Not that you could really blame her. Died in a car crash, dead drunk."

Eamon said, "You know what? Just forget about Bedford. Let's make tracks for Belmont, grab a bite along the way. Let's just get the hell out of here."

# *Eighteen*

~⌒~

*J*ared Cooper announced his presence with marvelous annoyance. "As you can see, this is quite an inconvenience."

He appeared in the ultramodern, ultrasoulless living room wearing only a monogrammed bathrobe. It was obvious that he'd just emerged from a shower, the way his rosy, whiskerless face and bald pate glistened. He was a small-featured, small-bodied man; in fact, he had smallness written all over him.

"I'm late as it is," Cooper said imperiously, glancing down at his watchless wrist.

The inspectors remained seated on the masculine, chocolate-colored, leather-and-chrome couch. Cooper's bodyguard, a silent, misanthropic ape, stood menacingly in the wide, doorless entranceway.

"Look," Bunko said in a tone that didn't leave room for debate, "you've kept us waiting for a good thirty minutes. Now we just want to ask you a few questions."

"Frank," Cooper said irritably, addressing his bodyguard, "go make a sandwich or something."

Cooper plopped himself down in one of the chocolate-colored, leather-and-chrome chairs. "Corbusier," he said, as if that might start a discussion.

The inspectors looked at him blankly.

"What do you think?" he said, not bothering to wait for a reply. "Quite a room, you'll have to admit."

Actually, they couldn't stand it. Neither postal inspector could see the beauty in a dramatic, black-floored, high-ceilinged, bleach white living space that had all the starkness and track lighting of a SoHo art gallery. They did not know what to make of the huge, abstract canvas that dominated one whole wall and looked to their eyes like nothing more or less than a floating parallelogram. The hanging African masks left them still further chilled. And as for that primitive wood sculpture of the pygmy with the long, narrow face and long, narrow penis—well, they were in critical agreement there, too.

Bunko said, "I gather the bodyguard is a recent addition."

"Quite a nuisance," Cooper said. "But then again, this whole business with my ex is more than a little trying. I mean, we all knew she had problems—but who'd have guessed the extent of it? Dear God, that chain letter made the national news last night, of all things. I tuned in just in time to see Connie Chung running off at the mouth about how it was a symbol of some undeclared war between the sexes. This whole women are mad as hell and aren't going to take it anymore nonsense. It was enough to make anyone ill. Thank God they left Lila's name out of it."

Bunko said, "And that's the way we'd like to keep it for right now."

"Look, I've already been all through this with the FBI."

"Do you have any idea what set her off?"

"Like I keep telling anyone who'll listen, I haven't had any contact with Lila in over two years. And I've been divorced from her for over four years. I have not the faintest idea of what's gotten into her screwed-up little head. Believe me, I wrote that cunt off for good after that incident with Meggy's boyfriend. Dismembering the boy, dear God."

"Is Meggy here?"

"I'm happy to report she's in Europe this summer. A little graduation present. Off to Vassar in the fall, you see."

"Do you have any idea where Lila is at present? Or where she might be likely to go?"

"Not a clue, I'm relieved to say."

Bunko, tiring of Jared Cooper's regal, petulant ways, was ready to turn the reins over to Eamon. Before doing so, he remarked, "You know, it wouldn't kill you to try a little harder."

"Look," Cooper said, rising from his Corbusier chair, "you're the ones who show up unannounced at my home on a Friday evening. As it is, I'm going to be late for a rather important dinner engagement—"

"Was your ex-wife always prone to violence?" Eamon asked, not wanting to let him leave just yet.

"Do you think I would have married her if that had been the case?" Cooper said, settling back down. "No, the Lila I knew was very dear. A quiet little bird, really. A woman of precious little appetite and simple wants. A woman to be proud of, you can be sure."

"Did Lila ever show an interest in firearms?"

"My word, no. Lila used to write poetry, for goodness sake. Collected art. Loved minimalism. But guns? Dear God, the woman had the soul of an interior decorator. Spent most of her time at home, arranging flowers, studying cookbooks."

"We understand she went bankrupt several years ago. Do you know where she might be getting money from right now?"

"Haven't the slightest."

Cooper took a moment to shove his bare feet up on the chrome-and-glass coffee table, causing his mono-grammed terry robe to fall partially open. The inspectors were unhappy to learn that he wasn't wearing underwear.

"How about her family?" Eamon continued, feeling embarrassed and wishing he'd just cover up.

"Lila's an only child. The parents are down in Palm Beach. And although they're quite well off, I sincerely doubt that they're giving her anything."

"Why is that?"

"Basically they've disowned her. Want nothing to do with the cunt—and who can really blame them?"

Eamon suddenly noticed that a teenage girl who was maybe fourteen or fifteen had entered Cooper's dramatic, Bauhaus living room. She was at that awkward age, a skinny, gangly thing still in pigtails and braces and a Snoopy T-shirt.

"Yes, what is it, Emily?" Cooper said impatiently. Then for the benefit of the inspectors. "My youngest daughter, gentlemen."

She seemed quite bashful, the way she kept her eyes glued to her sneakers. "I was wondering if I could stay over at Darlene's house tonight?"

"My answer is no," Cooper said, unabashedly scratching at his crotch. "There's too much to do around here, as you well know. Besides, I may need you later on."

"Yes, sir," she said in a voice that was practically inaudible, still keeping her gaze locked on the sneakers.

Eamon realized that Emily was more than just shy; she was actually scared of her father. As he watched her scamper away, he wondered what Cooper had meant about needing her later on.

Cooper rose from his dark, masculine chair. "Look, I hope you catch that crazy, lying cunt. Actually, I hope you shoot her. The world would be better off."

They were silent and grim-faced as he led them to the door. No, they didn't like him, that was for damn sure. They didn't like his taste in art and they didn't like the pompous, weasely way he talked. And they sure as hell didn't care for that open robe of his or the fact that he hadn't had the simple decency to cover up. No, he'd played with his balls right there in front of them. And right there in front of his own daughter.

It left them feeling more than a bit uneasy, for they both had some idea of what it might mean.

The somber inspectors came out of Cooper's ultra-modern, ultrasoulless house into a gentle, plum-ripe dusk, into a fine, jasmine-scented evening. They got into the rental car and backed out of the driveway. They weren't surprised to spot Cooper's coarse silhouette in one of the giant, second-floor window panels, watching them.

"Just take it around the block," Eamon advised.

"I was thinking the same thing, brother."

"We'll wait until he leaves, then talk to the daughter."

They drove up Concord Avenue, a road that seemed to run through early American history. Most of the houses were large, white-shingled, green-shuttered colonials, and most of these were set back on gener-ous, wooded pieces of property. There were also plenty of crude stone fences, the kind that Robert Frost described. The towns of Lexington and Concord were but a few minutes away.

Eamon was ashamed to realize how little history he knew. "Bunk, anything ever happen in Belmont? You know, any Revolutionary War battles or anything like that?"

"Kid, I'm like everybody else. I can't remember last week, let alone what happened two hundred years ago."

They came back around and parked a half a block from Cooper's futuristic concrete and glass fortress, which looked so out of place among its more refined and traditional neighbors. Cooper's car was still in the driveway. They lit up cigarettes and sat quietly as a wonderfully cool New England night settled over them. Fireflies flickered in the livid darkness.

"You know," Bunko said, interrupting the unfamiliar quietude, "there are women who think that all sex is rape. Did you know that?"

"Bunk, that's nuts."

"I'm not making it up," Bunko said, almost as if in a trance. "That's what this Dworkin woman says. All heterosexual sex is rape. And then there's that other one, this MacKinnon lady, who teaches law somewhere. I read she thinks it ought to be a crime for men to masturbate to pornography. Can you believe that?"

"Easy, big guy. I'm sure your *Playboy* collection is safe for the time being."

"Christ, it's all I have. Especially since Franny stopped talking to me. Christ, imagine if this MacKinnon lady got her way and they got rid of all the men's magazines. Imagine what that would do."

"Create a terrible void in your life?"

"No, you don't get it. It's a natural form of release, don't you see? Christ, the last thing you want to do is take that away. Then you'd have all these pent-up male powder kegs walking around. No telling how they'd vent their frustrations out on society."

"Don't worry, Bunk. The First Amendment covers the right to read *Hustler.*"

"Not according to this MacKinnon woman. Not only does she think it's a crime for men to masturbate, it's her esteemed legal opinion that we shouldn't even be able to think those kind of objectifying sexual thoughts about women. Jesus, what next? How about a law against wet dreams, or impromptu erections?"

"Mind telling me what brought all this on?"

Bunko let out a heavy sigh. "I'm just sick and tired of it, buddy boy. The whole blaming men for everything. Just look at this case we're working on. Just look at this Lila Cooper weirdo. I don't even care what happened to her anymore. I know I should feel sorry for her. But still, I don't see what gives her the right to go out there and mow down every male chauvinist pig who makes the mistake of opening his big fat mouth."

"Well, maybe if you'd been raped or—"

"Yeah, yeah," Bunko said, plowing on, "I say get a life, stop blaming everybody else for your troubles. Like these women who kill their husbands because they claim the bastards were beating 'em up. Christ, walk away, get a divorce—"

"That's not fair, Bunk. And you know it. A lot of times these women don't have the financial or emotional resources to just walk away. They have kids, they—"

"I tell ya, I don't care. No woman's got the right to shoot her husband—" Bunko stopped midsentence, seeing Cooper and his bodyguard coming out of the house. "Though maybe you'd have to make an exception in this case. Christ, imagine being married to that. What a world-class prick."

They ducked as Cooper's high beams passed over them.

"Strange that he took the bodyguard," Eamon said, after his BMW was gone. "Leaving the daughter alone."

"That's because she's not the one with anything to worry about."

Emily made them wait awhile on the front stoop. But they kept knocking and ringing the doorbell until she finally came, spying them through the peephole.

"Open up," Bunko commanded.

"I'm not supposed to let anybody in," a small, meek voice returned.

"But we forgot something," Bunko said.

After a long moment's hesitation she relented and unlocked the door.

"Yeah," Bunko said, stepping inside, "we forgot to talk to you."

This seemed to stun the pigtailed girl with the freckled face. Standing next to her in the foyer, they were both suddenly aware of how emaciated she was. Her arms and legs were mere matchsticks. Her Snoopy T-shirt was practically clinging to her rib cage. Before, they'd thought she was just another skinny, gangly kid. Now they guessed anorexia nervosa.

"I'm not supposed to talk to anyone," she said, her eyes still pinned to those damn sneakers.

"Don't worry," Bunko said, trying to sound reassuring, "this won't take much time."

"He doesn't like it when I talk to anyone," she repeated numbly.

Bunko tried tossing out an easy lob: "How old are you, Emily?"

"Thirteen."

"Do you know why we're here?"

"I guess," she answered weakly.

"Your dad tell you anything about your mom?" Bunko continued, still working the perimeter, still playing it safe.

"He didn't have to."

"What do you mean?"

"I talk to her all the time."

They were dumbfounded.

"She calls me collect," she said, suddenly looking up at them. She had pale, watery green eyes, like her mom. "I know she's done some bad things. But, you know, she's got her reasons."

"What reasons?"

"She saw us," she said, not bothering to hide a thing. "When I was like maybe nine years old. I guess she heard some sounds. Coming from my bedroom. Dad was on top of me. That's what he does."

She surprised them by seeming very calm and old beyond her years. "I want it to stop. Please help me make it stop. Will you do that?"

They nodded gravely. Bunko put his arms around the little girl. There were tears in his hardened eyes. But, strangely, there weren't any in hers.

"I want to show you something," she said, still the grown-up.

Bunko released his grip and they followed her

upstairs to her bedroom, a sanctuary that was tattooed with posters of the very tanned and very youthful cast of "Beverly Hills, 90210."

"Your favorite show?"

"Sometimes I daydream that it's real and that I'm one of those kids," she said, staring at a poster of Luke Perry. "I like to dream that I'm in Brenda Walsh's family. They just look so normal and nice and everything."

"What did you want to show us?" Bunko asked, all of the usual gruffness drained from his voice.

Emily went over to her dresser and pulled open the top drawer, the one containing her underwear.

"I wanted you to see this."

It was filled with satin and lace, with garter belts and midnight passion. The lingerie in this drawer—thong bikinis and push-up bras—came straight out of the Victoria's Secret catalog.

"That's what he buys for me," she said matter-of-factly. "Mom saw it, but she didn't do anything. I tried to talk to her, but she made believe she didn't hear me. So we never bring it up anymore."

"You know where she is now?" Bunko asked.

"You won't hurt my mom, will you?"

"I need to use your phone," Bunko said.

"There's one across the hall, in his bedroom."

Eamon knew his partner was going to call Masterson to find out how to proceed. Find out what the hell to do now.

"You look like a good person," she said when Bunko had left.

Eamon took out his cigarettes, not knowing anything worth a damn.

"You're going to help me, right?"

He nodded his head again, way past the use of words. He could hear Bunko in the other room, exclaiming "Jesus!" and "Not again!" and "Christ, I can't believe it!"

She said softly, "I was hoping you would come

back. I wished for it real hard. I just kept wishing until I made it come true."

He nodded one more time, still at a loss.

Bunko reentered her bedroom. He addressed Eamon first. "Not going to believe this. We got two more. Two more bodies. And you're not going to believe where they are. Right here in Beantown. For once, we're right where we're supposed to be. FBI and everybody else with badges are over at the Revere, this downtown hotel."

Then he faced the little girl in the Snoopy T-shirt. "What was the name of that friend of yours? The one where you wanted to stay over and your father wouldn't let you?"

"Darlene's?" she said, half a question, half an answer.

"Yeah, right. Darlene's. Well, how would you feel about staying the night and maybe even the weekend there?"

"Promise me you won't hurt my mom. Promise me."

Again they were forced to remain silent. Again they looked into those pale green eyes with something akin to sorrow.

193

# Nineteen

~~~

As befitting its good name, the Revere turned out to be a stately white-marble, buffed-brick presence on Copley Square in Back Bay. The hotel stood defiantly in the shadow of the city's tallest skyscraper, the sixty-story John Hancock Tower.

Neither Eamon nor Bunko had ever been to Boston before. From the car, it had seemed a tale of two cities, present and past. There was the new Boston, a shining skyline of towering glass, where banks and insurance companies reigned supreme. Then there was Old Boston, a stained-glass cathedral, a place of architectural worship, where wooden steeples and Gothic spires and gold-leaf domes were reflected back in the giant, Thermopane panels of Hancock and Prudential and Shawmut.

It was after nine in the evening when they checked in. The Revere's posh lobby—which had the look and feel of a rich man's private club, replete with over-stuffed armchairs and lingering cigar smoke—was crawling with G-men. But it was a strangely animated

194

species of G-man: These standard-issue blue suits, immaculately groomed and looking so much like a 1960s advertising campaign for Vitalis and Aqua Velva, were for the most part grinning broadly and behaving like happy, back-slapping conventioneers.

Everyone but Tony Montrez, that is. The gray man.

Montrez had the handsome, chiseled features of a Hollywood hero, the kind of commanding face that would always be asked to lead the calvalry into battle. Eamon had known him since Quantico, ever since he'd been in Montrez's document identification class. He was a little older now, and kindly crinkles had taken root around the wary blue eyes. But the thick, unruffled hair had always been—at least as far back as Eamon could remember—the color of gray slate.

"Agent Wearie and Agent Ryan," Montrez said, addressing them in his FBI mode. "Glad to have you aboard."

"I think you've got it all confused," Bunko said, sounding testy. "You're the ones hopping on for the ride."

"Maybe so," Montrez said, smiling wanly. "But of course it's not about getting credit, is it now, Agent Ryan?"

"Tell that to Del Masterson."

"Speaking of Del," Montrez said, smiling largely now, "you boys will be pleased to know that your boss is flying in tonight to join the posse."

Their faces fell in unison.

"Yes," Montrez said, understanding perfectly, "always a pleasure to work with Del. The man's just a ray of sunshine."

"Not that it really matters," Bunko said, noting the crowded, animated lobby. "Looks like you've invited every available field agent to the party. I see Phil Boze is here and Shefield. Even Annie Gunn."

"We've got all our female agents here. Less conspicuous. Perhaps even less dangerous. Although that's just a guess. Right now I've got them checking out every hotel and motel in the entire city. We know Lila Cooper is here somewhere."

"Why're you so sure? No one's filled us in yet."

"She left her calling card," Montrez said. "No chain letter this time. Just a business card with that special kissy seal of hers. Left it next to the bodies of Snowman and Flake. Rap singers. Shot with a Sig Sauer P226 in a downtown coffeehouse late this morning. Six or seven witnesses. All of them describing a miniskirted woman in a red wig."

"I don't get it," Bunko said. "Why these snowmen guys?"

"I don't know, but at the moment Snowman and Flake have the number one rap song in the country. They're what they call hard-core rappers. Do something called 'gangsta rap.' Their new album is called *Hose the Hos.* Hos, for your enlightenment, means whores. It's also, in rap parlance, everyday slang for women in general. Believe me, this has all been a learning experience for me, too."

"I'll stick with my Sinatra, thank you very much."

"I suppose I'll keep the needle on Charlie Parker," Montrez added.

Eamon made a mental note about that. It was just that he knew so little about the gray man. In fact, even after a decade of crossing paths, Eamon knew only two other personal details about him: that he collected duck decoys and that he was partial to Italian cooking. Now he could add Charlie Parker to that growing list.

"What about those witnesses?" Eamon asked. "Did anyone get a good look at our girl?"

"Flake's girlfriend had the best view. She's in the hotel bar, if you want to talk to her."

"Right here?"

"We brought her in for questioning earlier. She still hasn't left. I don't even know if she'll make much sense at this point. Her name's Jersey."

"Taking it real bad, huh?"

"Worse than that, I'm afraid."

They had no idea what Montrez meant. Before they could pursue it, he said, "There are some other things you should know. Lila Cooper, or at least this woman in the red wig, tried to kill somebody else this afternoon. Made an appointment with a Dr. Oswald Jericker, a Beacon Hill plastic surgeon. His specialty is breast implants. Quite notorious, really. A real butcher, it seems. Under investigation for reusing silicon implants. Putting old, leaky unsterilized gel bags into new patients."

"Sounds like our Lila made a good choice at least," Bunko remarked.

"Maybe so," Montrez said grimly. "But the gun jammed. Jericker was left unharmed. Cooper made a mad dash through the waiting room. Witness descriptions match those from the earlier incident at the coffee shop."

"Christ, where does it end?" Bunko said.

"I don't know, Agent Ryan. But it's accelerating out of control. We haven't released Cooper's name yet. She's too damn dangerous. We don't want members of the general public intervening. So far the news organizations are playing ball with us. But for how much longer, I can't say."

"What do you want us to do?"

"You might want to go out to Provincetown tomorrow. We've traced those collect calls that Lila Cooper made to her daughter."

"Already? We only called that in a couple of hours ago."

"We can light right into AT&T. And we don't need anybody's permission on something like this. Several of the most recent calls were made from Baltimore, at varying pay phones. But in the preceding months many more were made out of Provincetown. From the same number. Unfortunately, it didn't lead us to a residential address as we had hoped. A bar called

Ladyfingers. A ladies-only bar, if you catch my drift. I think somebody should check it out."

"You're just trying to get rid of us," Bunko complained. "The party's here in Boston. And you damn well know it."

"Well, I'm sorry you feel that way, Agent Ryan. But we're trying to make a concerted team effort here. There's no room for that kind of ego."

With that the gray man took his leave.

"I'll tell you what," Bunko said to Eamon, "I'm going to go take a shower and freshen up. Meet you in the bar in half an hour."

Eamon decided to skip the freshening up for now. He went into the King George lounge, which was a dark, woody pub off the lobby, looking for this Jersey woman.

She wasn't hard to find. Truth to tell, Jersey was the only woman and the only black at the small, crowded mahogany bar. Even though the King George was three-deep with conservative banker types, nobody seemed to want to sit on either side of Jersey. They left those stools suspiciously vacant.

"Hello," Eamon said, sitting down, "mind if I grab this one?"

She took a moment to look him over. She was a twenty-something hip-hop beauty in a red beret. The luminous eyes and elegant, high-cheekboned face were offset by a gaudy assortment of hoop earrings. This wasn't to mention the fuchsia lipstick or the fact that she was sporting a pair of the world's clunkiest boots. The laceless pole climbers, just like the kind telephone repairmen strapped on, were an interesting match for the denim shorts and black leather vest. The vest was worn without benefit of a shirt, and the short shorts were held in place with a swashbuckling-pirate's belt.

"Buy me a drink," Jersey said.

"What do you want?"

"Somethin' expensive."

198

Eamon called for the barkeep, who seemed reluctant to attend to their needs. Finally the old-timer, a frosty-haired gent with waxed handlebars, approached with caution.

"What can I get for you today, sir?" he asked with professional courtesy.

"I want one of those big old glasses of cognac," Jersey interrupted.

"I'm sorry, young lady, but you're cut off," the old man said tightly.

"It's because I'm black, isn't it? Because you don't like black people, that's what it is."

"No, it's because I don't like rude people," he said, trying to maintain control. "Rude people who keep scaring all my customers away."

"Well, in case you didn't know, something bad happened to me today. Some white bitch shot my boyfriend. Killed him dead, she did."

"I know all about it, miss. And I'm sure we are all very sorry for your loss."

"Get her that drink," Eamon ordered. "And get me a Bass Ale, while you're at it."

The old man simply shrugged, not wanting any trouble, and then went off to fetch their drinks.

"Now you're a real gentleman," Jersey said smiling at him. "Not like all the other assholes I met today."

She sure didn't seem all that broken up about the death of her boyfriend. She was more than a little tipsy, but even that didn't wholly account for such a poor show of grief.

"Know why they call me Jersey? 'Cause Flake and me met at this concert in Trenton. Oh, yeah, we had us some good times, baby. Now it's over. Goes round and round, you know."

Eamon said, "I'm sorry to intrude, but I've got to ask you a few questions. I'm a federal investigator."

"Some bitch did my boyfriend, that's what. Just sitting there minding our own business, you know."

"What did she look like?"

"Big, red hair that wasn't close to being real. Had a body like a boy's, nothing on that girl. No ass to speak of."

"What about her face? The color of her eyes?"

"I don't know. She had a white woman's face. You know, white-woman eyes. That kind of thing."

Eamon began to realize that he wasn't going to get very far with this. "Did she happen to say anything before she opened fire?"

"She looks at me and goes, 'Sister, I'm doin' you a favor.' You believe that? *Doin' me a favor?* Yeah, right, maybe in her bony-white-ass dreams. Snowman and Flake just startin' to hit it, baby. Money was on its way. Things were gonna be different. Why you think I'm hangin' around with those boys, puttin' up with all their tired shit?"

The barkeep arrived with the drinks. She drank her cognac back the same way anyone else might've taken a beer.

"That's not half-bad," she said, wiping her mouth. "I'll tell you, Flake not an easy man to live with. Always goin' on about how things gonna get better. So I put up with it. What am I gonna do? He got me with child. So I just look the other way, make believe I don't see those other trix and hos. I'm not even tellin' about the drinkin' and the flakin'. Why you think they call him Flake anyway? Man liked his pleasures, just like the next one."

Her tone was conversational, totally removed.

"Anyways, got to scoot. Got to figure what to do with the bodies. Arrangements, you know. Just goes to show you, I guess. Thanks for the drink, baby."

Jersey kissed him on the cheek.

"Maybe I'll see you around," she said.

He gulped back his beer and called for another.

"What did I tell you?" the old barkeep said, sliding it over. "That one's on me."

It had been a long, tiring day. It had started at dawn with a flight out of BWI. They'd landed in Providence, Rhode Island, and driven to New Bedford, the state loony bin. After consulting there with Dr. Freud they'd worked their way over to colonial Belmont and the child-molesting Jared Cooper. Now, several hours later, at the King George, after meeting the delightful Jersey, Eamon was ready to knock the beers back, one after the other.

If ever a day cried out for the Jack Daniel's . . .

No doubt he and Bunko were destined to arrive in that smoky part of Tennessee a little later on. But for now he was content to sip his beer and fade into the bankers' gauche din, into the harsh, determined sounds of a Friday night. He studied the Union Jack that hung over the bar and the many Beefeater figurines that were positioned among the bottles, lost himself in that.

He had trouble getting Jersey out of his mind. He was meeting more and more Jerseys lately, people with an almost sociopathic lack of feeling. It didn't matter what color they were. The Jerseys of the world were just as likely to be white as they were black or yellow, or whatever. Color and sex had nothing to do with it. It was about the cheapening of life in America, not just by guns but by our own perverse reactions and attitudes. Eamon saw it on the television news practically every night. Empty-headed bystanders being interviewed about some little sixth grader gunned down in the school yard, in the crossfire: "Yeah, shudda watched his ass. Kid got smoked but good." Neighbors being interviewed about the little old lady next door, the one who got strangled the night before: "Totally bogus, man. Didn't deserve that, nohow."

Eamon—drowning in thoughts of America's moral decline—was startled to find himself on the receiving end of a kiss. He was gladdened by the sight of Mary Seppala.

"You look like you could use some company," she said.

"What are you doing here?"

201

"Briefing Boston homicide."

"God, you're a sight for sore eyes," he said.

"Believe it or not, so are you," she said, returning his tender gaze.

"How about a drink?"

"Eamon Wearie, you spend entirely too much time in bars. How about a walk in the good fresh air instead?"

"I don't know, Bunk's supposed to join me."

"I'm sure he can manage without you for one evening."

"How about Kelsey? He come up with you?"

"No, I'm on my own—on the prowl. Better watch out, mister, I may just take advantage of you tonight."

"I'm sorry, Mary, I'm not that kind of boy. I don't know what you've heard, but—"

"Actually," she said, pulling him off his bar stool, "I've heard you're a real slut."

"Who says?"

"All the girls. The word is, you're an easy lay."

"Just idle boasts," Eamon said, acting indignant. "Foolish locker-room talk. God, you know how horrible girls can be. Always making up stories to prove their femininity."

"But, babe, if you really loved me," Mary said, doing her best imitation of a big, dumb jock, "you'd prove it."

At that they both broke out laughing.

Eamon was surprised by Mary's friskiness, especially after how they'd last parted. Neither one brought up that hard, sobering slap across the face.

They stepped out into a splendid night, full of starlight and cool, lavish breezes. They started up Boylston Street, to points unknown. They passed the Boston Public Library, a whole city block of ornate, Renaissance-style stonework, and several oppressive-looking Gothic churches besides. The ancient churches seemed to grow like weeds—just as plentiful and just as stubborn—among the modern glass and granite towers.

"So you'll never guess who I had lunch with today," Mary said as they walked along.

"Lila Cooper," he guessed. "She wanted to know where to find me. She's eager to deliver another personal, semiautomatic message."

"You just seem to have that effect on women."

"It's a gift."

"It must be, judging by Christy Gertz's reaction. I took her for hamburgers at the Inner Harbor. Talk about infatuated. That girl's really hung up on you. Has some foolish notion that you might be her knight in shining armor. So I took the opportunity to set her straight."

"What did you tell her?"

"I told her you were no bargain. Listed a few of your less endearing qualities. When that failed to work, I was forced to take drastic measures. I took out my Beretta 92FS and said, 'Back off, sweets. He's my man.'"

Eamon laughed. "What's got into you tonight? You're so . . ."

"Different? Is that what you were going to say? I don't know. I guess I just feel more and more comfortable with you."

She took his hand into hers, causing a nice, warm feeling to spread through him.

She said, "You'll be glad to know that I've made Christy my personal reclamation project. There's definitely hope for her. She even had quite a few questions about the work I do. By the end of lunch she was actually talking about becoming a cop someday."

"I hate to say it, but she starred in the adult-entertainment classics *Police Brutality* and *Men with Nightsticks*."

"God, you're kidding me. I suppose you were forced to watch them."

"Just part of the job, ma'am."

"And did it turn you on?"

The question was knotted with some hostility—not just toward him but toward his entire sex. He knew better than to try to answer it.

"It's just such a sick and hopeless world," she said. "The exploitation and abuse of girls like Christy will probably still be going on a thousand years from now."

"Maybe so," he ventured. "But that doesn't mean we should stop fighting it."

"Think about it, that's just what Lila Cooper's doing. Fighting back with everything she's got."

"She's a cold-blooded killer. I have no empathy whatsoever."

"I wish I could say the same," Mary said, sounding troubled. "Unfortunately, this is the first time where I've found myself empathizing with the killer and had some trouble feeling for the victims."

"I know you don't really mean that."

"*I do* mean it, though. It's been there all along. Starting at the Ackerman crime scene. God, remember that bludgeoned, eyeless thing lying in its own blood and feces? The former Lou Ackerman, porno distributor and general all-round scumbag. Usually your thoughts attach themselves to the victim. But instead I kept trying to imagine the woman who could do that to a man—gut him like that. Why such an ugly revenge? What has her life been like? What kind of ugliness has she been put through? What have men done to her?"

"But she killed a human being. Not just one, but—"

"I'm sorry, but Lou Ackerman was not a human being."

"Of course he was. I'm not saying he was a shining example of our kind, but he was flesh and blood, nonetheless. Your job, just like mine, is to enforce the law. You're not supposed to make exceptions."

"I'm not so sure," she said. "Lila Cooper has helped Christy Gertz in ways you could never imagine. Ackerman's death has freed her, given her retribution and justice. The kind of real justice that's lost on our own judicial system."

"You're making me very nervous," Eamon said.

"I'm just trying to be honest with you."

They came upon Boston Common, the oldest public park in America. Not that they were aware of that, or the withering fact that those forty-eight acres were set aside in 1634 for the common good, which mostly meant the grazing of cattle. Nor did they have to know that the floodlit, gold-leaf dome in the distance belonged to Charles Bulfinch's State House. No, in truth, it wasn't all that important to know any of these things. Like the thousands of young lovers who'd come before them, Eamon and Mary were just grateful for the respite, for a park bench situated among the fluttering trees.

And like so many before them, they were content to while away the time in slow, gentle pursuit. They caressed and kissed and nuzzled. Eamon was careful not to overwhelm Mary, not to let his natural voraciousness get the better of him. If anything, though, she seemed the more ardent of the two. It surprised him to have it returned like that, to know that it could be that way.

The only real awkwardness came early on, adjusting to the guns secured under their navy blazers. It was strange to kiss a girl who was holstered down, to be reminded of why they were in Boston in the first place.

On the walk back to the Revere they were unnaturally quiet. He knew that she was his, if that's truly what he wanted. But there was another part of him that wanted to show her that he could bide his time, that he was indeed capable of gentlemanly restraint.

He dropped her off at her room. It was hell to kiss her out in the hallway like that and then just turn around and leave abruptly. He didn't want to give her the chance to invite him in. After all, a man could resist only so much temptation.

Eamon returned to his own room, to the plush, old-world charm of a four-poster bed and heavy, vermilion drapes. It was lovely, really, so much the opposite of the kind of anonymous, sanitary-wrapped accommodations the inspectors were used to. Instead of paintings of sad clowns or pastel sunsets, the Revere presented elaborately framed Gilbert Stuart reproductions. In place of the standard bolted-in color television, the Revere had merely set two fine, gilt-edged, English Regency armchairs in front of the open, eighth-floor window. Instead of the anonymous hum of air-conditioning, Eamon listened to the rustling of those vermilion drapes, which swayed and danced on the shifting night currents, lulling him fast to sleep.

It was late, just past two in the morning. He was totally exhausted; he didn't even have the strength to dream.

He hadn't been asleep twenty minutes when the phone rang.

At first, hearing her distinct enunciation, he had some trouble grasping that it was real and that he wasn't in the throes of some topsy-turvy nightmare.

"It's no secret that you're quite the baseball fan," Lila Cooper said. "What I have to tell you should interest you greatly."

"How did you find me?"

"Mama always knows," she said queerly.

"What have you done this time?"

"I had a little date this evening with Bo Dallas."

"The Yankees catcher?"

"He really shouldn't have got so fresh with me."

"Where is he?"

"You'll find the big, dead slugger in his room at the downtown Holiday Inn."

"God, no—"

"Such a shame, too. On the last night of his life, he

went three for four. But Bo always did love to play in Fenway. Had his batting average right up around .300, too. God, life can be so unfair."

"Why did you call me again?"

"I find it very erotic, darling. Don't you?"

"I don't know what the hell you're talking about."

"Your rich, masculine voice. Oh, it makes me all warm and tingly."

"You're a very sick woman. You need help desperately."

"No, that's where you're wrong. It's the male penis society that's all sick and desperate and tormented. It's the penis men who equate sex with violence, who get off on such a twisted conjoining."

"Maybe we can still help you—"

"You're the one in need of help, Eamon Wearie."

"Let's arrange a place to meet, to discuss this."

"How quaint, these foolish attempts of yours to cajole me. It's such a shame that our little game of cat and mouse must come to an end."

"You going to kill me, is that it?"

"No, I promised a special little someone that I wouldn't."

"Who'd you promise? Christy? Who?"

"It's not your concern."

"You spoke to your daughter tonight, didn't you?"

"I must be going now, really I must."

"How did you get to her? How did you know she was staying at her friend Darlene's?"

"Oooh, Mister Mouse, you're just too darn, darn smart for your own darn, darn good," she said in a strange, childlike voice. "You making the big puddy cat very, very mad, Mister Eamon Mouse."

It was a chilling transformation; he was left speechless.

"Daddy a big, bad, mean man," the little girl said, sounding even younger now, if that were possible. "I don' like his i-cream cone."

Then little Lila Cooper hung up, leaving him more confused than ever.

He debated calling Tony Montrez.

Mister Eamon Mouse was just so very, very tired. All he wanted to do was hide under the covers until morning, or at least until all the big, bad monsters had gone away.

# Twenty

*B*o Dallas, the Yankee catcher, had been accused of raping a nineteen-year-old barmaid in Fort Lauderdale, Florida, during spring training. The trial was to have taken place in October, at the end of the baseball season. But Judge Lila Cooper had moved it up on her own private docket. Her verdict had not included the chance of parole.

The scene inside Bo's hotel room was ghastly bright with police flash and crimson splashings. Eamon and Bunko, along with Masterson, Montrez, and Mary Seppala, stood in the corridor, out of the way, leaving it to Boston's finest to sift through the carnage.

"Worst I've ever seen," Montrez commented.

"Right up there, for damn sure," Del Masterson said. "I've only seen a few mob hits that even came close. Stuffing a guy's private parts down his throat is about as bad as it gets."

Bunko said, "I wonder if he was alive for any of it."

"God, what a thought," Eamon said.

All four men shook their heads in grim, empathetic consideration.

Looking to Montrez, Mary said, "What now?"

"We redouble our efforts," said the gray man.

Masterson said, "Easy for you to say. You got a hundred some odd agents combing the city. What about the rest of us?"

"Provincetown needs to be checked out," Montrez said. "That bar. Ladyfingers. Where all the collect calls were made."

"Bullshit, hear me?" Masterson barked. "Fuckin' mop-up work. Postal's damn sick and tired of being treated like second-class citizens."

"I'll go out to Provincetown," Eamon said, thinking quickly. He wasn't so much volunteering for an assignment as he was attempting to escape Masterson's company.

"I'd be willing to accompany Lieutenant Wearie," Mary said.

"I'll bet you would, sweetcakes," Masterson muttered.

"You mind repeating that?" Mary said, glaring.

Trying to head off World War III, Eamon said, "Well, I don't know, Mary. Bunk and I are a team. We always work together."

Bunko said, "That's all right, kid. Me and Del will take it from this end. All the action's in this part of the world."

Eamon couldn't believe his ears; he knew Bunko couldn't stand Masterson and vice versa.

"It's settled then," Montrez said, eager to get on with it. "Agent Wearie and Detective Seppala will head out to Provincetown this morning."

Masterson grunted.

Bunko flashed Eamon a victorious smile.

Suddenly it dawned on Eamon that his partner had made the ultimate sacrifice for him.

"Now then," Montrez continued, "we've succeeded in tracing Lila Cooper's call to Agent Wearie. She used a phone booth not two blocks from here. But we're still not sure how she made contact with her youngest daughter. To that end I've sent agents out to Belmont to reinterview Emily Cooper. It's a long shot, but we're hoping that Emily knows her mother's whereabouts.

"However, I can tell you how Lila Cooper discovered Agent Wearie's whereabouts. She called Dead Letters and succeeded in convincing an Agent Santos that she was Wearie's mother and that she needed to contact him on some urgent matter.

"I should also tell you that we've been able to establish that Cooper was in the Holiday Inn lounge tonight. Several of Dallas's teammates have been able to identify her from our photographs and photographic enhancements. Our eyewitnesses say that Lila Cooper approached Bo Dallas at the bar sometime around midnight. This in itself was a somewhat unusual occurrence of late. Ever since that rape accusation the ladies have pretty much left Bo alone. Let's face it, he was practically a pariah.

"Now then . . ."

Tony Montrez was just about through briefing them. It was four-thirty in the morning, but you would never know it by looking at the gray man. Eamon had nothing but admiration for his freshly shaven appearance at this ungodly hour: Looking splendidly awake, he was turned out in a wrinkle-free, royal blue cotton suit. Eamon and his unshaven, sleep-deprived cohorts had not even managed a necktie among them. Mary Seppala, on the other hand, was a match for the gray man, with her subtly made-up face and crisp Calvin Klein linens. Eamon's heart practically leaped at the sight of her. It was a strange feeling for a crime scene, this newfound exuberance.

"I owe you," Eamon told Bunko as their little briefing broke up.

"Big time," the big man said.

* * *

Rush Limbaugh railed out against the "feminazis," his coinage for ugly, fatty, emasculating lesbian abortionists.

Mary Seppala asked Eamon if he wouldn't mind changing stations or turning the radio off altogether. They were on Route 6, just past Yarmouth, twenty miles outside Provincetown. They'd left the Revere at just after eight, and now it was a little after ten in the morning. Eamon had managed two whole hours of sleep last night. He swigged coffee from a thermos. The scenery didn't help matters. The road ran through the middle of the Cape, just service stations and billboards and turnpike motels. He wondered where all the water was.

"I thought Cape Cod was supposed to be such a big deal," he said.

"Maybe it will be," she said, patting his free hand reassuringly. "There's no way to know yet."

It was a gorgeous, sun-kissed, cerulean day. Eamon knew the season didn't hold too many more of these beauties. He felt a kind of sadness, one born of regret, in the summer's passing, in its last, great, waning moments. He hadn't even made it to the beach this year, no, not even that. The closer they came to Provincetown—catching glimpses of the emerald Atlantic and the bleached, rough-hewn shore—the more the pangs increased, and the more white and ungainly and unhealthy Eamon began to feel.

Just on the outskirts of town now, they passed dozens of motels, most of them facing out on Cape Cod Bay and almost all of them flashing No Vacancy on a Saturday morning. Eamon thought it was almost as if he and Mary were on vacation; it was a notion that he knew he'd best resist. But it was no secret that everything had worked out better than he had any right to hope. Here they were, together after all, following the yellow-brick road to Provincetown, a spit of pavement now bordered by the jewel green sea on two sides.

The town turned out to be congested with too many cars, tourists, and trendoids. All three were backed up on Commercial Street, a jam-packed stretch of bars, chowder houses, art galleries, gift shops, and T-shirt outlets. The crowded, festive boulevard belonged to the young, to their passing whims and quixotic desires. The young Bohemians strutted about in all their bright plumage—in their tangerine and lime swimsuits; with their sapphire- and ruby-tinted sunglasses; in their Malcolm X caps and earthy Birkenstocks— with their jejune faces registering either muted contempt or flagrant interest, one or the other, as if the entire range of human complexity in between eluded them.

But it was hard not to appreciate all those tiny saltboxes and Cape Cods, painted as prettily as a rose garden, so many yellows and pinks besides the mainstay white. It was hard, too, not to like MacMillan Wharf, which was still a real working pier, where the big commercial fishing boats still parked alongside the whale watchers and pleasure cruisers. For all its artsy-fartsy trendiness and overt gayness—yes, that, too; Eamon couldn't help noticing the same-sex couples who were everywhere, strolling blissfully, obliviously, hand in hand—Provincetown still retained enough brininess and historic anchorage to please any jaded old salt.

Parking was nearly impossible. Eamon just blocked a private driveway off Pilgrims Way, one of the many tightly squeezed side streets off Commercial, not having the patience for anything else. "Wait here," he told Mary. "I'll check it out." Ladyfingers was just across the street, a dark-looking hole in the wall. His spirits plunged at the locked front door, where the hours were clearly posted.

Open 6 P.M. to 3 A.M. (or until the Last Dyke Staggers Out)

He returned to the car, at a loss what to do next.

"Jesus, what a waste," he said to Mary through her

passenger-side window. "Should've figured something like this. Should've called ahead, damn it."

"It's not the end of the world," she said, looking up at him with the glimmerings of possibility. "At least we have each other."

"Jesus, I'm so tired," he moaned, not hearing her. "What the hell do we do now? Can you tell me that?"

"We'll go swimming," she said simply and decisively.

"I'm sorry to disappoint you, but I didn't bring my swimming trunks."

"Even better," she said, smiling deliciously.

Before he knew quite what was happening, she had got out of the car and was leading him by the hand into one of those all-purpose pharmacies. There, they had no trouble purchasing swimsuits and the appropriate, vampire-numbered sunblock. They also picked up towels, sunglasses, breath mints, and the local papers. It seemed that they were ready to go, but then Eamon decided he couldn't do without the Boogie board. It was all downhill from there as they loaded up on paperback novels; decided they couldn't pass up those really nifty-looking Red Sox caps; and came to the joint realization that they'd be needing an Igloo cooler for all the food that they'd soon be loading into it.

At the register Mary prevented Eamon from using his American Express card. "Not on your life," she said. "This one's on me."

They had one more stop to make before they hit the beach. The gourmet deli. Where they indulged in the paté de foie gras and a tub each of the tangy marinated shrimp and cold lobster salad. Of course this constituted only a partial list, not including the hunk of Camembert, or the sourdough baguettes, or the herbed potato salad made of precious, rosy new potatoes. Eamon also threw in a six-pack of Sierra Pale—since the gourmet deli seemed to carry only a selection of pricey gourmet beer—thereby causing

Mary to frown noticeably. She herself made do with a quart-size bottle of Orangina.

Then it was just a short hop to the Cape Cod National Seashore, miles of magnificent, uncrowded, unspoiled ocean beaches. They changed in one of the public facilities and then made their way past the monster dunes to the sharp, clear, deep green water.

Eamon couldn't help staring at Mary in her string bikini. It was just difficult to ignore that outrageous figure, just as it was hard to ignore his own strong, tender feelings for her. They rubbed lotion on each other with all the purposefulness accorded any other sensual act.

Eamon didn't wait long, though, to run down to the sea. There, bobbing up and down amid the giant swells, he gave in to aquatic abandon, thrashing about with the kind of high-spirited solar energy that had so long been denied him. Here, in the bracing, salt-charged surf, he had no trouble forgetting that he hadn't had sleep in two days.

Then Mary joined him, and they played like seal pups, inventing their own version of underwater tag, suddenly flapping away from each other but then just as suddenly charging back together for friendly, slippery kisses. They were children again, and their squeals of unhindered delight seemed to echo from the faint shores of other, more distant summers.

There may never have been a better day in their lives, or in anyone else's, for that matter. So many times they reentered the sparkling, absolving sea. So many times they let the hot sun dry them off. So many hours they spent caressing and talking in the safety of this memory-dipped day.

"I've never been so happy," she said from her towel.

He looked up from his book, one of those paperbacks they'd bought earlier. The sleek girl-woman with the dark mane, now soft with curls and natural highlights, had contentment radiating from every pore.

"What are you reading?" she asked.

"Called *Secret Survivors*. About incest and repressed memories. Got another one here, too. *The Courage to Heal*. Ever hear of them? Both self-help books are huge, huge best-sellers. I gather there's a lot of people out there who're convinced that their adult problems come from being abused as children. Even if they can't remember any of it."

"And I'm gathering this has something to do with our Ms. Cooper."

"Well, ever since talking to that Dr. Slavitt, I'm a bit more curious about all this. What gets me is the sheer, mind-boggling numbers. This woman who wrote *Secret Survivors* says that it's probable that more than half the nation's women are victims of childhood sexual abuse. Doesn't that sound absolutely unbelievable? I just can't see how that can be. It's just too bizarre, don't you think?"

"I believe it," Mary Seppala said shortly.

"No way," he said, not inclined to believe his country was that sick.

"It's interesting that while you find this ugliness so hard to accept, I have no such trouble. I guess that's just one more difference between being a man and a woman."

"I don't understand."

"It's just that women grow up hearing other women's horror stories. We know the secrets our sisters keep. We know what goes on out there. I can't tell you how many of my friends have confided their private traumas, their personal nightmares. Really, I can't tell you how many of my girlfriends have been raped, or have just barely escaped being raped. I can't count the number of friends who've told me about that kissy-kissy uncle in the family or the touchy-feely minister or the good-natured neighbor who turned out to be a major sex pervert. There's so much of it out there. You just don't know."

Not too far away someone's portable CD player was

spinning the Beach Boys' greatest hits. "Fun, Fun, Fun" came out sounding tinny and dated, its sweet, infectious naiveté laid bare by the pounding surf of time.

"Did anything ever happen to you?" Eamon asked Mary, suddenly hearing a discordant chord in all that blithe harmonizing.

"Yes. No. Maybe. I don't know anymore. God, it's so hard."

She started to choke up. Then just as quickly she refrained, becoming instead a model of resolve:

"Uncle Donny. The son of a bitch. When I was twelve. Came into my bedroom. Ostensibly to say good night. Started to fondle me. I let out a wretched howl. My mother came running. Fortunately, she believed me."

He put his arm around her, just as she started to choke up again. This time Mary didn't do anything to stop it, and before long she was full-blown sobbing.

"I miss her, my mom," she said, gulping it back. "And my dad's so good. He never doubted me for an instant. And he hasn't spoken to his brother since. God bless my father."

The Beach Boys segued into "California Girls." It sounded like just more of the same old, easy lies. Oh, Eamon knew there would always be a place for this kind of music, that it would never lose its innocent appeal entirely. The tawny girls would forever parade about in their citrus bikinis and jejune faces, just as the young surfer dudes could forever be counted on to ogle them, from now to the end of humankind. But for Eamon, who was so much older now, this sweet, carefree harmonizing was somehow the sound of lost innocence, about what was no longer and about a world that may never have been in the first place.

# *Twenty-one*

The burly male bouncer didn't budge until Eamon produced his badge. "Yeah, I guess," he said sheepishly.

Inside, k.d. lang was crooning "Save Me" from a vintage, rainbow-lit Wurlitzer. An elegant, middle-aged couple slow danced in its otherworldly glow. Upon seeing him, they simply came to a standstill, in obvious wonder. All the conversation in the joint also came to a puzzled halt.

Ladyfingers was not at all what he expected; after all, its dark, faceless exterior hardly matched its rich, dowager interior. The smoky-mirrored art deco bar was a priceless fixture, just as the antique slate billiard table with the leather pockets was another perfectly conditioned, one-of-a-kind piece. This was not to mention the Tiffany lamps, or the bordello-style paintings of naked, Rubenesque beauties in various states of repose.

He approached the bar, which was enveloped by a dozen or more women, including Mary Seppala, who had arrived a half hour earlier as part of the plan.

"Ladies, I'm sorry to be intruding," Eamon announced, "but I'm a federal agent working with the FBI on an urgent matter. We are looking for a former patron of this establishment. We know her by the name Lila Cooper, although it's possible you may know her by an entirely different name. If anyone knows anything, anything at all, I need to talk to you. Lives are at stake. Rest assured, I will not betray your confidentiality."

He proceeded to pass photographs of Cooper down the length of bar. There was a lot of head shaking. Mary was careful not to make eye contact with him, and he was just as careful not to linger on her. She was strictly backup tonight. The plan was, if nothing materialized with him, maybe she'd overhear something after he left.

"I've seen her before," the waiflike bartender said, examining one of the glossies. "Yeah, used to drop by here. But I haven't seen her in a few months now."

"What do you know about her?"

"Not much," said the elfin woman with the short, slicked-back hair. "Come in for a single drink, never attempted to make conversation."

"Did she ever come in with anyone? Or leave with anyone, for that matter?"

"Usually just ordered her vodka martini and then went to make a call, using the phone by the restroom. Then she'd just down the drink and leave. Not much more to tell, other than the fact that she always left a decent tip."

Eamon sighed, more than a little frustrated at this point. "Let me give you my card. You never know."

"I'll keep an eye out," she assured him.

"Now I could go for a stiff drink. How 'bout some Jack on the rocks, okay?"

"I don't know if that's such a good idea," she said, scanning her hushed, all-woman bar.

"Just a quick one, trust me. I want to give everyone

a chance to mull it over. Maybe something will occur to them in the next few minutes."

She didn't look all that thrilled about it, but she poured him one and he drifted off to a quiet corner. The unnatural hush didn't last long, fortunately, and before he knew it the pleasant hum of bar conversation was once again rising over k.d. lang's mellifluence. That elegant, older couple went back to their slow swaying as k.d. swooned over "Miss Chatelaine."

The well-heeled crowd, Eamon noticed, was for the most part in their thirties and forties, and they were costumed in a wide array of fine evening wear, everything from pearls and gold lamé to men's double-breasted suits. The clothes seemed to make the woman, stressing either the masculine or the feminine, as if somehow meant to convey one's psychic gender. He watched, fascinated, as the most mannish-looking women in lapels and pants came on to the dresses and skirts, buying them drinks and exhibiting a certain cocky aggressiveness.

In fact, he couldn't help but notice the tall, handsome k.d. lang look-alike who was paying particular attention to Mary Seppala. The man-tailored woman with the rumpled, just-awakened look and Elvis-inspired hairdo was staring directly into Mary's eyes with nothing less than ardent desire. What bothered Eamon was that Mary was doing nothing to discourage it. Quite the opposite, it seemed, as she met those lustful eyes head-on. He watched in astonishment as Mary agreed to a dance with the handsome stranger. The real k.d. lang sang "Constant Craving" as her double held Mary's waist and boldly led her through the motions.

He didn't care if she was just playing along for the sake of the case. Eamon still didn't like it one bit. His irritation only mounted watching them dance cheek to cheek. He almost lost it when the stranger put her goddamn hands on Mary's ass. And he couldn't believe it when Mary made no move to stop it. Christ, she'd never have let him get away with that. What in the name of God was she thinking?

He swallowed the rest of his Jack and stormed out, not at all sure that he wanted to hear the answer to his own question.

He went across the street to another bar, Lucy's Dive, their foreordained meeting place. He didn't know whether it was gay or hetero, or what, and he didn't give a damn as long as they poured the Jack and didn't waste any time doing so.

The bartender was a gorgeous grungette with a huge, ornate Byzantine cross around her alabaster neck. "Hey, dude," she said by way of greeting.

"Hey yourself," he said, grabbing a stool at the deserted bar.

"What can I get you for?"

"A double Jack over ice."

"Living dangerously, huh?"

"No more than any other night," he said, laying a twenty on the ill-used bar, a slab of graffiti-gouged oak that had been worked over pretty good by someone's pocketknife.

"I haven't seen you in here before," she said, showing palpable interest.

He looked her over closely. She had long, unwashed blond hair and a long, lithe body. The arms were tattooed with blue snakes, and her alabaster coloring obviously came from an unhealthy, vampirish existence. But it was her face, her killer face, the face of an exquisitely young Bardot, that made you feel like you were missing out on something.

"You look like you caught some rays today," she commented.

"Yeah," he said, suddenly feeling tired and sun-drained.

"It suits you," she said, not giving up.

He took out his cigarettes—and, before he could strike a match, she had a light waiting.

"You want to hear some music?" she asked.

221

He watched her saunter over to the CD-playing juke. Watched her make her selections in the tainted blue. Lucy's was a real hole, just a slab of beat-up oaken bar and some old blinking Christmas lights. The first one out was Berlin's "Sex," this old new-wave song. The female singer said she was a slut and a goddess and a one-night stand, and a few other things.

"You like this song?" she asked, getting back behind the bar.

"It's okay, I guess."

"I think it's great. I think it captures the whole thing, you know. That we're not, like, just one kind of person, that we all need, like, the freedom to explore other sides of ourselves."

"Yeah, right."

Eamon swallowed back the whiskey. She poured another before he had a chance to decide for himself.

"Do you have a girlfriend?"

"I thought I did. Now I'm not so sure."

"That's the way it goes sometimes."

"Left her in Ladyfingers," Eamon confided. "Left her dancing with some strange woman."

"I once lost a boyfriend to some guy," she sympathized. "That kind of thing happens a lot in this town."

Blondie replaced Berlin on the juke with "Heart of Glass."

"So what's your name anyway?"

"Trace. At least that's what they call me."

"You been in Provincetown long?"

"Long enough to know better."

"What do you mean?"

"It's like Sodom and Gomorrah, you know."

"I don't follow."

"It's all about finding a warm body, nothing more than that."

"I'm losing you," he said, shaking out another cigarette.

"Men, women, what's the difference," Trace declared, holding the lighter out again. "Whatever's warm, whatever feels good."

"I hate to disagree with you, but I'm kind of partial to women."

"Hate to tell you, dude, but so am I."

"But I thought you were—"

"I'm bi, not that it matters much. Everything happens in your own head anyway. Don't think it doesn't. You could hump parking meters if you had a mind to."

"Maybe that's my best bet," Eamon said. "Finding a sincere, attractive parking meter."

"A person could do worse. I'd take a meter over some of the guys I've been with. You better believe it, dude."

"You like women better than men?" he asked, oddly curious.

"I wouldn't put it that way. It's just that women would never think to pull half the stunts guys do. Guys think they own you. Think they can force you to do stuff. Women always ask nice if they want something special. There's a difference, sexually speaking. Men are more interested in the technical aspects. Just want to know about what buttons to push, how to get you off, you know. It's like you're this thing, *just this thing* to them. And that's how they like to keep it, like having feelings would just ruin it for them."

He pondered it over the whiskey, throwing back another tumbler of the black stuff as the juke kicked in with R.E.M.'s "Losing My Religion."

"I've been with over a hundred men," she suddenly professed.

"Why so many?"

"Because that's the way it had to be."

"I don't understand."

"I didn't feel like I was worth anything," she said.

"I still don't understand."

"I kept having sex with losers because it was my way of verifying my low self-esteem. At least that's what

223

my therapist says. You see, I was molested when I was very little."

"Did you just recently remember it?"

"What?"

"Did it just come back to you in therapy or—"

"I don't know what you're talking about. I never forgot it in the first place. How could I ever forget my brother doing those things to me?"

"Some people can," he said. "You'd be surprised."

"Yeah, I guess. But my problem, dude, is not remembering, but forgetting. Because, believe me, I'd love to forget all about it."

"Have you ever confronted your brother?"

"I don't talk to him anymore. Or anybody else in my family for that matter. What's the point? They're all sick. They say it never happened, you know."

"Even your brother? Does he say it never happened?"

"Yeah, can you believe that? Like he thinks I'm making it all up or something."

"Just what we were talking about," Eamon said. "People being able to block anything."

"Yeah, that's so weird," Trace said.

"I want to show you something," he said, reaching into his jacket pocket for a photo of Lila Cooper, now that she was back on his brain. "Ever see this woman before?"

"Wow, you know Emily?"

"Emily?" he repeated, remembering that that was Lila's daughter's name.

"That's not her name, is it?" Trace said. "I should've guessed."

"What are you talking about?"

"Her gold cigarette lighter. A gift from Patricia. It was engraved, you know. I was always picking it up and looking at it."

"What was on it?"

" 'To L.C., love always, Patty.' I never could figure

that L.C. part. Thought it was a nickname or something."

"Who's Patty?"

"Patricia Fall. Emily's girlfriend. They were an item. But I haven't seen them in a while. Why do you want to know anyway?"

"I'm looking for Emily. That's not her real name. But that's who I'm looking for."

"Why? What's she done?"

"Why do you say that?" Eamon asked. "Why would she have had to do anything?"

"That's just the way she was. A real bitch. Everyone knew to stay clear when she was in one of her famous moods."

"Tell me about Patricia Fall."

"She had some money, inherited, you know. Not a bad person, really. Just messed up. Lonely, searching. Just like everybody else. Emily just zeroed in on her, you know. Like she was some kind of target."

"Were they living together?"

"Yeah, somewhere in town."

"You got a phone directory?" Eamon asked.

Trace handed him the white pages from behind the bar. But he couldn't find any listing for a Patricia Fall.

"Probably unlisted," she said. "You know how the rich are."

Eamon went right over to the wall phone next to the juke and punched up Tony Montrez at the Revere. Percy Sledge was wailing "When a Man Loves a Woman."

"Patricia Fall, whatever you can find on her. She was living with Cooper. Somewhere in town."

"Okay," the gray man said, "sit tight. I want you and Seppala to stay in Provincetown and await further instructions. Check back in in one hour's time."

Mary Seppala walked into Lucy's Dive just as Eamon was hanging up the phone.

"What were you doing? Talking to your girlfriend?" Mary said, ribbing him.

225

"Speaking of girlfriends, what happened to yours?" Eamon said without any of the good humor. "What, she find somebody else?"

"Oh, God," Mary said in disbelief. "You've got to be kidding me. I was just working all the angles."

"I'll say."

"The bad news is that I came up short in there. No one was very forthcoming."

"You had some woman who looks like a man with her hands all over your ass. I don't know what the hell you call it, but I'd call that very forthcoming."

"Why, Lieutenant, you're starting to sound a tad homophobic."

"Not in the least. I have nothing against homosexuals. As long as they leave me alone, I'll leave them alone."

"Oh, how awfully big of you," Mary said mockingly. "Letting them walk the earth with you, letting them breathe the same air—"

"C'mon, give me a break. I'm not prejudiced. I've got nothing against them."

"You should really hear the way you sound. It's just so patronizing."

"She's right, dude," Trace said from the bar, having overheard everything. "What's all this them and us stuff?"

"Yeah, okay, all right," he said, giving in to their point.

The Righteous Brothers erupted into "You've Lost That Lovin' Feeling."

"God," Eamon said, turning to Trace, "why'd you have to pick this tune?"

"I've loved it ever since *Top Gun*. Remember that movie, where Tom Cruise and Kelly McGillis are dancing to it in that bar? It was just so, so romantic, don't you think?"

"Yeah, I guess."

"Want to dance?" Trace asked.

"No, that's okay," Eamon said, slightly embarrassed and feeling the sting of Mary's eyes.

"I see you've got your own new friend," Mary said, not letting it go by.

"Yeah, well," he said with some ill-advised huffiness, "while you were swaying with your gal in Ladyfingers I was in here trying to solve the case. And with the help of Trace here, we may have made some headway. . . ."

After filling Mary in on the details, Eamon added, "And I came up with Patricia Fall's name without resorting to dirty dancing or sexual favors or—"

"I guess we'll need some rooms in town tonight," Mary said, interrupting the sarcasm.

"Lots of luck," Trace said. "Saturday night in Provincetown is impossible."

"Tell me about it," Eamon said.

# *Twenty-two*

❧

*T*hat bartender had been right about finding rooms on a Saturday night. After a while those No Vacancy signs were like a blinking nightmare, as they continued to prowl the outskirts of Provincetown in search of lodging and relief. It was a quiet, anxious ride that was short on conversation and long on frayed nerves. Eamon imagined Mary was just disappointed in him, nothing new there. He'd made an ass of himself again, a jealous homophobic ass of himself. But there wasn't much he could do about it now, except to keep his mouth shut and hope for a pardon in the morning. Right now, though, he just wanted to hit the sack and make up for lost sleep. He could feel the afternoon's sun burning its way into his skin, tiring him still further.

"Look, over there!" Mary exclaimed, her first words in ages. "We're in luck."

"It's probably a mistake," he said doubting the red-lit Vacancy, its neon taking on all the properties of a mirage at this point.

Nevertheless, he swerved into the parking lot of the

228

Mysterious Pleasure Cove, a ramshackle grouping of weather-beaten cabins facing out onto Cape Cod Bay.

In the manager's office, a tall, skinny, disinterested kid with a ponytail and diamond-studded earrings told them there'd been a cancellation.

"Have only the one cabin. Take it or leave it."

"We'll take it," Mary said quickly, hearing the office door open, its jingle bells announcing another tired, anxious, disbelieving couple.

One hundred and fifty dollars had bought them a room with a view, not much else. Their cabin was cramped, dingy, and not altogether sanitary. The previous occupants had left the remains of a pizza and a dozen not exactly empty beer cans. They'd also left sixty-seven cents in the envelope for the maid, which may have offered a partial explanation for the damp, sand-sprinkled carpeting and soiled bedding and the general all-round disheveled appearance of the cabin.

There was only one bed, a sagging, coil-piercing queen that should've been taken off the active-duty roster.

"I'll see if I can get a cot," Eamon said gallantly. "Otherwise I'll just sleep on the floor."

"Whatever," Mary said dispassionately, disappearing into the bathroom.

He rang up the manager's office, and the ponytail told him to just go for it. "What do you need a cot for," he said, "when you got a babe like that? Besides, we don't have one anyway."

Then he called Tony Montrez.

"The trail's still cold," the gray man said. "I'll be in touch."

Eamon sat on the edge of that sagging bed, looking out the screened windows at the utterly placid, moon-lit sea. He heard the shower running, could imagine Mary's divine nakedness. He was exhausted, yet sort of horny and sort of sad all at the same time. Here he was in this honeymoon cabin, with the keeper, the real thing, getting ready to stretch out on the floor without her. His cells, his very DNA, everything that made him *him,* cried out for a very different ending, for consummation, nothing less.

He stole a pillow and a threadbare blanket and tried to make himself as comfortable as possible on the damp carpet. He could hear the gentle lap of the tide, and he concentrated on that, on its soothing, sleep-lulling rhythm. Damn you, Mary, he thought, drifting off.

Moments later Mary Seppala emerged from her shower wearing only a skimpy towel. She nudged him with her foot. "What are you doing on the floor?" she asked, towering over him.

She let the towel fall off her before he could say a word.

It would be useless, serve nothing but the most prurient interests, to describe that wondrous body or Eamon's own concupiscence. To say that he desired her, or that he even loved her, would not really say much, save what was so readily apparent. But love, that specious and slippery word, was not the only thing Eamon Wearie was feeling. Love didn't wholly capture the miraculous—the cleansing of original sin, the sweet eradication of sorrow. Old anxieties and newer worries fell harmlessly to the wayside. For a short, precious while, the terrible, bountiful cruelties of the world simply dissipated.

He felt truly reborn.

Sex and love, that was something, all right. But it hardly compared to the feeling of being saved from the abyss.

It wasn't quite coitus interruptus.

But Tony Montrez's phone call, coming in at five in the morning, just as Eamon and Mary had finally collapsed into mutual satiation, certainly qualified as an unwanted interruption.

"We've got a reading on Patricia Fall," the gray man

said. "She lives at Thirty-four Liberty Road. You writing this down, Agent Wearie?"

"Yeah, right," he said groggily, grabbing stationery from the nightstand drawer.

"The good news is that Patricia Fall left us a plastic trail to follow. Her Mastercard and Mobil receipts match Lila Cooper's known whereabouts. We've got hotel and restaurant verification that place her at crime scenes in Baltimore, Annapolis, and Boston. The dates and places match up, but the signatures seem a little queer. Our identification gurus are putting them to the test as we speak. It's our guess, though, that Patricia Fall is no longer with us."

"According to the plastic, where was Fall last?"

"At Bo Dallas's Holiday Inn. Right under our noses. Checked out this morning. Either Patricia Fall is riding shotgun with Cooper or she's dead and Lila's just using her cards and checking accounts."

"Do we have a make on the car yet?"

"Fall's got a registration for a ninety-three Honda Accord. Color: metallic blue. Massachusetts plate number: RKL two-two-two-nine."

"Where did it last fill up?"

"That's just it. On the Cape. Two days ago. Mobil station in Harwich, off Route 6. We don't know if Cooper, or this Patricia Fall, or whatever, made a visit to thirty-four Liberty Road, but we need to find out."

"We're on it," Eamon said, the adrenaline taking over.

"We want you to rifle through that house and see what you can come up with. And we want you to do that immediately."

"What about a warrant?"

"We've got one. You just have to pick it up. A federal judge by the name of Francis. On vacation. Right in town. Eight seventeen West Vine. I can't tell you how thrilled he was to get our wake-up call."

"Is it possible that Cooper and Fall are there?"

231

"We don't think so. The phone is disconnected for nonpayment. But we don't know. Play it safe and call for backup if you see the Accord in the driveway or any sign of activity inside."

"Detective Seppala is backup enough."

"I suppose," the gray man said. "What's her room number? I'll fill her in, if you like."

"That won't be necessary," Eamon said, smiling broadly.

"Very well then. Exercise extreme caution."

"Take no prisoners and shoot the wounded."

"We've trained you well, Agent Wearie," the gray man said.


It was a redolent, pink dawning, fragrant with promise and new beginnings. The sleepy-eyed lovers picked up their warrant from an ill-tempered, bathrobe-clad Judge Francis and then proceeded to Thirty-four Liberty Road, which was just another eighteenth-century saltbox nestled on Provincetown Harbor.

The daffodil-bright house was a tiny, two-story affair that, like its equally scrunched neighbors, was virtually yardless. There was no driveway, just curbside parking, and neither he nor Mary saw any sign of a metallic blue Accord in the vicinity.

All the windows were closed, all the shades were drawn. And there wasn't an air-conditioner in sight, all of which pointed to abandonment. Eamon checked the one garbage can—just to confirm that it was indeed empty.

Mary questioned the papergirl, a heavyset teen on a bicycle loaded down with Sunday papers.

"Nope, ain't seen those two since the spring," she said. "Still owe me ten bucks. Just pisses me off, really. Right out of my own pocket."

It was exactly six A.M. as they approached the front door with their guns drawn and their ears cocked.

They rang, then rapped loudly. Nothing, not a sound in there.

"Should I kick it in?" Eamon asked. "Or just break a window?"

"Men," Mary Seppala said, shaking her head good-naturedly and taking out some funny-looking keys.

In less than a minute she had the door unlocked.

"Not bad," he said appreciatively.

"I can't cook or clean," she said, "but I can pick locks, apprehend suspects, and shoot to kill."

"I like that in a woman."

They stepped inside and were staggered by the lack of light and pervading mustiness, as if the previous spring were still bottled up in there. As their eyes adjusted to the dimness they saw that they were in the living room, which was done up in a Southwestern motif, a pleasant enough sampling of Navajo rugs and cactuses that went nicely with the matching set of Indian-print couches. There were also two dazzling paintings of desert flowers, one over the decorative adobe fireplace, the other dominating a whole wall. Each was in extraordinary close-up, and the artist had taken pains to render the stamen, pistils, ovaries, and other organs with a dewy, almost human sexuality.

"Georgia O'Keeffe," Mary said, checking the artist's signature. "Big bucks for these."

Eamon's attention was lodged on the fancy photo—the frame was inlaid with silver and turquoise—above the fireplace. Lila Cooper and another woman, most likely Patricia Fall, were snapped at the beach with their arms around each other. They were in big, wide-brimmed straw hats and they were smiling. But it was Fall who drew his attention, a small, pert brunette with a troubled face. It was captured in the blink of a camera, a lifetime of unhealed psychic wounds and trashed self-esteem. It was even there in the fleeting smile, which, when you came in close, had a feeble, undeveloped quality about it.

He realized that Patricia Fall was dead. Her tragedy was somehow foretold in the picture, somehow glimpsed in its very composition, as if all her cells were in the process of photodisintegration.

"God," Mary said, "all these cactus plants are dying."

"I thought they could live through anything."

"I guess even a cactus needs a little sun and water," she said.

They moved on to the kitchen, which completed the downstairs portion of the tiny house. It was a spotless, purely functional space with a drippy, stainless-steel sink and blond-wood cabinetry. A no-frills wall calendar—courtesy of Porky's Seafood—hadn't advanced beyond the merry month of May.

A skylighted bedroom and bath made up the entire upstairs.

"Nothing to this place," Eamon said.

"Well, makes our job that much easier," Mary said.

Still, the sun streaming through the skylights was certainly pleasing, especially after the preternatural conditions downstairs. Eamon was just tired, overwhelmingly tired. He hadn't been to sleep now in three days. He tried to focus on the job at hand, tried to take inventory: two single beds pushed together. Some bookshelves crammed with women writers— Virginia Woolf, Jane Austen, the Brontë sisters, a few others. A French, Louis-the-something writing table and chair . . .

Jesus, he was just too damn tired.

He went into the bathroom to splash his face with cold water. He felt awful, looked awful. The face in the mirror belonged to an unemployed drifter, an ax-murderer: The hard stubble. The bloodshot eyes. The uncombable, ocean-crusted hair. Christ, what did Mary see in him anyway? He opened the medicine cabinet in a hunt for mouthwash, but instead came across a prescription graveyard. Mostly antidepressants and anti-anxiety pills. Patricia Fall, in all her craven insecurity, had made sure that she was never going to run out of Prozac or Xanax. The bottles were labeled with the names of several doctors and several pharmacies. Eamon found only one prescription for Lila Cooper, an acne ointment dated six months ago.

He came out of the bathroom to find Mary dabbing herself with perfume, something that had been left on the nightstand.

"Ralph Lauren's Safari," she said, as he came over to appraise.

"I like it," he said, instantly amorous.

"You like anything," she said.

"Only if it's on you," he said, putting his hands around her waist and nibbling at her earlobes.

"God, you're crazy," she said, falling back on one of the single beds.

"Crazy about you," he said, forgetting all about how tired he was and what kind of trouble they could both get into if anyone found out.

The hell with it, he thought, unzipping her jeans.

Twenty minutes of unbridled passion led to waking up in a fabulously disconnected state almost two hours later.

"Jesus Christ," Eamon said, seeing that it was nine-thirty by his watch.

Then he froze. He thought he heard something downstairs. Specifically, the front door. He shook Mary awake, putting his finger to his nose. She reached for her gun, the Beretta 92FS, which was in a mad tangle of clothing on the floor.

They heard nothing.

After a few minutes of hearing nothing, Eamon went for his own gun, the snub-nosed Smith & Wesson .38. Naked, he crawled across the wide-planked floor to the head of the stairs. There, he had a view of the front door below. Seeing and hearing nothing unusual, he stealthfully maneuvered the stairs, maintaining a sweaty-palmed grip on the gun.

Nothing.

Thank God, nothing.

The living room was the same, just the same.

He checked the kitchen, just to be sure.

He sighed relief, big time. Then headed back up to Mary.

"You had me going there," she said, fully dressed now.

"Christ, just so damn tired," he said, slipping back into his pants.

"Could've fooled me," she said, looking at him in the way of a lover, the conspiratorial mixing with the slightly goofy.

"I need some coffee," was all he could say.

"I'll tell you what, I'll go to a deli and get us some coffee and ham-and-egg sandwiches. I think we're in real need of sustenance here."

"You said it," he said, ready to fall back into bed again.

"Then we'll take this place apart, drawer by drawer."

"The fun never stops, does it?"

After Mary left, he couldn't seem to relax. His exhaustion was only mitigated by his jumpiness. In his mind he kept hearing the click of the front door, so close by, so unmistakable . . .

But was it the sound of somebody coming in? Or had somebody been in a hurry to leave? Was it possible that someone had been in the house with them?

God, banish the thought.

He needed to go through it again, room by room.

He just couldn't tell.

The living room *seemed* the same. The shades were still drawn. No lights had been turned on. The couches remained unfurrowed. The coffee-table magazines seemed unaltered. The cactuses were still dying. The *feel* was the same. But who knew for sure?

But something was different about the kitchen.

Something.

He realized the sink wasn't dripping anymore. Could that just stop by itself? Was that possible?

Then he saw it, the brown grocery bag.

On the floor.

Acting as an impromptu garbage bag.

No, he was almost sure that hadn't been there before.

Instinctively he placed his hand on his gun holster, just to make sure it was still there. Then, with some trepidation, he opened the refrigerator. There was an unopened carton of milk. Not to mention bacon, eggs, butter. All of it unopened, all of it dated for freshness.

Judging by the date on the milk they were lucky not to have got blown away in their sleep.

He needed to call for backup.

He remembered there was a phone in the living room.

He'd just forgotten that it was disconnected.

Before he could even think what to do next he heard someone using a key on the front door. He pulled his gun out and got into a crouch. He knew Mary hadn't been gone long enough.

He braced himself.

"Freeze!" he cried as Lila Cooper turned to face him with a strange, crooked smile.

"I should've known," she said, undaunted. "You've been such a thorn in my side."

Joan of Arc was looking gaunt and red eyed. She was in a silky, coral-colored suit that was stained with something dark on the pants. She was holding only an oversize Gucci pocketbook.

"I want you to drop the bag and raise your hands above your head."

She did this.

"I want you to kick the bag toward me. Don't try anything remotely funny. Believe me, I won't hesitate to shoot."

She kicked the bag over to him, much too hard, almost as if she were testing his resolve. When he didn't shoot, she bared another perverse smile.

"I want you to sit down now," he said, directing her to one of the Indian-print couches.

"You new at this?" she said, enjoying his discomfort.

"Just do it," he said, scooping up the Gucci bag.

He sat down opposite her. Only the coffee table separated them. He felt around in her bag, and it didn't take long to come up with the Glock.

"Kill anybody today?" he asked, careful to keep his own gun fixed on her.

"A girl needs protection in this crazy, penile world."

"The only one anybody needs protection from is you," he said.

"Ever kill anybody?"

"Yeah, as a matter of fact. So don't get any ideas."

"I thought it would be harder than it was," she said. "I thought I would really feel it, but it wasn't like that at all."

"Do I have to remind you that you're talking to a federal law enforcement officer, that what you say to me may be used against you in a court of law—"

"Oh, spare me, Mister Eamon Mouse."

She was smiling again, almost as if she were playing with him. It didn't seem to matter that he was the one holding the gun.

"I gather you bought that whole routine the other night?" she said.

"You mean, when you were talking in that little girl's voice?"

"Fooled you, didn't I?"

"I'll say."

"I'm good at that."

"Why did you pretend to be a little girl?"

"I'm not really sure," she said, sounding it. For

just a second uncertainty and vulnerability peeked through the emotional cloud cover.

"What happened to you? I've got to ask you that. What made you kill all those people?"

She didn't answer. She focused on him, hard. Like she was looking him over for signs of weakness, for something she could turn to her advantage. Even in the shade-drawn living room—not so dark, really, not with all that grainy light streaming down the stairwell—she didn't look so hot. Her skin had never been all that great, judging by the acne pits, but the hair, which had been blond, was now a henna-dyed disaster, as if it had been styled and restyled to the point of no return. He came to realize that she hadn't been to bed in a while, either. For one thing, the bleary green eyes were in serious need of Visine. But it was those dark spatterings on her silky pink pants that really gave her away. Blood stains—old blood stains.

"So what are we waiting around for?" she asked.

"Until I'm good and ready," he said, giving out as little information as possible.

He needed Mary's help. To cuff her, to tie her up, whatever. He wasn't taking any chances. He knew what this woman was capable of.

"How about a cigarette while we wait?" she asked.

"No way," he said, thinking what she might be able to do to him with a lit cigarette.

"You're no fun," she said, her voice shifting into another unsettling gear.

"So I've been told."

"Why don't you loosen up, baby?" she said, trying to make herself sound sexy. "We could have a good time together. I could make you happy, if you'd just let me, baby."

"You can just forget about that ever happening."

She started undoing her blouse.

"What the hell are you doing?"

She wasn't wearing a bra.

239

"Give me a break already. Just button that back up."

She cupped her breasts with her hands. "Oh, I know you want to feel them. Come here, baby. Touch me. You'll love it. Look at my nipples, look how aroused I am."

"You keep forgetting that I've seen what your boyfriends look like *after* you've got through with them."

"Oh, fuck you, Mister Eamon Mouse," she said, buttoning up and dispensing with all her sexual guile.

He wished Mary would just hurry back. This woman was more than any man could handle. And it didn't help that he was dead tired and that his nerves were shot. The gun was starting to feel very heavy.

"What's the matter?" she said. "You look so sleepy. Oh, poor baby. Not getting your recommended eight hours."

"You don't look so great yourself, Lila."

"My, aren't we getting personal now."

"I haven't quite forgiven you for the time you sprayed automatic gunfire all over my house."

"What a decidedly long memory."

"It seems my insurance doesn't cover bullet holes."

"It was just a warning. Because believe me, Mister Mouse, if I'd really wanted to exterminate you, you wouldn't be here right now."

"Thanks, I feel so much better knowing that."

"Christy would never have allowed me to do that. Not to mention my own daughter. They both like you so much. And now I can see why, you're such a sensitive, attentive young man."

"Please stop it."

Her voice was changing over again, to the sexual ingenue. "You want to put your fingers down my panties? It's okay, I'll let you. Your strong, masculine voice makes me so wet—"

*"What the hell happened to you?"*

"Oh, fuck you," she said, turning it off just as abruptly.

"Is it because of what happened with Whit Ellsworth? When you were at Wellesley? Is that what this is about?"

"It's conceivable."

"Did Whit really rape you in his car?"

"Even if he didn't, it happens all the time. Boys are always raping girls. It's what they do. It's happening even as we speak."

"What about your own father? Did he abuse you?"

"Same answer," she said. "Even if my father didn't, it goes on all the time. Fathers are always molesting their daughters. And even when they aren't, that doesn't mean they're not thinking about it."

"Why didn't you kill your husband? You knew that Jared was forcing himself on Emily."

"Believe me, we were getting around to him. We just wanted to make the little prick squirm."

"We?"

"Why, Patty and I. Why, who's house do you think this is, anyway?"

"I assume you killed Patricia, too."

"No, I loved Patty. She cared about me and I cared about her."

"Where is she?"

"Dead, I'm afraid."

"And you had nothing to do with it?"

"I had everything to do with it, that's the worst part."

Eamon didn't say a damn thing. He knew if he just waited long enough she'd tell him everything he needed to know. She wanted to come clean. She wanted to hear how it sounded at this point.

"We came up with the idea for that letter together. Patty wrote it. We were the Committee, just the two of us. We just wanted to put a scare into people. It was supposed to be a gag. Somehow it just got out of hand."

"Wasn't Dr. Dawkins your first victim? Didn't it all really start at that hospital in New Bedford?"

"Goodness, no. That hamster brain really did kill himself. I had nothing to do with it."

"Were you involved with him?"

"We fucked, if that's what you're asking."

"So you did have something to do with him, then."

She glared at Eamon. "Look, this is my story. And, if it's okay with you, I'll just tell it the way I want. The first person I killed was Whit. Let's set the record straight."

"Did Patricia help you?"

"Patty went with me to St. Michaels. Moral support. I wanted to scare the living shit out of that smug bastard. That's why I brought the gun. I hadn't intended to use it."

"I don't believe you."

"Okay, maybe I did plan to kill him. But Patty didn't know that. I told her it was an accident."

"What happened next?"

"We went to Baltimore. Neither of us had ever been there before. That's when it really started to go haywire."

"Eddie Dooley, the saloon keeper," Eamon said, talking in shorthand now.

"A big, fat spudhead. Stopped serving us drinks. Threw us out of his bar. Big, fat mistake."

"How did Patricia die?"

"It was right afterward, really. We decided to go after that judge and the woman district attorney. You remember them, don't you?"

"Judge Harold Draper and Assistant District Attorney Molly Webster."

"We remembered them from Court TV, from the rape trial."

"Governor Cowel's son, Graham," Eamon said, continuing to supply the missing links.

"The mistake was not taking out Graham Cowel," she said bluntly. "We should never have gone after

242

that Webster woman. We chose her because she had a long history of treating rape victims badly on the stand."

"I don't understand how this ties into Patricia's death."

"Patty had the assignment to kill Webster. Which she accomplished just fine. The problem was, she couldn't live with the guilt."

"Of killing someone?"

"Of killing a woman. That was our mistake. But the Committee was still in its formative stages and—"

Someone was at the door.

Mary. She dropped the coffee and sandwiches.

Eamon had looked in that direction for just a second. It was all Lila Cooper needed. She lunged at him, across the coffee table, shoving two bony fingers right into his eyes. He was temporarily blinded. He hadn't even been able to get off a shot. It didn't matter now, anyway. She had the gun and that was all the difference in the world. It was stuck right under his chin.

Mary had her own weapon raised. "Drop it," she commanded.

Cooper had forced Eamon up from the couch and was using him as a shield. She had one arm around his neck and the gun pushed hard into his throat.

"I said drop it."

"We're leaving now," Lila Cooper said coldly.

Eamon could only hear the voices. And he could only see stars.

"You're not going anywhere," Mary said.

"Well, neither is Eamon Mouse, then."

Eamon knew he was as good as dead. He had made one of those mistakes that you didn't get to do over. He had only looked away for one, unremarkable second, and now he was going to pay the eternal price.

He'd always heard that thing about your whole life flashing before your eyes. But for him it was just a single incident.

When he was eleven or twelve. At Fire Island with his family. His dad had told him not to go out too far because the water was particularly fierce that day. Riptide, a word he'd never heard before. But he didn't listen, of course, and before he even knew it he was being carried far from shore. It was a current you just couldn't fight. He struggled, but it did no good, and he was sent farther and farther out to sea. The beach and his family got smaller and smaller. He didn't even have the strength to yell for help. He was going to drown. He loved them. He had never really got to tell them that.

"I'm going to count to three," Mary said.

"Fine with me," Lila said, keeping the gun jabbed into him. "It's your loss."

He felt only hot shame at his failure. If only he'd listened to his dad. He was drowning, sucked into the ocean's terrible, unshakeable vortex. He was just a boy. God have mercy on his soul.

"I have to warn you I'm an expert marksman."

"I'll take your word for it."

There must be some mistake, he thought, like so many doomed men before him. Not me, not me . . .

"I'm going to start counting now," Mary said. "One—"

He heard the bullet. And he also felt it burn by him, pure heat.

Lila fell, clutching at him.

It was over, just like that.

"Are you all right?" Mary said, coming for him.

Just as that alert lifeguard had come for him so many summers before, coming from nowhere on that surfboard to save him.

"You screwed up the count," he said, still disoriented. "You never made it to three."

"I know," Mary said. "But I just couldn't afford to take that chance."

# *Twenty-three*

⤳

They were content to stay in the stern, away from all the pushing and shoving going on starboard. Maybe he was just getting too old for such things. It had sounded like a good idea earlier, getting out on the open water, out in the bracing sea air, watching for whales.

At fifteen dollars a ticket whale watching wasn't exactly cheap, but he thought it would be worth it to see those behemoths up close. The thing was, you couldn't see much. You'd see a dorsal fin, or an underwater flash of gray tummy, or if you were really lucky, a submerging black tail. You had to make do with these unsatisfactory glimpses, for these were creatures that knew better than to reveal themselves whole.

Right now everyone was crowding starboard to view a couple of giant sperm whales that were putting on a show with their spouting blowholes. The children somehow made it worthwhile, just seeing their wonderstruck expressions as they rode their daddies' shoulders and pointed at those delightful, unexpected geysers.

He saw that Mary's attention was also lodged on those young, ice-cream-smeared faces. "That's what it's all about, isn't it?" he said, taking the opportunity to place his arm around her.

"I want a whole bunch," she said. "I want to do it right. Raise happy, contented, normal kids. The way it's supposed to be."

"I want that, too. And I want it with you."

She went quiet, no doubt gauging his sincerity.

The moment was right. He took out the little velvet box.

"What in the world?" she said, looking slightly flustered. "I don't know about this," she said, opening it. "Oh, God," she exclaimed, "it's absolutely beautiful!" Then, eyeing the emerald ring with newfound suspicion: "But what's this for?"

"Mary . . ." he said, getting down on bended knee.

"Oh, I was afraid of something like this," she said, discomfitting him.

"Mary, will you marry me?"

"I don't know," said the woman of his dreams. "Just get up and we'll talk about it."

"Talk about it?" he said, hurt and dismayed.

"It's just not something to embark upon lightly."

"I know that," Eamon said, rejoining her. "But I'm sure that I love you. In fact, I've never been more sure of anything."

"I love you, too, Eamon. But let's face it, we haven't known each other all that long."

"Long enough," he said sullenly.

"Don't get me wrong," she said. "I haven't said no or anything like it."

They sat quietly for a while, looking out at the choppy, green Atlantic, the wind blowing pretty strongly five miles from shore. They were a handsome young couple, looking tanned and rested, looking to all the world as if they were on their honeymoon. And it had been a little like that, their week in Provincetown. Deciding to stay on after they were done with all that nasty business with Lila Cooper.

"I'm glad it's an emerald ring," she said. "I can't stand diamonds."

"I thought they were a girl's best friend."

"Diamond engagement rings. They're just such a sign of ownership, like a man is buying you like so much chattel. And we're just as bad, the way we're always parading them around, telling everyone how much it cost, as if our own worth could somehow be measured in carats."

"Then I guess I made a good choice with the emerald," he said, more than a little relieved.

"A wonderful choice. It's intimate, personal. I'll cherish it."

"So you will marry me, then?" he said in a rush of hopefulness.

"There are some things we have to get straight right now. Some conditions, if you will."

"Anything, you name it."

"You don't even know what they are yet."

"I don't have to. I already agree to them."

"I don't want a traditional wedding. I don't want to have to wear a white dress and walk down the aisle and be some kind of virgin-goddess sacrifice. I'm not something to be given away."

"I can live with that."

"I don't want to change my last name," she said. "I like Mary Seppala. It's me, I'm used to it."

"I can live with that, too."

"And Eamon, you'd have to make one very big change for me. You'd have to stop drinking so much. I don't want to have to live like that. I saw what my father's drinking did to my mother."

"That's a tough one," he said, sounding a lot less gung ho. "But I guess I could try to cut back."

"And I want our marriage to be a marriage of equals. I don't want the traditional marriage. I want us always to be friends first."

"No problem there."

"Okay, those are my conditions."

"So does that mean you'll marry me?"

"No, it means I need some time to think about it," she said.

"I don't understand," he said, crestfallen.

"I'm just exercising a woman's prerogative."